drawnandquarterly.com

FIRST DRAWN & QUARTERLY EDITION: AUGUST 2016
printed in china
10 9 8 7 6 5 4 3 2 1

ISBN 978-1-77046-264-9 (HARDBACK)

LIBRARY AND ARCHIVES CANADA CATALOGUING IN PUBLICATION

1. GRAPHIC NOVELS
I. TITLE

BARRY LYNDA -1956-
CAPRICORN, AUTHOR ILLUSTRATOR THE GREATEST OF MARLYS
originally published Seattle Sasquatch Books 2000
PN6727.B36G74 2016
741.5'973 C2016-900498-8
PUBLISHED IN THE USA BY DRAWN & QUARTERLY A CLIENT PUBLISHER OF FARRAR, STRAUS AND GIROUX. orders 888.330.8477

FORE STORY BACKWORD

ONE DAY, I WAS DRAWING MY WEEKLY COMIC STRIP, AND AS I DREW THE FRAME, I HAD A HALF-MEMORY OF BEING WITH MY COUSINS AFTER SEEING THE TORCH LIGHT PARADE.

GONNA THROW UP!

UGH

GRANDMA I'M GOING TO MAKE SUKA*

9 KIDS CRAMMED INTO ONE CAR- NO SEAT BELTS, 3 ADULTS SMOKING!

DON'T YOU DARE!!

DON'T, MY DEAR.

* "START BARFING"

1

AND SUDDENLY WE WERE ALL JUST THROWING UP PARADE FOOD AT THE SAME TIME. ON TOP OF THIS IMAGE WAS A HALF-MEMORY OF STAYING OVERNIGHT AT A NEIGHBOR'S HOUSE. NINE KIDS. THE MOM SAID THINGS LIKE, "HOLY BALLS!"

ASUS MARI- OSEP!!!*

HOLY BALLS!!!

* JESUS, MARY, JOSEPH!

2

WHEN I MAKE A COMIC STRIP, I LET THESE SORTS OF IMAGES LEAD AND COMBINE AS I MOVE MY PEN. I TRY TO LET ONE LINE LEAD TO THE NEXT WITHOUT PLAN. THE ONLY THING I HAVE TO DO IS STAY IN MOTION. THAT'S WHAT I WAS DOING WHEN I FIRST SAW MARLYS.

SHE WAS 7 OR 8 YEARS OLD

MY 1ST VIEW OF MARLYS

"MARLYS." IS THAT EVEN A NAME? SHE'S QUEEN OF "BUTT ISLAND"

OK.

in 1986 I WAS 30 YEARS OLD

THE NIGHT WE ALL GOT SK

SKRITZY SKRICH SKRIZZ

3

ONE OF THE RULES I MAKE IS TO FOLLOW MY HAND - I LET IT WRITE THE PICTURES AND DRAW THE WORDS --- I TRY TO STEP BACK TO THE POSITION OF OBSERVER.

"LAND OF MARLYS" ALSO KNOWN AS "BUTT ISLAND"

my 2nd View of Marlys

4

KIDS DO THIS ALL THE TIME WHEN THEY PLAY WITH DOLLS AND ACTION FIGURES. THEY ARE BOTH WATCHING THE SCENE UNFOLD AND RESPONDING IN REAL TIME. THIS IS JUST WHAT I WAS DOING THE FIRST TIME I SAW MARLYS. SHE SHOWED UP FASTER THAN I COULD HAVE THOUGHT HER UP.

DREAMING HER UP' IS MORE LIKE IT. WITH HER CAME ARNA, ARNOLD, FREDDIE, AND THE WORLD AROUND THEM. THAT WAS THOUSANDS OF VIEWS OF MARLYS AGO. IT'S STRANGE TO COPY THOSE FIRST PICTURES. MY HAND DRAWS HER DIFFERENTLY NOW.

THIS RELATIONSHIP IS MUTUAL. I BELIEVE MARLYS CONJURES ME AS MUCH AS I CONJURE HER. THE PORTAL BETWEEN HER WORLD AND MINE IS A PEN LINE MADE BY THE LIVING MYSTERY OF THIS HAND, THIS HAND THAT LOOKS LIKE YOURS.

SO BACK TO THAT HALF-MEMORY: WE'RE ALL LIVING TOGETHER IN A BIG, RUN-DOWN HOUSE; THE PARENTS SLEEP UPSTAIRS, US KIDS SLEEP ON TWO DOUBLE BEDS WITH GRANDMA, IT WAS THE NIGHT WE ALL GOT SICK, GRANDMA, TELL US THAT STORY AGAIN!

5

THE NIGHT WE ALL GOT SICK

BY LYNDA "BAD TO THE BONEY BUTT" BARRY © 1986

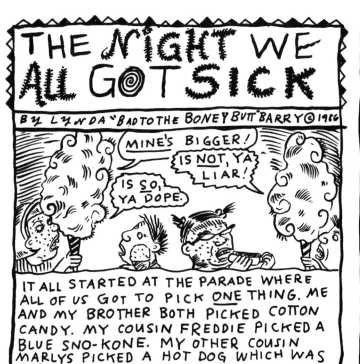

IT ALL STARTED AT THE PARADE WHERE ALL OF US GOT TO PICK <u>ONE</u> THING. ME AND MY BROTHER BOTH PICKED COTTON CANDY. MY COUSIN FREDDIE PICKED A BLUE SNO-KONE. MY OTHER COUSIN MARLYS PICKED A HOT DOG WHICH WAS A PERFECTLY STUPID PICK.

LATER WE ALL GOT TO SLEEP IN MY COUSIN'S HOUSE IN THE FRONT ROOM BUT <u>NO HORSEPLAY</u>. NONE OF US FELT LIKE IT ANYWAY BECAUSE WE ALL HATED EACH OTHER'S GUTS. ESPECIALLY ME AND MARLYS. SO WE ALL HAD <u>OUR</u> OWN TERRITORY WHICH WAS <u>OFF LIMITS</u>.

MARLYS STARTED IT BY SITTING UP AND BARFING AND PRETTY SOON ALL OF US WERE. MY BROTHER RAN TO GET AUNT SYLVIA AND SLIPPED AND FELL AND THREW UP. NONE OF US COULD EVEN LAUGH. EVENTUALLY AUNT SYLVIA AND UNCLE TED HELPED US AND TOOK TURNS ROCKING US IN THEIR BIG ROCKER AS SOON AS WE COULD STAND IT.

AFTER THAT NIGHT WE ALL HAD A SECRET WEAPON AGAINST EACH OTHER. ALL YOU HAD TO DO WAS SAY THE WORDS "SNO-KONE" TO FREDDIE AND HE'D PRACTICALLY START CRYING. MY BROTHER'S AND MINE WAS THE SAME SO WE NEVER USED IT. BUT MARLYS WOULD CALL UP OUR HOUSE AND ASK FOR ME AND WHEN I SAID HELLO SHE'D WHISPER "THE SMELL OF COTTON CANDY."
BUT EVEN JUST A <u>DRAWING</u> OF A HOTDOG WOULD MAKE <u>HER</u> BAWL. WHICH IS WHY I GOT TO BE SUCH A GOOD ARTIST.

6

the NEW YEAR

BY LYNDA BARRY © 1987

THIS YEAR IT TURNS OUT ME AND MY COUSIN MARLYS ARE GOING TO BE IN THE SAME ROOM, ROOM 9, MISS MARTLES'S CLASS. WE ARE DOOMED.

YOU HAVE YOUR MILK MONEY?

YEAH.

THANKS, MOM.

WE HAVE HEARD *STORIES* ABOUT MISS MARTLES FROM WHEN MARLYS'S SISTER MAYBONNE HAD HER IN THE SIXTH GRADE. WE HEARD THAT SHE THROWS HER CHALK WHEN SHE'S MAD AND PLAYS "WHEN JOHNNY COMES MARCHING HOME AGAIN" ON THE ACCORDION. AND THAT SHE MAKES YOU STICK YOUR FIST IN THE AIR DURING THE 'HURRAH HURRAH' PART AND YELLS "FEELING! MORE FEELING!"

YOU'RE SURE YOU HAVE YOUR MILK MONEY?

YES.

YOU'RE SURE.

YES!

LET ME SEE IT.

MOM.

WE'VE HEARD SHE MAKES YOU DO ABOUT A THOUSAND SQUAT JUMPS FOR P.E. AND ALSO THOSE MODERN DANCE EXERCISES THAT SHE GETS FROM A BOOK, WHERE YOU HAVE TO RUN ACROSS THE PLAYFIELD RIGHT BY THE LIBRARY WINDOWS AND PRETEND YOU'RE AN ANGRY TREE.

WHAT IF SHE MAKES US SIT IN ORDER OF HOW SMART WE ARE? THAT MEANS I'LL BE RIGHT UP FRONT BY HER DESK.

THAT'S NOT EVEN FAIR!

JUST 'CAUSE I'M A GIFTED CHILD!

MAYBONNE SAID THE ONLY GOOD PART ABOUT MISS MARTLES WAS HER PET BIRD DONALD WHO COULD HOLD A PENCIL IN HIS MOUTH. BUT THEN SOMEONE GAVE DONALD A MILK DUD. MAYBONNE WARNED US: DON'T YOU NEVER BRING NO MILK DUDS IN YOUR LUNCH. THIS IS GOING TO BE THE WORST YEAR OF OUR LIVES.

QUIT THINKIN' YOU'RE SO COOL JUST 'CAUSE YOU'RE A PATROL, ARNOLD.

I WAS ON PATROL LAST YEAR

I WAS A LIEUTENANT.

READY?

WA-ALK

STOP

7

WHO ARE THE DOGS?

LYNDA BARRY © 1 9 8 8

WHEN YOU COME TO A NEW PLACE, YOU WANT TO KNOW WHO ARE THE DOGS, RIGHT? HERE'S A MAP OF THE DOGS OF OUR STREET.

"VACU-FORM"

GARY HIRAKI'S DOG. GOT HIS NAME BECAUSE OF EATING THIRTEEN VACU-FORMS. HIS NAME USED TO BE "REX." HE ALSO CHEWS CRAYONS.

"HERMAN AND INEZ"

DOGS OF MRS. VORICE. THEY MOSTLY STAY IN THEIR OWN YARD BUT SOMETIMES THEY WILL COME OVER AND STARE AT YOUR GARBAGE CAN. THEY SMELL LIKE OLD BALONEY. I WOULDN'T GO PETTING THEM.

"TIGER"

DOG OF THE COUSINS WHO VISIT OUR ACROSS THE STREET NEIGHBORS. HE DOESN'T LOOK LIKE THAT BIG A DEAL BUT HE BITES LIKE CRAZY SO WATCH OUT! HE WILL GET PSYCHOLOGICAL IF YOU EVEN LOOK AT HIM! ONE THING HE LOVES IS WEARING DOLL CLOTHES, AND IF HE IS WEARING THEM YOU CAN PICK HIM UP AND HE'LL LICK YOU. WITH NO CLOTHES ON THOUGH, HE WILL CHEW VIOLENTLY!

PRINCE BUSTER

THE OWNER: MR. BAYLO

PURE POLICE DOG, MOSTLY TIED UP. IF HE GETS LOOSE HE WILL TRY TO DANCE ON YOU AND IF YOU TRY TO GET AWAY, HE GROWLS.

"CARLA"

NEVER PETTED HER IN REAL LIFE BECAUSE THE WOMAN OF HER, MRS. ALANZA, SAID MY HANDS CAN SPREAD DISEASE. YOU CAN ONLY SEE THIS DOG FROM THE WINDOW WHICH IS SAD. SHE LOOKS NICE.

"COOKIE"

OWNERS: THE MANNINGS

DON'T EAT FOOD BY THIS DOG. HE GRABBED MY SISTER'S FUDGSICLE OUT OF HER HAND AND RAN TO THE BUSHES. WE ALSO SAW HIM WITH A WHOLE LOAF OF BREAD AND HE KNOCKED DOWN A 3-YEAR-OLD FOR A PIECE OF HOT DOG.

"QUEENIE"

MAKES BREATHING NOISES THAT SOUND LIKE CHOKING BUT ARE NORMAL. HER OWNER, MRS. PATNOE, COOKS THE DOG FOOD: SCRAMBLED EGGS, HAMBURGERS, MIDGET MEATBALLS. SOMETIMES YOU'LL SEE QUEENIE IN THE WINDOW SLEEPING, SOMETIMES SHE'S IN THE YARD SLEEPING AND THAT IS HER WHOLE ENTIRE LIFE.

"MURRAY"

"THE CHEWER"

OWNER: BILLY HOOKS

DON'T LEAVE NOTHING YOU LIKE BY THIS DOG. HE IS DESTRUCTIVE!!! HE CHEWED THE COVERS OFF THE CAR SEATS OF MR. AND MRS. HOOKS, AND EVEN HONKED THE HORN! AND HE'S CHEWED A MILLION DOLLS UP! G.I JOE, BARBIE, TAMMY, CHATTY CATHY! CHEWS ANYTHING! THEY ARE TRYING TO FIND HIM A GOOD HOME!

Fine Dining

By chef LYNDA LaBARBEE © 1986

ALTHOUGH HARDLY ANYBODY HAD EVER GONE TO A GREAT RESTAURANT, ALL OF US HAD OPINIONS ON WHAT WAS A EXCELLENT MEAL. FOR MY BROTHER IT WAS 2 CHICKEN POT PIES WITH COLD SPAGHETTI-O'S RIGHT OUT OF THE CAN. I PREFERRED THE DELICATE TASTE OF FRIED BALONEY AND MAYONNAISE ON SUNBEAM BREAD.

LEAVE IT IN THE CAN PLEASE

'ETTI-O'S

INITIALS CARVED ON PIE

SOLE UTENSIL

MILK GLASS MUST HAVE HANDLE

TV TRAY: "A MUST"

FRY BALONEY UNTIL IT HUMPS UP. BURN EDGES. HIDE FRYING PAN UNDER BED SO MOM WON'T CREAM YOU FOR THE BLACK MARKS THAT YOU CAN'T SCRUB OUT.

AT EVERYONE'S HOUSE THEIR FAMILY ATE AT LEAST ONE THING THAT WAS SCARY.

DEENA'S — MUSTARD AND ONION AND RELISH SANDWICHES

THE TWINS — JELLY ON SPAGHETTI

OUR HOUSE — "DINOU-GOUAAN" (A.K.A. "MIDNIGHT MEAT" and "BLACK OUT")

MARLYS — "BAGOUNG" (SCARY PINK FISH CONDIMENT THAT THE SMELL WOULD MAKE YOU START RUNNING)

WALTER'S — SARDINES AND COOL WHIP (HE ATE THIS FOR SHOW OFF ONLY)

DICKY'S — FRIED PIG GUTS

OUR MAIN OPINIONS, HOWEVER, REGARDED THE WORLD OF DESSERTS. FOR EXAMPLE EVERYONE AGREED ANYTHING TASTED THE BEST WHEN YOU ATE IT IN YOUR CLASSROOM DURING A HALLOWEEN OR VALENTINES PARTY. EVEN THE WORST KOOL-AID WAS SIMPLY DELICIOUS IF IT WAS IN A PAPER CUP ON YOUR DESK WITH A CUPCAKE. (ESPECIALLY IF THE CUPCAKE WAS IN A BLUE PAPER HOLDER. THE WORST CUPCAKE HOLDER WAS THE YELLOW.) (YELLOW WAS ALWAYS BAD DUE TO P.)

REGARDING CANDY NATURALLY EVERYONE HAD ONE FAVORITE. BUT THERE WERE TWO THINGS WE ALL AGREED ON.

① CHUNKYS WERE A TOTAL RIP OFF

② THE WORST CANDY KNOWN TO THE ENTIRE UNIVERSE IS THOSE ORANGE MARSHMALLOW "PEANUTS"

ESPECIALLY WHEN THEY HAVE BEEN SITTING IN A BOWL SO LONG THEY HAVE DUST ON THEM BUT YOUR MOM FORCES YOU TO EAT IT BECAUSE IT WAS AN OLD PERSON WHO GAVE IT TO YOU.

THE CARNIVAL

BY LYNDA SWANG THANG BARRY © 1986

WE DECIDED TO HAVE A CARNIVAL SHOW AND WE DECIDED TO HAVE IT ON A DAY WHEN NO ONE'S PARENTS WOULD BE ANYWHERE EXCEPT AT WORK. OUR MAIN ATTRACTION WAS GOING TO BE: "THINGS LIGHTED ON FIRE". OUR MAIN PROBLEM WAS GOING TO BE: "MARLYS TELLING."

YOU THINK YOU'RE SO BIG.

YOU'RE NOT THE BOSS OF US MARLYS.

WHY DON'T YOU GO BACK INSIDE AND WATCH YOURSELF IN THE MIRROR SOME MORE?

THEN I'M GOING TO HAVE YOU PUT IN JAIL.

I'M GONNA WRITE DOWN EVERYTHING YOU DO.

1

MY SISTER AND DEENA WERE GOING TO DO A SPECIAL TUMBLING SHOW TO THE SONG "LOVE IS BLUE." TO GET THE MUSIC THEY HAD TO PUT IT ON FULL BLAST AND PUSH THE RECORD PLAYER OVER BY THE WINDOW. MARLYS WAS GOING TO TELL ON THEM FOR THAT TOO.

CAN YOU HEAR IT GOOD?!

LOUDER!

IT CAN'T GO NO LOUDER!

PUSH IT MORE BY THE WINDOW!

THERE'S NO MORE PLUG!

YOUR MOM SAID NEVER TOUCH HER RECORD PLAYER BUT YOU HAD TO DO IT, DIDN'T YOU?

I'M WRITING YOU A TICKET.

2

MARLYS WAS MAKING A HARD TIME FOR EVERYBODY TO THINK UP THINGS TO DO BECAUSE NO MATTER WHAT YOU THOUGHT OF, SHE SAID SHE'D TELL ON YOU FOR IT. AND SHE WOULD TOO. FINALLY SOMEONE HAD THE GENIUS TO ASK MARLYS TO BE THE STAR OF THE SHOW.

YEAH MARLYS! YOU CAN BE THE MAIN QUEEN!

YOU CAN HOLD THE MATCHES!

YOU CAN ANNOUNCE EVERYBODY!

YOU CAN WEAR MY MAMA'S HIGH HEELS!

WE'LL EVEN LISTEN TO YOU SINGING!

COME ON MARLYS!

YEAH! COME ON MARLYS!

3

FOR ABOUT ONE SECOND MARLYS STOOD THERE LOOKING AT US LIKE SHE NEVER EVEN MET US BEFORE. THEN SHE WENT OUT OF HER MIND AND YELLED "I HATE YOU, I HATE YOU ALL" ABOUT 600 TIMES UNTIL SHE WAS PRACTICALLY DROOLING. IT SCARED US AND DEENA AND MY SISTER STARTED CRYING ALONG WITH MARLYS WHO WOULDN'T EVEN LET US COME NEAR HER. AFTER THAT WE REALIZED IT WAS A LOT BETTER FOR MARLYS IF YOU JUST KEPT TREATING HER LIKE YOU HATED HER GUTS.

X

THE WORLD of ARNOLD

L Y N D A B A R R Y © 1 9 8 8

MY BROTHER ARNOLD HAS THIS IDEA ABOUT HOW HE IS GOING TO LIVE ON A DESERTED ISLAND. HE GOT THE IDEA FROM TV, YOU KNOW THE SHOW. BUT HE SAYS THAT IF ANYONE TRIES TO DISCOVER <u>HIS</u> LOCATION AND COME RESCUE <u>HIM</u>, HE'LL EXPLODE THEIR SHIP WITH A BAZOOKA.

HOW DO I KNOW IT? I READ IT IN THE SECRET BOOK HE'S WRITING CALLED "<u>MY ADVENTURES OF ARNOLD ARNESON</u>." THE STORY OF HOW AFTER HIS SHIP GETS BLOWN UP, HE IS SAVED BY A HALF SHARK-HALF DOLPHIN NAMED <u>KILLER</u> WHO BRINGS HIM TO A DESERTED ISLAND THAT MYSTERIOUSLY ALREADY HAS ELECTRICITY. KILLER ALSO BRINGS HIM THINGS THAT FALL OFF SHIPS: A COLOR TV, A DRAGSTER, A CASE OF CHOCOLATE MALT BALLS.

THEN A BEAUTIFUL MOVIE STAR COMES RIDING BY ON A SURFBOARD THAT'S BEEN UNCONTROLLABLE SINCE HAWAII, AND SHE'S SCREAMING AND ARNOLD RESCUES HER AND SHE'S SO THANKFUL SHE SERVES HIM ORANGE CRUSH IN HER PAJAMAS. THEN THEY'RE GOING TO GET MARRIED UNTIL THE TRAGEDY OF KILLER ACCIDENTALLY EATS HER. IT'S KIND OF A SAD STORY, IN A WAY.

MY BROTHER GOES UNDER THE PORCH SOMETIMES AND PRETENDS HE IS ALREADY THERE ON HIS ISLAND. YOU CAN SEE HIM NOW IF YOU LOOK THROUGH THIS CRACK, BUT SHHH. I WATCH HIM ALL THE TIME. HIM LYING ON THE PILE OF WOOD, LOOKING THROUGH HIS BINOCULARS, WATCHING FOR THE APPROACHING ENEMY.

.TALENT. SHOW.

By LYNDA BUDDY GUY BARRY © 1986 Seattle

SOMETIMES LIKE ON A SUNDAY AND YOU'RE STUCK AT YOUR COUSIN'S AND THERE AIN'T ONE DECENT THING TO DO BESIDES WATCHING DUMB STUPID "ROMAN THEATER" (— ONE MILLION BLACK AND WHITE MOVIES ABOUT GLADIATORS —) WELL WHY NOT HAVE A TALENT SHOW OR SOMETHING?

TESTING TESTING LADIES AND GENTLEMEN FOR NOW LET ME INTRODUCE THE GREAT MARLYS GONNA DO SOME TUMBLING FOR YOU NOW. LET'S HEAR IT FOR MARLYS!

LIKE YOU CAN DO AN ACTING OF YOUR FAVORITE MOVIE.

OR YOU CAN DO SOME INCREDIBLE THING TO MAKE PEOPLE AMAZED BY YOU.

I VANT TO SUCK YOUR BLOOD. BETTER WATCH OUT BECAUSE I VANT TO SUCK YOUR BLOOD!

I WILL NOW EAT THE SIX RAW HOTDOGS WITHOUT STOPPING 'TIL THEY ARE GONE. THE MUSIC TO IT WILL BE "REVOLUTION" BY THE BEATLES.

YOU CAN DO A DEMONSTRATION OF AN EXCITING TRICK YOUR DOG LEARNED.

OK. MARTY. GOOD BOY. OK. NOW WHICH HAND HAS THE WAD OF BOLOGNA IN IT MARTY? USE YOUR MYSTERY POWERS AND TELL US WHICH HAND HAS

A LOAD OF BOLOGNA ALL INSIDE?

BUT PLEASE, JUST NO SINGING.

NA NA NA NANANANA HEY JUDE. NUH NA NA NANUHNUH NA HEY JUDE. NA NA NA NUH NUH-NUH NUH HEY JUDE NUH NUH —

WHEN'S THIS SUPPOSED TA BE DONE MAN? DANG!

SHUT UP! NOW I GET "DO OVERS" AGAIN BECAUSE YOU TALKED.

HEY JUDE DON'T MAKE IT BAD

WORST HAIRCUTS
BY LYNDA "SKITCHHEAD" BARRY © 1986

ABOUT THE WORST HAIRCUT I EVER SAW WAS THE ONE ME AND MY COUSIN MARLYS GOT BY HER MOM ONE TIME WHEN I HAD TO STAY OVER THERE.

Before | After

WHO'S FIRST?

MARLYS?

NO WAY MAN.

YOUR MOM PROMISED WE'D LOOK LIKE MODELS FROM FRANCE AFTERWARDS!

SHUT UP.

SHE SAID A PIXIE HAIRDO WAS THE LATEST STYLE!

SHUT UP.

I HATE EVERYTHING.

WE STARTED CRYING THE MINUTE WE SAW THE FACT THAT SHE WAS GOING TO USE A PLUG-IN DOG HAIR RAZOR ON US. IT HAD THE SAME SMELL AS BURNING THOSE PLASTIC ARMY MEN AND IT WOULD GET SO HOT SHE'D DROP IT ON US AND WE'D JUMP OFF THE CHAIR AND TRY TO RUN BUT SHE'D SNAG US BACK.

The "at home" Haircut

YOUR MEAN COUSIN HOLDING A MIRROR TO TRY AND MAKE YOU CRY

PLENTY O' BALD SPOTS

CLOTHES PIN

HAIR DOWN SHIRT

96 TEARS

WATER DRIPPING DOWN BACK

OLD SMELLY TOWEL

DOG CLIPPERS

RE-READING INSTRUCTIONS

YOUR AUNT

CIG

WOMEN'S DAY MAGAZINE ARTICLE THAT GAVE HER THE IDEA

COMB

MORE INSPIRATION

ALL YOUR BEAUTIFUL HAIR

TACOMA

SEATTLE

PHONE BOOKS

HOW TO CUT YOUR CHILD'S...

BEER

AFTER SHE WAS DONE SHE'D MAKE US STAND NEXT TO EACH OTHER AND SHE'D LOOK AT US AND TILT HER HEAD BACK AND FORTH LIKE A GERMAN SHEPHERD HEARING A WEIRD NOISE, WATCHING FOR SOME HAIR SHE HAD MISSED. WHEN WE WERE FINALLY TOTALLY BALD SHE'D PUT A RIBBON ON US.

AUNTIE ARDIS SCOTCH TAPE LOOKS FUNNY ON A HEAD.

NONSENSE! SCOTCH TAPE IS TOTALLY INVISIBLE!

BESIDES! HOW ELSE CAN YOU EXPECT TO HOLD THESE ADORABLE RIBBONS ON?!

BE STILL MARLYS!

WHEN I GROW UP I'M GONNA GROW MY HAIR DOWN PAST MY BUTT.

SO EVEN THOUGH IT WAS A MILLION DEGREES OUTSIDE ME AND MARLYS WORE SKI JACKETS BECAUSE IT WAS THE ONLY THING WE HAD WITH HOODS. AND EVEN THOUGH WE HATED EACH OTHER WE SORT OF FELT LIKE BEST FRIENDS UNTIL WE GOT SOME HAIR AGAIN.

HEYA STUPES. DONCHA EVEN KNOW IT'S SUMMER?

SO?

BIG DEAL, MAN.

AIN'T YOU GUYS HOT?

NOPE.

NOPE.

13

SCIENCE

BY LYNDA GOLF BALL BARRY ©1987

FOR OUR SCIENCE PROJECT, ERNIE BARTA BROUGHT A GRASSHOPPER IN A BAND-AID BOX. HE HAD NAMED IT "BRUCE LEE JR."

WHOSE YARD DID YA CATCH IT AT?

I CAUGHT IT UP AT THE CHURCH.

ERNIE TOLD THE TEACHER HE HAD TRAINED THE GRASSHOPPER TO SMOKE A MINIATURE CIGAR. WE COULDN'T WAIT TO SEE IT.

IT TOOK A LONG TIME BUT IF AT FIRST YOU DON'T SUCCEED, TRY TRY AGAIN.

MRS. BROGAN SAID SMOKING IS BAD ENOUGH, BUT TEACHING A GRASSHOPPER TO SMOKE IS TOTAL CRUELTY TO ANIMALS. ERNIE SAID IT'S NOT A REAL CIGAR BUT MRS. BROGAN MADE HIM LET THE TALENTED BRUCE LEE JR. GO. AT RECESS WE SADLY WATCHED IT JUMP THROUGH THE FENCE AND INTO THE STICKERS.

I KNOW YOU'RE UPSET NOW ERNEST, BUT ONE DAY YOU'LL THANK ME. YOU'LL SAY "BY GOLLY, MRS. BROGAN WAS THE BEST TEACHER I EVER HAD!" AND YOU'LL WANT TO SEND ME FLOWERS.

MRS. BROGAN SAT AT HER DESK AND ASKED US TO THINK ABOUT WHAT VALUABLE LESSON HAD WE LEARNED THAT DAY. THE ANSWER WAS "WHATEVER YOU DO, NEVER SHOW NOTHING GOOD TO MRS. BROGAN."

BORN FREEE AS FREE AS THE WIND BLOWS...

BAD FOR YOU

BY LYNDA ORSON WELLES BARRY ©1989

MRS. BROGAN TOLD THE LIGHT MONITOR TO TURN THE LIGHTS OFF, THEN SHE SWITCHED ON THE OVERHEAD PROJECTOR AND *SHOWED* US ABOUT 40 PICTURES OF ROTTEN TEETH AND SAID THE *SUBJECT OF THE DAY WAS POP.*

A LOT OF YOU WILL END UP WITH TEETH EXACTLY LIKE THIS.

SHE SAID OF ALL POP, COKE WAS THE WORST AND IF YOU HUNG A HUNK OF MEAT IN A CAN OF COKE IT WOULD ROT RIGHT OFF THE STRING IN <u>ONE</u> DAY. SO THINK OF WHAT IT DOES TO YOUR STOMACH.

HOW MANY OF YOU LIKE THE THOUGHT OF BIG HOLES IN YOUR STOMACH LINING?

WHEN ARNOLD ARNESEN SHOWED UP THE NEXT DAY WITH A THERMOS FULL OF COKE AND A HOT DOG FLOATING IN IT MRS. BROGAN SAID "OK, WE SHALL <u>SEE</u> WHAT HAPPENS" AND PUT THE THERMOS ON A TABLE BY ITSELF WITH AN INDEX CARD TAPED TO IT THAT SAID "EX-PERIMENT."

Experiment

THIS IS NOT A TOY

ALL DAY WE WONDERED ABOUT THE HOT DOG TRAPPED IN THE THERMOS WITH THE COKE. WHAT A HORRIBLE WAY TO GO.

AFTER 24 HOURS MRS. BROGAN TOOK US ALL OUT TO THE STORM DRAIN WHERE SHE WAS GOING TO POUR OUT THE COKE, AND SHE POURED IT AND THE HOT DOG FELL OUT IN PERFECT CONDITION.

FOR SOME REASON ALL OF US KNEW THIS WAS ABOUT THE SADDEST THING WE HAD EVER SEEN. ESPECIALLY MRS. BROGAN.

16

BELIEVE IT OR NOT

BY LYNDA BARRY ©1987

OUR FAVORITE BOOK OF ALL TIME WAS BY RIPLEY CALLED RIPLEY'S BELIEVE IT OR NOT. WE ENJOYED A LOT OF THE PICTURES AND STORIES. IN OUR OPINION THAT'S THE BOOK THEY SHOULD TEACH READING WITH.

(PALL MALL)

FRANK BROWN WOUNDED SOLDIER CAN SMOKE A CIGARETTE THRU A HOLE IN HIS FOREHEAD.

1

IN THIS BOOK YOU CAN LEARN ABOUT A LOT OF INTERESTING PEOPLE.

A MAN WHO PLAYS POOL WITH HIS NOSE

THE HUMAN PIN CUSHION

THE MAN WITH FINGERNAILS 22¾ INCHES LONG

THE BABY CYCLOPS

THE FORK-TONGUED FRÄULEIN OF FRANKFORT

A GUY THAT COULD YELL SO LOUD YOU COULD HEAR HIM FOR THREE MILES

A MAN WITH LONG ARMS

2

ALSO THERE WERE MANY INTERESTING ANIMALS TO EXPLORE.

A CHICKEN WHO LAID TWO SQUARE EGGS

A FISH THAT CAN CLIMB TREES

THE MAN-EATING CLAM

A BIRD CALLED "THE LAUGHING JACKASS"

THE PEG-LEG COW

A TOAD THAT HOPPED 75 MILES IN FIVE DAYS

THE WONDER WEENIE AN 885-POUND HOT DOG THAT WAS HALF A MILE LONG

3

ALL OF US DREAMED OF SOMEDAY BEING IN THAT BOOK.

ARNOLD: JUMPED OFF THE PORCH 37 TIMES WITHOUT STOPPING. -COULD HAVE DONE MORE BUT HIS MOM MADE HIM QUIT.

FOUND: A PEANUT WITH THREE THINGS IN IT.

FOUND: TWO M&Ms STUCK TOGETHER (GREEN)

ARNA: COULD FIT A LOT OF MARBLES IN HER MOUTH

CHEWED: 1 PIECE OF GUM, 11 DAYS STILL GOOD

MADE: RUBBER BAND CHAIN ONE BLOCK LONG

ALL THE LIVE LONG DAY ♩♫

FREDDIE: CAUGHT 19 BEES IN ONE JAR

MARLYS: SANG "CAMP TOWN RACES" 100 TIMES IN A ROW ON A LONG CAR TRIP BUT HAD TO HUM THE LAST 72 TIMES OR HER MOM SAID SHE'D GET IT.

X

17

SEARS CATALOG PART ONE

LYNDA "EARL AVENUE" BARRY © 1987

THE FIRST TIME I EVER GOT ANYTHING FROM THE SEARS CATALOG, IT WAS A BABY TINY TEARS. BABY TINY TEARS CAME WITH A WHOLE WAD OF ACCESSORIES WHICH IS THE BEST PART OF ANY DOLL.

MINIATURE WASHCLOTH
"MOLDED" HAIR
DIAPER
PACIFIER
SCARY MOUTH
LITTLE SPONGE
TINY BAR OF SOAP
IVORY
BOTTLE
Tiny Tears
DRESS
BONNET
MIDGET KLEENEXES
BOOTIES THAT WON'T STAY ON
TINY TEARS TISSUE
SHRIMPY BUBBLE PIPE

1

SHE HAD THIS KIND OF MOUTH WITH A TINY HOLE IN IT THAT YOU COULD STICK THE END OF A PENCIL IN AND MAKE IT LOOK LIKE SHE WAS SMOKING. THE BAD THING WAS IF YOU TRIED TO USE A PEN AND YOU MISSED.
ONCE YOU GET BLUE BALLPOINT INK ON A DOLL HEAD, THAT'S IT. IT'S WRECKED FOR LIFE.

CIGARS? CIGARETTES? TIPARILLOS?

UH-OH.

2

THE OTHER THING WAS THAT SHE WOULD "WET" OUT OF HER SHOULDERS, HER NECK, AND HER EYEBALLS IF YOU ACCIDENTALLY HUNG HER UPSIDE DOWN AFTER YOU FED HER.

OH NOT AGAIN!

3

YOU WERE SUPPOSED TO ONLY LET HER DRINK WATER BUT SOME OF US FELT SORRY FOR BABY TINY TEARS AND LET HER DRINK MILK. THIS WAS A BIG MISTAKE, ESPECIALLY IF IT WAS SUMMER AND YOU LET HER TAKE A NAP IN THE HOT SUN FOR ABOUT FIVE HOURS AFTERWARDS. I TELL YOU, YOU WILL NEVER PLAY WITH THAT DOLL AGAIN.

SEARS CATALOG

BY LYNDA BOUNCY SPRINGS BARRY © 1987

PART TWO: MARLYS PICKS

I TRIED TO WARN MARLYS THAT THEM RUBBER GLAMOR WIGS WEREN'T GOING TO BE NO GOOD. I MEAN ONE LOOK AT THE PICTURES IN THE CATALOG AND ANYBODY WOULD KNOW.

SEARS EXCLUSIVE MOLDED RUBBER GLAMOUR WIGS FOR YOUR YOUNG LITTLE MISS. SOPHISTICATED STYLES, WASHABLE, LIFELIKE, EASY TO WEAR.
BLONDE, BRUNETTE, REDHEAD..........
3 PC SET........$3.98

HER MOM SAID SHE COULD ORDER PRACTICALLY ANY TOY AND SHE PICKS THE <u>WIGS</u>. WHY NOT "MR. FREEZE" SO WE COULD MAKE SNO-KONES? OR A DOLLHOUSE 5 ROOMS COMPLETELY FURNISHED?

YOU COULD SET UP YOUR OWN SNO-KONE STAND AND MAKE 'BOUT A MILLION BUCKS!

I CAN'T HEAR YOU
I CAN'T HEAR YOU
I CAN'T HEAR YOU
I CAN'T HEAR YOU

YOU GET THAT DOLL HOUSE AND ALL THE GIRLS WHO HATE US WILL WANT TO COME OVER AND WE'LL BE POPULAR!

WHEN THE WIGS FINALLY CAME THEY WERE ABOUT FIVE HUNDRED TIMES WORSE THAN I EVER COULD HAVE IMAGINED. MARLYS STARTED CRYING AND FOR ONCE I DIDN'T BLAME HER. THEY LOOKED LIKE A BATHING CAP WITH A BAD INFECTION. LIKE KAL-TIKI THE IMMORTAL MONSTER. LIKE OLD GUM IN THE DIRT.

CAN YOU EVEN BELIEVE IT?!

THE MINUTE MY BROTHER SAW THEM THOUGH, HE FIGURED OUT A WHOLE GAME WITH THEM BASED ON A MOVIE WE ALL LOVED CALLED "DIE, MONSTER, DIE!" WHERE YOUR HEAD GETS TOTALLY DEFORMED. AND THOSE SEARS WIGS WERE ABOUT THE BEST DEFORMED THINGS WE EVER SAW. IT TURNED OUT TO BE THE FAVORITE GAME OF OUR LIFE.

K'MON MARLYS, YOU ALWAYS GET TO BE BORIS KARLOFF

NO FAIR.

WHOSE WIGS ARE THEY, HUH? I'M BORIS KARLOFF FOR LIFE.

K'MON MARLYS!

DANG.

19

SEARS CATALOG

BY LYNDA BEEFARONI BARRY © 1987

PART THREE
ARMY MEN

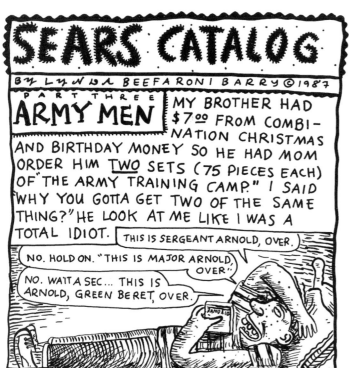

MY BROTHER HAD $7.00 FROM COMBINATION CHRISTMAS AND BIRTHDAY MONEY SO HE HAD MOM ORDER HIM TWO SETS (75 PIECES EACH) OF "THE ARMY TRAINING CAMP." I SAID "WHY YOU GOTTA GET TWO OF THE SAME THING?" HE LOOK AT ME LIKE I WAS A TOTAL IDIOT.

THIS IS SERGEANT ARNOLD, OVER.

NO. HOLD ON. "THIS IS MAJOR ARNOLD OVER."

NO. WAIT A SEC... THIS IS ARNOLD, GREEN BERET, OVER.

WHEN THEY FINALLY CAME HE TOOK ABOUT TWO HOURS TO FIX IT ALL IN A LONG ROW OUT ON THE FRONT SIDEWALK.

GUYS MARCHING

ONE GUY SALUTING

GUYS SHOOTING

KNEELING GUYS WITH BAZOOKAS

LAYING DOWN GUYS WITH RIFLES

GUYS THROWING GRENADES

GUY WITH BAYONET

GUYS WITH BINOCULARS

TENTS THAT NONE OF THE GUYS COULD FIT INTO

FLAG-POLE THAT WON'T STAND UP

FENCE THAT WON'T STAND UP

JEEP NONE OF THE GUYS CAN RIDE IN.

FREESTANDING GUNS THAT YOUR DOG CHEWS

LIGHTER FLUID

THE NEXT DAY HE SETS UP A WHOLE WAR OUT IN THE GARDEN. HE MADE A REALISTIC LAKE FROM A MIRROR PART BURIED IN THE DIRT. HE MADE A RIVER FROM THE GARDEN HOSE. HE MADE PARACHUTERS OUT OF HANDKERCHIEFS. HE HAD THE WHOLE THING SET UP PERFECTLY, THEN HE GOT A BOWL OF CEREAL AND ATE IT OUT ON THE GRASS AND JUST LOOKED AT IT ALL. THEN HE TOOK HIS BOWL IN THE HOUSE, CAME OUT AND BLEW THE WHOLE THING UP WITH DIRT BOMBS.

AAGGGH!

BLAM-BLAM-BLAM!

KA-BLOOEY!

NO! NO! NOOOOO!

RATA-TAT-TAT-TAT-TAT-TAT

I'LL GET YOU YOU DIRTY LITTLE

BLASH!

BLAM!

HELP! HAVE MERCY!

BLAM!

DUCK!

KER-PLUNK!

BLAMMO!

ON THE THIRD DAY I SMELL A TERRIBLE BURNING SMELL AND I CAN HEAR MY BROTHER UNDER THE PORCH WITH HIS MEN. I SNEAK AROUND AND SEE HIM WITH THE LIGHTER FLUID, MATCHES AND HE HOLDS UP THIS ONE GUY HE JUST LIT ON FIRE AND PART OF IT MELTS ON MY BROTHER'S HAND AND HE YELLS AND HE STILL HAS THE SCAR FROM THAT TOO.

YOUCH!

HEY MAN NO FAIR!

OW-OW OW-O-W OOOW!

CHHHHHH!

SEARS CATALOG

BY LYNDA SPRAY 'N' WASH BARRY © 1987

Part Four: MISC.

—HERE ARE SOME TOYS OUR MOM REFUSED TO EVER BUY US, AND WHY.

ICE GOES IN HEAD
SPECIAL SPOONS
CRANK IT
OUT COMES SHAVED ICE TO MAKE SNO-KONES

Mr. Frosty Freeze

MOM: "A LADY I WORK WITH GOT THAT FOR HER KIDS AND THEY ENDED UP THROWING UP FOR TWO DAYS."

BALLERINA WATCH "HER LEGS TELL THE TIME"

MOM: "YOUR COUSIN HAD ONE, AND THOSE LEGS FELL OFF IN LESS THAN A WEEK."

THE SPARKLING ELECTRIC BURP GUN. — shoots sparks

MOM: "EVERY TIME I SMELL ONE OF THOSE THINGS, I THINK THE TV IS BURNING. I DON'T NEED THE HEARTACHE. BESIDES, IT TORMENTS THE DOG."

THE LITTLE RED SCOOTER

MOM: "YOUR COUSIN FREDDIE WENT OVER THE ROCKERY AND BROKE HIS COLLARBONE RIDING ONE OF THOSE."

MODEL FARM SET WITH STEEL BARN AND ONE PLASTIC TREE AND ABOUT 25 ANIMALS

MOM: "THAT'S HOW COME ONE OF NORMA'S KIDS ENDED UP IN THE HOSPITAL. HE WAS SUCKING ON ONE OF THOSE PLASTIC CHICKENS AND HIS BROTHER HIT HIM IN THE BACK AND THAT CHICKEN LODGED IN HIS WINDPIPE. I TELL YOU, IT'S A WONDER HE SURVIVED."

RUBBER TIPPED DART GUN SET.

MOM: "OH NO. I KNOW ALL ABOUT THOSE THINGS. YOU KIDS SUCK ON THE ENDS OF THOSE DARTS TO MAKE THEM STICK BETTER, THEN THERE ARE SPIT RINGS ALL OVER THE WINDOWS AND TV SCREEN. ALL OVER THE WALLS. FORGET IT. BESIDES I READ IN THE PAPER WHERE A BOY PUT HIS EYE OUT WITH A GUN LIKE THAT."

PACESETTER "CONVERTIBLE" WITH BALL BEARING PEDAL DRIVE

MOM: "THOSE THINGS ARE GREAT UNTIL YOU GO DOWN A STEEP HILL. THEN THOSE PEDALS WILL RIP YOUR LEGS OFF."

"MUSICAL JACK-IN-THE-BOX"
PLAYS "POP GOES THE WEASEL"

MOM: I'M TELLING YOU, ONCE I GET THAT SONG IN MY HEAD I CAN'T GET IT OUT AND I JUST HEAR IT FASTER AND FASTER UNTIL I FEEL LIKE I'M IN AN INSANE ASYLUM. THAT TOY SHOULD BE AGAINST THE LAW. AND DON'T EVER LET ME CATCH YOU SINGING IT."

MAYBONNE'S ROOM

By LYNDA MUDDY HEADED BARRY © 1987

THE MAIN TEENAGER OF MY LIFE WAS MY COUSIN MARLYS'S SISTER, MAYBONNE, WHOSE NERVES WE GOT ON. SHE WOULD ALWAYS LEAN DOWN ABOUT ONE INCH FROM YOUR FACE AND YELL "BUG OFF, MAN!" WHEN YOU FOLLOWED HER AROUND. BUT THIS NEVER STOPPED HER FROM BEING MY IDOL.

KNOCK IT OFF OR I'LL CREAM YA!

"KNOCK IT OFF OR I'LL CREAM YA"!

HAIR STYLE
WHITE GLASSES
PIERCED EARS
BRA STRAP
FROSTED LIPSTICK
BEADS
BELT

THE ONE THING WE WERE NEVER SUPPOSED TO DO WAS GO IN HER BEDROOM WHICH WE DID ANYWAY. IT WAS WORTH HAVING HER YELL AT US, FOR IT WAS THE COOLEST PLACE I EVER SAW. HOW COME TEENAGERS CAN DECORATE EVERYTHING SO PERFECT?

GUM WRAPPER CHAIN THAT WENT ALL AROUND THE WHOLE ROOM
MIRROR WITH HER FAVORITE SAYINGS
WRITTEN LIPSTICK
COOL SAILOR HAT
TINY DRIED FLOWERS
"SOLID!" "TUFF!" "MOD" "GO-GO" "WICKED" "BOLD 'N' BRASSY!"
A MILLION NECKLACES
POSTER OUT OF 'TEEN MAGAZINE
STATIONERY THAT SMELLS LIKE STRAWBERRIES
OP-ART JEWLERY BOX
OP-ART POSTER
GO-GO RING COLLECTION
BRIGHT GREEN FLOWERED CONTACT PAPER
MAYBELLINE EVERYTHING
WHITE GO-GO BOOTS
DRAWER FULL OF UNDERWEAR
DRAWER FULL OF NOTES FROM GIRLFRIENDS
DRAWER FULL OF SOCKS
DRAWER FULL OF "TOMISINA" COLLECTION
PINK GO-GO BOOTS

SHE HAD HER OWN RADIO AND WE WOULD SPY ON HER ACTING OUT SONGS IN FRONT OF THE MIRROR. IF A SAD SONG CAME ON SHE'D GET RIGHT UP CLOSE TO THE MIRROR AND TRY TO SEE HOW SHE LOOKED WHEN SHE WAS CRYING. OTHER TIMES SHE'D PULL HER SHIRT UP AND STARE AT HER BRA FOR NO REASON.

WHY'S SHE KEEP ON DOIN' THAT?
CUZ SHE THINKS SHE'S COOL BUT SHE'S NOTHING BUT A FOOL
LOOKING THROUGH A CRACK IN THE DOOR
SHE THINKS SHE'S SMART BUT SHE'S NOTHING BUT A FART

ABOUT THE BEST NIGHT OF MY LIFE WAS WHEN MAYBONNE WAS GROUNDED FOR A WEEK SO WE WERE HER ONLY CHOICE OF WHO TO HANG AROUND WITH. ONE NIGHT SHE EVEN LET US SLEEP IN HER ROOM. SHE TAUGHT US THE GREAT DANCE OF "THE HITCHHIKER" AND WE ALL THREE DID IT IN A LINE IN FRONT OF THE MIRROR. AND I WILL NEVER FORGET THAT NIGHT BECAUSE MAYBONNE KEPT THE RADIO ON AND IT WAS THE FIRST TIME I EVER HEARD MUSIC WHEN YOU'RE JUST LYING THERE WITH YOUR COUSINS IN THE PITCH DARK.

A-HEY HEY HEY--- THAT'S WHAT I SAY.... I CAN'T GET NO..... A-NO-NO-NO..... A-HEY-HEY-HEY NO SA-TIS-FAC-TION....

BATON

BY LYNDA SHILLY SHALLY BARRY © 1987

UP AT THE SCHOOL, ON SATURDAY MORNINGS IN THE SUMMER WAS <u>BATON LESSONS</u> TAUGHT BY TWO GLAMOROUS TEENAGERS, LILA AND BARB, OUR PERFECT IDOLS, THE MOST PERFECT GIRLS IN THE WORLD, OUR TOTAL HEROES.

HAIR SPRAY
MAKE-UP
NAIL POLISH
LIP-STICK
RATTED
DEVELOPED
TERRIFIC UNIFORMS
SPARKLING
SHINING
PANTY HOSE
HOT PINK FRINGE
GLOWING
LIME GREEN SEQUINS

1

TO BE IN THE CLASS, YOU HAD TO GET YOUR BATON FROM THE PAY 'N' SAVE AT THE BOTTOM OF THE HILL, WHERE THEY HAD BEEN ESPECIALLY ORDERED. FROM THE SECOND YOU GOT IT, YOU FELT TOTALLY DIFFERENT.

THANK YOU THANK YOU LADIES AND GENTLEMEN

AND NOW HERE'S LILA!!

NO MAN I'M BARB

CAN'T YOU EVEN REMEMBER WHO'S BARB?

OH YEAH I MEAN "BARB"

SAY IT AGAIN. THAT DIDN'T COUNT.

SEARS BATHING SUIT

SEARS BATHING SUIT

2

THERE WAS SOMETHING ABOUT EVEN <u>HOLDING</u> A BATON THAT COULD GIVE YOU THE MYSTERIOUS EXCITED FEELING. ALMOST LIKE IF YOU JUST HELD IT LONG ENOUGH YOU WOULD AUTOMATICALLY GROW INTO A GORGEOUS BEAUTY PAGEANT WINNER, FULLY DEVELOPED.

3

IN THE MEANTIME, WHAT YOU DID WITH IT, WAS THROW IT UP IN THE AIR AS HIGH AS YOU COULD, TWIRL AROUND, THEN TRY NOT TO MOVE WHEN IT LANDED ON YOU. WE GOT HIT ABOUT A MILLION TIMES BUT IN OUR OPINION IT WAS WORTH IT.

THIS ONE HARDLY EVEN HURTS. DOES YOURS HURT?

HECK NO!

WHY SHOULD IT HURT?

NO REASON.

X

25

BIKES

By LYNDA HIPPY-MAN BARRY © 1 9 8 7

THIS IS A STORY ABOUT OUR BIKES. LIKE MY FIRST ONE, ASSEMBLY NOT INCLUDED, WITH TRAINING WHEELS, FROM SEARS. IF YOU HAVE TRAINING WHEELS EVERYONE WILL YELL "BABY" AT YOU, SO BETTER GO AHEAD AND TAKE THEM OFF AND JUST MAKE SURE YOU'RE BY SOME BUSHES WHEN YOU START TO WIPE OUT.

WHERE YOU ARE NOT SUPPOSED TO RIDE YOUR FRIENDS.

HORN

STREAMERS

REFLECTOR

THIS MEANS IT'S A BOY'S BIKE

"BABY" WHEELS

THE "JR. ROADMASTER"

1

THE NEXT BIKE, ME AND MY BROTHER HAD TO SHARE. A SEARS STINGRAY "SPYDER" ALL GOLD WITH BUTTERFLY HANDLEBARS, A LEOPARD SKIN BANANA SEAT AND A GIANT SISSY BAR. WE PUT TONY THE TIGER HANDLES ON IT AND ABOUT A HUNDRED CLOTHESPINS WITH PLAYING CARDS ON THE WHEELS TO MAKE IT SOUND LIKE A ACTUAL DRAGSTER. YOU COULD TELL IT WAS THE BEST BIKE IN THE WORLD JUST BY LOOKING AT IT.

HEY MAN, POP A WHEELIE!

NOW YOU CAN RIDE SOMEONE PERFECT

GEAR SHIFT KNOB

BIG DADDY ROTH STICKERS

KUSTOM FENDERS

TWO CURB JUMPER TIRES

GOLD REFLECTORS ON PEDALS

2

OUR THING TO DO WAS GO UP THIS ONE HILL AFTER DARK WITH OUR BIKES AND TWO POP CANS WHICH YOU STEPPED ON SIDEWAYS REALLY HARD SO THEY MOLDED TO THE BACK OF YOUR SHOES. THEN EVERYBODY GETS IN A LINE AND WHEN THE GUY AT THE BOTTOM YELLS "NO CARS!" YOU TAKE OFF DRAGGING THOSE CANS ON THE STREET AND IT MAKES TERRIFIC SPARKS FLYING ALL OVER. WE CALLED THIS "THE TORCH-LIGHT PARADE."

TIMES!! MY CAN IS COMING OFF. YELL FOR HIM TO HANG ON A SEC.

OK?!

NO CARS!!

3

OF COURSE SOMETIMES YOU JUST DON'T LISTEN TO ADVICE ON GOOD BIKE SAFETY ABOUT "DON'T RIDE YOUR FRIENDS DOWN THAT ONE PERFECT HILL THAT GOES TO THE A+P WITH NO BRAKES." THE ONLY LAW WE HAD ABOUT WIPING OUT WAS AFTER YOU WIPED OUT, NO MATTER HOW MUCH IT HURT, YOU HAD TO YELL "RUPTURE!" FIRST, WHICH WOULD USUALLY MAKE YOU START LAUGHING AT THE SAME TIME YOU WERE CRYING BECAUSE YOU'RE BLEEDING AND MAN LOOK HOW WRECKED-UP YOUR BIKE IS.

BIKE UPSIDE DOWN WITH WHEEL STILL SPINNING

RUPTURE!

RUPTURE!

RUPTURE!

OW

DANG!

4

26

LUNCH

BY LYNDA HIP HUGGER BARRY © 1987

ONE THING ABOUT OUR AUNT. SHE MADE THE WORST SANDWICHES IN THE UNIVERSE. HER IDEA OF A SANDWICH WAS A PIECE OF BOLOGNA ON A PIECE OF BREAD, THEN A HUNK OF COLD MARGARINE IN THE MIDDLE, THEN SMASH THE OTHER PIECE OF BREAD ON TOP. WHEN YOU BITE A WAD OF COLD MARGARINE YOU CANNOT FORGET IT FOR ABOUT TWO HOURS.

DAMN IT! NOW WHERE'S THEM SANDWICH BAGS?!

ONE FOR MARLYS

ONE FOR FREDDY

WON BREA

BOLOGNA

CROCK OF MARGE

MARLYS AND FREDDY HAD TO LUG THESE TERRIBLE SANDWICHES OUT OF PAPER BAGS IN THE LUNCHROOM AND BE SITTING BY THIS ONE GIRL, DELORES, WHO HAD THE GORGEOUS BLACK VINYL BARBIE LUNCHBOX AND INSIDE WERE THE MOST PERFECT SANDWICHES YOU EVER SAW, POTATO CHIPS IN SARAN WRAP, BOTH TWINKIES, A THERMOS FULL OF CHOCOLATE MILK, A NAPKIN WITH ANIMALS ON IT AND A CHOCKS VITAMIN IN A TINY BOX. WELL IT WOULD KILL YOU TO SEE IT ALL, ESPECIALLY IF YOU WERE MARLYS.

FLOWERED HEADBAND

TRADE YA.

MILK

ME AND MY BROTHER GOT THE HOT LUNCHES AND MARLYS AND FREDDY WOULD COME AROUND TRYING TO TRADE THOSE LUMPY SANDWICHES FOR SOME OF OUR MEAT BLANKET. WE ALWAYS SHARED BECAUSE THEY'RE OUR COUSINS, BUT WE NEVER TRADED. YOU COULDN'T EVEN FAKE EAT A SANDWICH LIKE THAT.

THAT DELORES THINKS SHE'S SO BIG JUST 'CAUSE HER LUNCH PAIL LOOKS LIKE A PURSE FROM FRANCE.

SHE WOULDN'T EVEN TRADE ME FOR ONE POTATO CHIP.

FORGET HER.

CHEAP.

MILK

LATER, MARLYS ALWAYS SAID THAT IT WAS PARTLY BECAUSE OF THOSE SANDWICHES THAT HER WHOLE LIFE WAS WRECKED UNTIL JR. HIGH SCHOOL. AND YOU KNOW, I HAVE TO AGREE WITH HER.

HOLY BALLS! THEY FORGOT THEIR DAMN LUNCHES AGAIN.

Marlys M. Room 6

Freddy M. Room 2

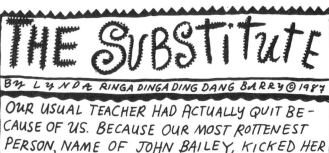

THE SuBStitute

By LYNDA Ringa Ding a Ding Dang BaRRy © 1987

OUR USUAL TEACHER HAD ACTUALLY QUIT BE-
CAUSE OF US. BECAUSE OUR MOST ROTTENEST
PERSON, NAME OF JOHN BAILEY, KICKED HER
LEGS AND YELLED "YOU'RE NOT THE BOSS OF
ME!" MISS ANASLY STARTED CRYING AND
WALKED OUT. THEN WE HEARD SHE HAD TO
MOVE TO NORTH DAKOTA WHERE CHILDREN
HAVE BETTER RESPECT.

I AM MISS BEVENS,

YOUR SUBSTITUTE.

MISS BEVENS WAS OUR MAIN PUNISHMENT
FOR BEING SUCH A AWFUL CLASS. SHE HAD
THIS CRUSTY PITCH PIPE WHICH SHE WOULD
BLOW, THEN MAKE US SING THE WORST
SONGS YOU EVER HEARD IN YOUR LIFE.
ALSO SHE HAD A BIG POINTY BOSOM AND
FAKE TEETH THAT FLIPPED AROUND.

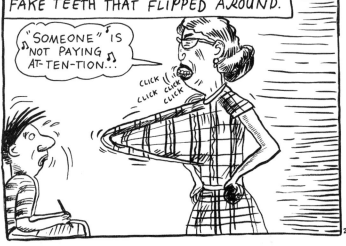

"SOMEONE" IS NOT PAYING AT-TEN-TION...

CLICK CLICK CLICK CLICK CLICK

SHE ALSO HAD A SPECIAL SMELL, A
PERFUME SMELL THAT PRACTICALLY CHOKED
YOUR HEAD OFF WHEN SHE WAS BY YOU.
AND SHE DIDN'T EVEN CARE IF YOU SAW
HER EAT. DURING A MATH TEST WE SAW HER
TRY TO EAT A CHICKEN LEG. EVERYONE
GOT AT LEAST MINUS 8 ON THAT MATH
TEST.

ON A FRIDAY MISS BEVENS TOLD US THE
SCHOOL HAD GOT US A PERMANENT TEACHER,
SO THIS WAS HER LAST DAY. SHE ASKED
US FOR A SPECIAL FAVOR WHICH WAS TO
SING HER HER FAVORITE SONG OF "JOHN
BROWN'S BODY LIES A-MOULDERING IN THE
GRAVE." WE STOOD UP AND SANG IT AND IF
WE HATED HER SO MUCH HOW COME A LOT
OF US STARTED CRYING?

READY? HERE'S OUR NOTE...

OTHER PLANETS

BY LYNDA BARRY ~~~~~ ©1987

EVERYONE IN OUR CLASS LOVED the Solar System. ESPECIALLY DRAWING IT. IT WAS SO PERFECTLY GORGEOUS.

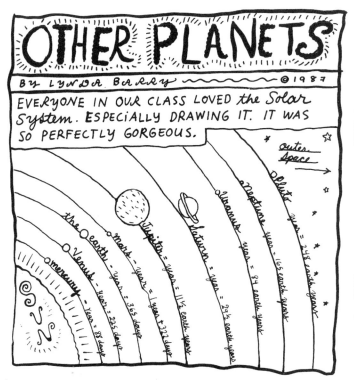

ONE OF THE MAIN OBJECTS WAS TO GET THE NUMBER OF MOONS RIGHT FOR EACH PLANET. WE COULDN'T HELP FEELING GYPPED BY HOW EARTH ONLY GETS ONE. JUPITER GETS SOMETHING LIKE ELEVEN MOONS AND NO ONE EVEN USES THEM.

Darla Martles
May 3   Extra Credit Report
The Moons of the Planets
1. Mercury O (0) no moons
2. Venus O (0) no moons
3. Earth O° (1) one moon
4. Mars O°° (2) two moons
5. Jupiter O (11) eleven moons
6. Saturn (9) nine moons
7. Uranus O (4) four moons
8. Neptune O° (1) one moon
9. Pluto o (0) no moons
Total of Moons = 28 moons

OF COURSE EVERYONE'S FAVORITE PLANET WAS SATURN BECAUSE IT TRULY LOOKED LIKE THE WORLD OF OUTER SPACE. IT WAS THE HARDEST PLANET TO DRAW ALTHOUGH A COUPLE PEOPLE WERE EXPERTS AT IT.

Darla Martles and Howard Grimes. The world's best drawers of Saturn

The Planet of SATURN

SATURN OUR 6TH PLANET

FOR THE ASSEMBLY OUR CLASS GOT TO ACT OUT THE SOLAR SYSTEM FOR THE REST OF THE SCHOOL. ONE GIRL CRIED BECAUSE ALL SHE GOT TO BE WAS A DISTANT STAR AND TWO BOYS GOT INTO A FIGHT OVER WHO GOT TO BE SATURN AND ONE GOT A BLOODY NOSE.

HEADS DOWN, CLASS. I'M ASHAMED OF YOUR BEHAVIOR THIS AFTERNOON.

IF OUR SOLAR SYSTEM BEHAVED THE WAY YOU DID TODAY WE'D ALL BE IN BIG TROUBLE.

YOUR HOLIDAY PROJECT

BY LYNDA BARRY © 1987

HOW TO MAKE A PERFECT PICTURE OF A TURKEY BY MARLYS
FOR THANKSGIVING

FIRST YOU JUST TRACE YOUR HAND. IT DON'T EVEN MATTER WHICH ONE. GO SLOW OR YOU'LL MESS UP. THIS IS NOT A RACE.

WHAT YOU CAN USE TO DRAW WITH:

PENCIL
PEN
CRAYON
EL MARKO

WHAT YOU CANNOT USE

A DYMO MARKER

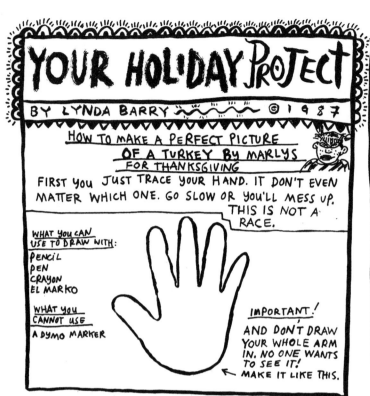

IMPORTANT!
AND DON'T DRAW YOUR WHOLE ARM IN. NO ONE WANTS TO SEE IT!
← MAKE IT LIKE THIS.

THEN PUT ON SOME LEGS. LIKE A Y UPSIDE DOWN WITH A THING IN IT. DON'T MAKE THEM TOO LONG OR THEY WILL LOOK STUPID. GO AHEAD AND PUT ON THE BEAK LIKE A SIDEWAYS V. PUT IN THE NOSE HOLE. THEN DRAW THE RED RUBBER THING HANGING FROM THEIR HEAD.

RIGHT HERE'S THE HEAD PART

THIS IS TOTALLY WRONG ↓

DRAW A LINE IN THE BEAK

YOU CAN DECORATE THIS WITH DOTS OR WHATEVER

MAKE THEM SHORT LEGS
YOU CAN PUT ON TOENAILS

THEN THE EYE BUT DON'T GO PUTTING ON EYELASHES. AND DON'T PUT IT SMOKING A CIGARETTE LIKE MY COUSIN ARNOLD DID OR THE TEACHER WON'T PUT IT UP. TO MAKE IT REALISTIC DECORATE THE FINGERS TO BE FEATHERS.

USE YOUR IMAGINATION THIS IS THE HARDEST PART TO GET RIGHT →

NO SMOKING!

FOR EXTRA CREDIT YOU CAN PUT A WING IN IF YOU ARE GOOD AT ART. IF YOU ARE TALENTED. IF YOU ARE NOT YOU PROBABLY ARE GOING TO WRECK IT UP.

PERSONALLY I LIKE TO PUT ON A LITTLE HAT. THAT'S WHY I GET AN (A+) BUT IF YOU DO IT THAT'S COPYING.

THIS IS A PERFECT DECORATION →

WHERE YOU CAN PUT THIS UP:

AT SCHOOL
THE LUNCHROOM
THE OFFICE
THE HALLS
ON THE DOOR
OVER THE CHALKBOARD

AT HOME
THE KITCHEN
THE FRONT ROOM
THE BEDROOM
THE FRONT DOOR

WINTER MARLYS

HOLIDAY BAZAAR

BY LYNDA BARRY ©87

ON THE FREEZING MORNING OF THE SCHOOL'S HOLIDAY BAZAAR, EVERYONE COMES TO THE GYM CARRYING A TRAY OF SOMETHING THEIR MOM MADE WRAPPED IN TINFOIL, WAX PAPER, OR MAGIC CLING WRAP. WALK CAREFUL BECAUSE IF YOU DROP IT: THE END.

IF I DROP THIS IT'S YOUR FAULT ARNOLD

FLAKE OFF

IT'S YOUR FAULT FOR WALKING IN FRONT OF ME.

THE TEACHER'S HELPERS POINT YOU TO THE RIGHT TABLE DEPENDING ON WHAT YOU BROUGHT. THERE'S A LOT OF COOKIES, ALL KINDS: NORMAL ONES LIKE OATMEAL, GRANDMA ONES LIKE "MOLASSES JINGLES," GORGEOUSLY DECORATED CHRISTMAS ONES YOU FEEL BAD FOR EVEN EATING, AND KINDS YOU NEVER EVEN HEARD OF BEFORE LIKE "YULA MYSTERY BALLS" WHICH LOOK LIKE DIRT CLODS.

THERE'S A LOT OF CUPCAKES, ALL COLORS OF FROSTING. THE BEST ONES HAVE THE LITTLE SILVER METAL BALL DECORATIONS THAT WHEN YOU BITE THEM, YOUR TEETH FEEL LIKE CRACKING. THE SADDEST ARE THE ONES WHERE THE FROSTING GOT YANKED OFF BY THE MAGIC CLING WRAP. THEY BETTER PUT THOSE ON SALE HALF PRICE.

WHAT ARE YOU GOING TO DO WITH THAT FROSTING THAT JUST CAME OFF? I'LL TAKE IT TO THE GARBAGE FOR YOU, OK? OK? HUH?

YOU HAVE TO WAIT UNTIL TONIGHT AFTER THE PAGEANT TO BUY ANYTHING SO QUIT WASTING TIME BY PUTTING ON DIBS. TEACHER'S HELPERS DON'T TAKE NO DIBS. AND WHAT'S OUR OPINION OF WHAT'S GOING TO JUST SIT THERE, NO BUYERS? THE PRUNE-FILLED YAM SQUARES, ICE BOX BARLEY LOGS, CANDIED HOLIDAY FRUIT LOAF, AND THE YULA DIRT CLODS.

HOW MUCH WOULD I HAVE TO PAY YA TO EAT ONE OF THESE?

PSSST

CHRISTMAS PAGEANT

LYNDA BARRY © 1987

"OH HOLY NIGHT THE STARS ARE BRIGHTLY SHINING" MARLYS SINGS OVER AND OVER FOR PRACTICE AS ALL OF US WALK IN THE DARK OVER THE FROZEN MUD IN THE ALLEY ON OUR WAY UP TO THE SCHOOL. ARNOLD JUMPS AND BUSTS ALL THE ICE HE CAN FIND. IT'S THE NIGHT OF THE SCHOOL PAGEANT.

WHEN WE TURN THE CORNER, WE SEE THE WHOLE SCHOOL JUST COMPLETELY LIT UP. CARS ARE DRIVING UP AND DOWN DROPPING PEOPLE OFF AND THERE'S EVERYBODY EVERYWHERE YELLING "HI! HI! HIYA!" ARNOLD SEES HIS FRIEND STEVE AND TAKES OFF RUNNING.

MARLYS AND FREDDY REPORT TO THEIR ROOMS BUT I'M NOT NOTHING IN THE PAGEANT THIS YEAR SO I CAN JUST GO WALKING AROUND THE HALLS NOTICING HOW BEING IN YOUR SCHOOL AT NIGHT MAKES EVERYTHING FEEL LIKE IT'S ON ANOTHER PLANET.

I CLIMB THE STAIRS TO THE 2ND FLOOR AND LOOK OUT THE WINDOW AND SEE THEM SHUT THE DOORS TO THE GYM. OH NO. IT'S STARTING. I RUN DOWN THE HALL, DOWN THE STEPS, DOWN THE HALL AND SKID IN FRONT OF THE BOYS' LAVATORY. NOBODY'S AROUND ANYWHERE. I DARE MYSELF TO GO INSIDE. I OPEN THE DOOR AND SEE THEIR STALLS, THEIR SINKS, THEIR MIRROR. THEN WHO KNOWS WHY I SCREAM "MERRY CHRISTMAS FROM ARNA ARNESON!" AND TEAR OUT OF THERE, OUT OF THE SCHOOL AND ACROSS THE BREEZEWAY INTO THE GYM.

THIS VASE

BY LYNDA BARRY

IT WAS WINDY AND POURING RAIN THE AFTER-NOON OF FRIDAY OUR ART PERIOD. THE HARDEST RAIN YOU EVER SAW. YOU KNOW WHEN YOU SIT THERE AT YOUR DESK AND IT'S LIKE TONS OF BBs ARE JUST POUNDING OFF THE WINDOWS?

WE WERE ON CLAY. THE COIL METHOD. EVERYONE WAS ROLLING OUT THEIR MILLION LITTLE SNAKES CURLING THEM AROUND AND AROUND ON TOP OF EACH OTHER. AND THE RECORD PLAYER WAS GOING. WHAT WAS THAT SONG? THAT ONE ART PERIOD SONG?

EVEN WITH THE LIGHTS ON, OUR ROOM WAS DARK AND ALL THE DESKS WERE GANGED UP TOGETHER AND I KEPT STARING AT MY HANDS ON THE CLAY GOING BACK AND FORTH, BACK AND FORTH LIKE A PURE HYPNOTISER.

I WAS ROLLING THE CLAY WHEN MY TEACHER BENT DOWN AND PUT HER WARM HAND ON MY SHOULDER AND I DIDN'T STOP.
   YOU KNOW HOW SOMETHING CAN FEEL SO PERFECT YOU CAN'T EVEN BLINK?
   THAT WAS THE DAY I MADE THIS VASE FOR YOU.

34

HOME-EC.
with Mrs. Vorice
BY LYNDA BARRY © 1 9 8 7 ...

MRS. VORICE WAS MY FIRST PERIOD TEACHER AND HER SUBJECT WAS THE COOKING PART OF HOME EC. ON THE FIRST DAY SHE PASSED OUT THESE TRIANGLE SCARVES AND TOLD US NOTHING TAKES THE JOY OUT OF A CAREFULLY PREPARED MEAL MORE THAN FINDING A BIG WAD OF HAIR IN IT. SO PLEASE, WEAR YOUR SCARVES.

I CAN THINK OF WAY WORSE THINGS THAN HAIR.

SHHH.

DON'T GET ME IN TROUBLE.

HAIR IS NOTHIN' COMPARED TO WHAT I CAN THINK OF.

OUR FIRST COOKING PROJECT WAS: THE TANGY BREAKFAST SQUARES. THE FIRST STEP WAS MIX INSTANT TANG WITH 3 TBSP. OF PEANUT BUTTER, QUAKER OATS, A RAW EGG, AND SOME RAISINS. SOME GIRLS AUTOMATICALLY STARTED COUGHING FROM ALL THE TANG POWDER FLOATING IN THE AIR. IT WAS WORSE THAN POWDER BUBBLE BATH.

I DON'T GET HOW THIS IS EVEN SPOSTO MIX TOGETHER.

COME ON! HOLD THE BOWL BETTER!

I'M HOLDIN' IT PERFECT. YOU JUST DON'T KNOW HOW TO STIR ANYTHING DECENT.

THEN, WHILE YOUR PARTNER IS PREHEATING THE OVEN AND GREASING THE COOKIE SHEET, YOU CUT THE CRUSTS OFF SOME BREAD. MY PARTNER WAS MARLYS WHO DIDN'T LISTEN WHEN MRS. VORICE SAID ALWAYS CHECK INSIDE THE OVEN BEFORE YOU TURN IT ON. IT'S MAINLY BECAUSE OF THAT OUR TANGY BREAKFAST SQUARES MAINLY HAD THE FLAVOR OF A BURNT UP RUBBER ERASER.

HOW WAS I SUPPOSED TO KNOW, MAN?

JUST AS IMPORTANT AS THE FLAVOR IS THE PRESENTATION OF THE FOOD. MRS. VORICE SAID WE MUST ALWAYS STRIVE TO MAKE OUR MEALS LOOK ATTRACTIVELY BEAUTIFUL. BUT YOU KNOW WITH TANGY BREAKFAST SQUARES I JUST DON'T THINK THERE'S ANY WAY.

I JUST DON'T THINK THAT CUTTING THEM UP INTO THE SHAPE OF THE CROSS IS REALLY GONNA HELP.

YOU WATCH. NO ONE GIVES ANYTHING LESS THAN A B- TO THE SHAPE OF THE CROSS.

BOOK REPORT

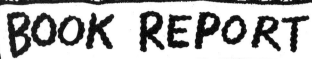

By Lynda Barry © 1987

Book Title: What is a Rodent?
Author: Alita Wescott and Carlotta Scott
Copyright: 1962   Pages: 48

by Freddie Room 2

The book tells What is a rodent? They are mammals. There are a lot of kinds. They all want to chew up things.

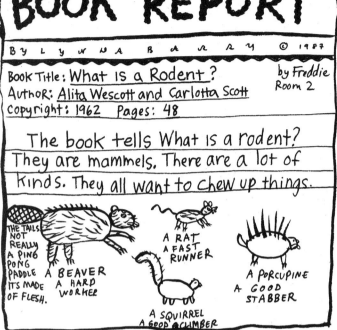

THE TAIL'S NOT REALLY A PING PONG PADDLE ITS MADE OF FLESH.

A BEAVER A HARD WORKER

A RAT A FAST RUNNER

A SQUIRREL A GOOD CLIMBER

A PORCUPINE A GOOD STABBER

The reason is the teeth keep on growing. They have to chew their teeth down or they'll grow and take over their heads.

What would happen if a rodent forgot to chew.

BOOHOO

Oh No not again

IS IT HARMFUL TO MAN OR A HELPER?

harmful	Helpful
① Can eat the crops.	① We can make a fur coat
② Can kill a tree	② Beavers can build a dam
③ Can run in the grocery store	③ We can do science experiments on them

THIS IS GOOD!

HEY STOP IT

MY DARLING ITS BEAUTIFUL

TIMBER

AHHHHH

GOOD Boy

IM NOT BUYING NO MORE FOOD HERE AGAIN!

YOU STILL GOT NINE MORE CIGARETTES TO GO

What was the author trying to say? That rodents are exciting.

The End

DRAWING FOR EXTRA CREDIT. This is not a trace

Theresa WATFORD

LYNDA BARRY ©1987

YOU KNOW WHO I MEAN WHEN I SAY THERESA WATFORD, DON'T YOU? THE SISTER OF KENNY WATFORD? THE ONE THAT LIVES AT THAT GREEN HOUSE ON 22ND WITH THE REFRIGERATOR IN THE YARD? ALL SHE EVER DOES AT RECESS IS BOUNCE ON THE FENCE, BOUNCE ON THE FENCE, BOUNCE ON THE FENCE.

EVERY YEAR SINCE FIRST GRADE THAT IS HER WHOLE LIFE. SHE'S OUR WORST PARTICIPATOR. MY COUSIN ARNA TRIES AND TRIES TO MAKE FRIENDS WITH THERESA JUST LIKE SHE TRIES TO MAKE FRIENDS WITH ALL THE DOGS SHE SEES, ESPECIALLY THE ONES THAT ARE CHAINED UP. WELL IT'S BECAUSE ARNA'S GOAL IN LIFE IS TO ACTUALLY IMPRESS JESUS.

SO OK. IT'S FIRST RECESS, FIRST DAY OF SCHOOL AND THERE GOES THERESA TO THE FENCE AND BOUNCE BOUNCE BOUNCE, YOU KNOW, AND THERE GOES MY COUSIN ARNA WALKING VERY SLOW, THEN SHE'S TALKING TO THERESA, STANDING BACK FAR SO THE SPIT WON'T GET ON HER BECAUSE I FORGOT TO TELL YOU, THERESA SPITS. BUT THE ONLY ONE SHE EVER SPITS AT IS ARNA. IF SHE SPIT AT ME, I'D PUSH HER OVER, I'LL TELL YOU THAT MUCH.

AND LIKE EVERY YEAR, WE'RE STANDING THERE WITH THE BALL, ME, DIANE AND BARBARA, WAITING FOR THERESA TO HURRY UP AND SPIT SO THAT ARNA CAN GIVE UP AND COME BACK AND PLAY FOUR SQUARE, BUT THIS YEAR THERESA WATFORD WON'T SPIT. SHE WON'T. AND IF SHE DOESN'T SPIT, ARNA'S GOING TO GET STUCK BEING HER FRIEND AND SHE'LL BE RUINED. AND I'M RUINED BECAUSE I'M HER COUSIN AND THEN DIANE AND BARBARA-- SPIT, THERESA! SPIT OR I SWEAR TO GOD I'LL CREAM YOU!!

HI THERESA WATFORD.

HI.

HI AND EVERYTHING.

HI.

HI.

BEAN PLANTS

BY LYNDA BARRY ©1987

ALL YOU NEED FOR LEARNING ABOUT THE PLANT KINGDOM IS: YOUR MILK CARTON THAT YOU SAVED FROM LUNCH, SOME DIRT, SOME WATER, SOME BEANS, SOME SARAN WRAP, SOME RUBBER BANDS AND YOUR TEACHER MRS. BROGAN YELLING AT YOU TO NOT GOOF UP IN ANY WAY.

COVER IT WITH THE SARAN WRAP TO KEEP IT WARM AND THE WONDER OF EVAPORATION.

REMEMBER: THESE ARE THE EARTH'S NATURAL RESOURCES SO BE RESPONSIBLE CITIZENS AND DON'T MAKE A MESS. MR. BEAN IS DEPENDING ON YOU TODAY FOR A GOOD HOME.

YOU WILL HAVE A GREAT FEELING WHEN YOUR BEAN STARTS TO GROW. YOU WILL HAVE TO SHARPEN YOUR PENCIL A LOT JUST FOR AN EXCUSE TO PASS BY IT.

ARNA! THE PENCIL SHARPENER IS NOT A TOY.

SOMEONE GOT THE IDEA TO NAME THEIR BEAN PLANT AND PRETTY SOON EVERYONE DID IT.

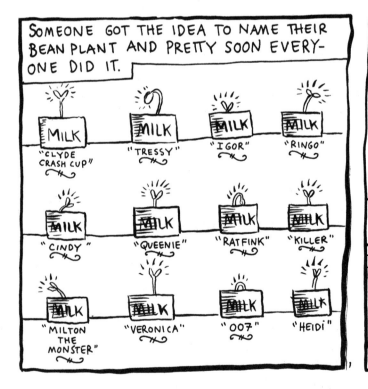

"CLYDE CRASH CUP"

"TRESSY"

"IGOR"

"RINGO"

"CINDY"

"QUEENIE"

"RATFINK"

"KILLER"

"MILTON THE MONSTER"

"VERONICA"

"007"

"HEIDI"

FINALLY ON THE LAST DAY OF SCHOOL YOU GET TO TAKE YOUR BEAN PLANT HOME. AFTER SHE GAVE US ALL OUR PLANTS, MRS. BROGAN STOOD AT THE FRONT OF THE ROOM TO SAY GOODBYE. SHE TOLD US WE WERE A LOVELY CLASS AND SHE WILL MISS US VERY MUCH. AND SHE STARTED TO CRY WHEN SHE TOLD US TO BE SURE TO REMEMBER TO WATER OUR BEANS.

RRRIIINNGGGGG

IF YOU WANT TO BUY CANDY

BY LYNDA BARRY © 1987

NUMBER ONE, BUY YOUR CANDY AT FRED'S NOT AT BLUMA'S. BLUMA'S GOTS THE CANDY IN A GLASS CASE AND HE WON'T LET YOU EVEN TOUCH IT UNTIL YOU PAY. EVERYBODY JUST HATES BLUMA. HIS STORE SMELLS LIKE LYSOL.

YOU TAKE TOO LONG! OUTSIDE UNTIL YOU KNOW WHAT YOU WANT!

MAN I'M JUST LOOKING! CAN'T A GUY EVEN LOOK?

FRED'S GOTS THE GOOD CANDY AND YOU CAN PICK IT UP AND PUT IT BACK AND TAKE YOUR TIME MAKING YOUR DECISIONS. BLUMA'S GOTS OLD CHOCOLATE SANTAS WAY UNTIL JULY 4TH AND HE DON'T EVEN REDUCE THE PRICE. BLUMA WEARS A HAIRNET. A MAN WEARS A HAIRNET.

YOU KIDS!

YOU THINK I AM JOKING YOU?! OUT! OUT! OUT!

HAIR IN EARS

YOU WANT ME TO BOCKLE YOUR HEAD!?

ALSO BLUMA RUNS OUTSIDE AFTER YOU YELLING WHERE DO THE WRAPPERS GO! WHERE DO THE WRAPPERS GO! FRED JUST SITS THERE SMOKING. FRED DON'T HARDLY MOVE FOR NOTHING NOT EVEN IF YOUR BIKE BASHES AGAINST HIS WINDOW WHEN YOU LEAN IT DOWN. BUT BLUMA DON'T LET NO BIKES EVEN TOUCH HIS STORE. HE'LL HIT YOU WITH THE FLY SWATTER, HE DON'T CARE.

FRED

FRED HOW MUCH FOR THESE MONSTER CARDS

10¢

CREEPY MONSTER

BLUMA

NO BIKES!

NO BIKES!

NO BIKES!

WHO MADE THIS GARBAGE!

THE ONLY THING ABOUT FRED'S IS THAT IT CAN MAKE YOU SORT OF SAD BECAUSE OF THE WAY HE NEVER TALKS. AT LEAST WITH BLUMA HE'LL CHASE AFTER YOU AND YOU GET TO SEE HIS GIANT BUTT AND LEGS. NO ONE IN THE WORLD HAS EVER SEEN THE LEGS OF FRED. OUR MOM SAYS HE DON'T TALK BECAUSE OF HIS WIFE LEFT HIM. WHAT A DUMB STUPID LADY.

HI FRED! HOW ARE YOU FRED. HI.

HI FRED.

HI AND EVERYTHING

HI FRED

FOUND A PEANUT

BY LYNDA BARRY ©1987

THAT SONG, "FOUND A PEANUT" WAS ABOUT OUR NUMBER ONE SONG. IT WAS A FUN SONG TO SING.

OK NOW WATCH MY MAGIC HAND WHILE I SING SO YOU CAN FOLLOW THE NOTES.

NO MAN, JUST TELL ME THE PART THAT GOES AFTER "CRACKED IT OPEN, IT WAS ROTTEN."

FIRST WATCH MY MAGIC HAND.

FORGET IT, MAN. WATCH MY MAGIC BUTT.

I'M TELLIN'!

MARLYS MADE A BIG DEAL ABOUT HOW SHE KNEW ALL THE WORDS. WE WANTED HER TO TELL US BUT WE DIDN'T WANT TO HAVE TO WATCH HER STAND ON A CHAIR DOING THAT MAGIC HAND THING WHICH SHE LEARNED FROM WATCHING MISS DORIS ON SCHOOL TV THE GOAL OF MARLYS'S LIFE WAS TO BE THE STAR OF HER OWN SHOW LIKE ON MISS DORIS TIME.

MARLYS PARTICIPATING WITH HER IDOL MISS DORIS

MAGIC HAND

(CLOSE UP OF MISS DORIS ON TV)

MY HOME'S IN MONTANA, I WEAR A BANDANA

2

THE WAY WE FINALLY ENDED UP KNOWING THE WORDS WAS BY SNEAKING LOOKS THROUGH THE CRACK IN THE DOOR, SEEING MARLYS DO THE WHOLE MISS DORIS SHOW BY STANDING ON THE TOILET AND WATCHING HERSELF IN THE MIRROR. AFTER A WHILE WE DIDN'T EVEN CARE ABOUT THE SONG "FOUND A PEANUT" ALTHOUGH IT WAS MARLYS'S SPECIALTY. TURNS OUT WE JUST LIKED WATCHING MARLYS. SHE SHOULD GO IN A TALENT SHOW.

GOOD MORNING BOYS AND GIRLS! I'M SO GLAD YOU'RE HERE TODAY! LET'S SING "I'M A LITTLE TEA POT" SHALL WE? GOOD. WATCH MY MAGIC HAND! REMEMBER DON'T STICK YOUR BOTTOMS OUT SO MUCH OR YOU'LL LOOK LIKE A STUPID IDIOT, OK? NO, WAIT A SEC. LET'S SING "DRILL YE TARRIERS DRILL." NO, LET'S DO "FOUND A PEANUT." IS EVERYBODY READY? MR. PITCHPIPE, WILL YOU GIVE US OUR NOTE? ONE TWO THREE.

3

WE SECRETLY KNEW THAT MARLYS SECRETLY KNEW WE WERE WATCHING BUT NOBODY EVER SAID NOTHING UNTIL THE TIME MARLYS TRIED TO DO THAT GO-GO DANCING SONG AND FELL OFF THE TOILET AND THE SEAT CAME FLYING OFF AND SHE SPRAINED HER MAGIC ARM AND GOT SOME MAGIC BRUISES. HER MOM CAME RUNNING IN AND SPANKED EVERY ONE OF US AND WANTED TO KNOW WHY WE HAD TO LEARN EVERYTHING THE HARD WAY? ESPECIALLY MARLYS.

x

PETS in our LIVES

BY LYNDA BUSHMILLER BARRY © 1987

Part One: REPTILES

WE HAD A COUSIN COME FROM IDAHO ONE TIME BY THE NAME OF MELTON AND HE BROUGHT HIS PET SNAKE CALLED "JOHNNY QUEST THE 2ND." JOHNNY QUEST THE FIRST DIED FROM EATING A WHOLE ROLL OF LIFE SAVERS ACCORDING TO MELTON WHO WAS A MAJOR LIAR.

WE EACH GOT A TURN AT HOLDING JOHNNY QUEST THE 2ND BY THE TAIL AND IF YOU HAVE NEVER HELD A SNAKE BEFORE, WELL, IT IS TOTALLY WORTH IT. THE SAD PART IS THAT ONLY CERTAIN KINDS OF MOMS WILL LET YOU HAVE A SNAKE AND OURS WAS NOT ONE OF THEM.

C'MON YOU GUYS WATCH ME! I WATCHED YOU WHEN YOU HELD HIM!

WATCH ME!

WATCH ME OR I'M TELLIN!

IT TURNED OUT MELTON'S MOM WAS NOT A FRIEND TO SNAKES EITHER AND HAD A FIT WHEN SHE CAUGHT MELTON SHOWING OFF HIS SNAKE AND FOUND OUT SHE DROVE CLEAR FROM IDAHO WITH A SNAKE IN THE CAR. SHE SAID IF THAT SNAKE HAD GOTTEN LOOSE SHE WOULD HAVE DROVE STRAIGHT INTO A TREE AND THEY'D ALL BE DEAD AND HOW WOULD MELTON LIKE THAT FOR A CHANGE?

ANSWER ME!

MELTON HAD TO LET HIS SNAKE GO IN THE STICKERS IN OUR ALLEY AND EVEN THOUGH HE WAS SOMETHING LIKE 13, HE CRIED. HE SAID NOBODY WOULD LIKE HIM ANYMORE WITHOUT THAT SNAKE WHICH WAS TRUE. WITHOUT HIS SNAKE MELTON WAS NOTHING BUT REGULAR. THAT NIGHT WE ALL SNUCK OVER TO THE STICKERS AND MELTON WHISPERED "HERE BOY. HERE JOHNNY." I TOLD HIM I READ WHERE SNAKES CAN'T HEAR, AND HE TURNED AROUND AND SLUGGED ME.

DANG MELTON!

I CAN'T HELP IT IF I KNOW SCIENCE.

Pets in Our Lives

BY LYNDA BARRY © 1987.

PART 2: SOME MORE REPTILES

IT WAS A GREAT DAY THE DAY WE GOT OUR TURTLES AND THEIR GORGEOUS HOME CALLED TURTLE ISLAND. WE GOT THEM AT THE WOOLWORTHS AND IT TOOK A LONG TIME TO PICK OUT THE PERFECT ONES OUT OF ABOUT TEN THOUSAND.

LADY!

THAT'S THE WRONG ONE!

NOT THAT ONE!

THAT'S NOT IT!

THE OTHER ONE!

THEY'RE ALL EXACTLY THE SAME.

1

TURTLE ISLAND WAS A DREAM HOUSE. IT CAME WITH A PLASTIC PALM TREE AND A PLACE TO SWIM AND A PLACE TO JUST GOOF OFF. WE EXPECTED OUR TURTLES TO GOOF OFF A LOT MORE THAN THEY DID THOUGH.

MINE JUST KIND OF MOVED AGAIN.

I WONDER CAN YOU TRAIN THEM.

2

MY BROTHER INVENTED THE GAME CALLED ESCAPE FROM TURTLE ISLAND AND HIS TURTLE NAMED HARRY MOSCOW WAS THE STAR AND MY TURTLE NAMED QUEENIE WAS HIS GLAMOROUS ASSISTANT. ALL IT WAS WAS THEM CRAWLING ON THE KITCHEN FLOOR WHILE MY BROTHER SANG GOLDFINGER.

GOLD FINGA! NUH-NUH-NUH! HE'S THE MAN, THE MAN WITH THE GOLD FINGA! NA-NAH-NA HE'S THE MAN, THE MAN WITH THE GOLD FINGA!

3

OUR TURTLES STAYED AT OUR AUNT SYLVIA'S WHEN WE WENT ON VACATION AND THAT WAS THE END OF OUR TURTLES. OUR MOM TOLD US LATER AUNT SYLVIA NEVER WAS THAT GOOD WITH ANIMALS. YOU WOULD LIKE TO KNOW WHAT HAPPENED TO OUR PETS BUT NO ONE WOULD TELL US. AUNT SYLVIA JUST GAVE US EACH A DOLLAR AND OUR EMPTY TURTLE ISLAND WITH A BIG CRACK IN IT.

YOU JUST WAIT 'TIL SHE GETS A TURTLE, MAN.

X

42

BEDROOMS OF OUR DREAMS

BY LYNDA BARRY © 1987

DREAM BEDROOM OF FREDDIE

SNAKE

MAGIC ROPE LIKE ON JOHNNY QUEST

BUILT IN TV ...

WHOLE WALL OF A REPTILE ZOO BUT THEY CAN ESCAPE ALL THEY WANT

MICRO-SCOPE

TALKING BIRD NAMED ELVIN

BUILT-IN GIANT ANT FARM

PYTHON

GEKKO

DOORS FOR ANIMALS TO COME ON IN

LIVE TRAINED MONKEY I ORDERED FROM A COMIC BOOK

IN OUT

HAMMOCK FOR A BED

HAMSTER

REAL GRASS FOR THE RUG

SPECIAL HATCH

UNDER HERE IS A FIRE POLE TO KITCHEN

TV

P.S. SECRET COMPARTMENTS ARE EVERYWHERE!

DREAM BED ROOM OF ARNOLD

CUSTOM BLOODY EYEBALL WALL-PAPER

POP MACHINE (FREE)

GIANT BUILT-IN TV UP ON CEILING

CANDY MACHINE (FREE)

ROPE LADDER TO ROOF

I-SPY TV SCREEN WHERE YOU CAN WATCH WHAT EVERY-BODY'S DOING EVERYWHERE

DRAWER FULL OF COMICS AND MADS.

DRAWERS FULL OF MONSTER CARD COLLECTIONS ARMY MEN, WEAPONS, MATCHES, GOT A PLAYBOY TOO IN THERE TOO IN CERTAIN ONE

CONTROL PANEL FOR WHOLE ROOM

CLIMB ROPE TO GET ALL THIS

PERISCOPE

WALKIE TALKIES

MY BED: LOOKS LIKE A DRAGSTER, CAN ACTUALLY TAKE OFF PLUS LAY A PATCH.

REAL SMOKE IS COMING OUT

DOOR WITH ELECTRIC SHOCKERS FOR IF PEOPLE COME IN WITHOUT ASKING

2-WAY MIRRORS

LIGHTS COME ON

DIRT CLODS

FLOOR IS OF REAL DIRT!

OPEN THIS HATCH AND RIDE GIANT SLIDE FOR ONE MILE.

IMPORTANT WARNING! THIS ROOM HAS A LOT OF BOOBY TRAPS!

TRAP DOOR

ESCAPE HATCH

2

DREAM BEDROOM OF ARNA

HIGH UP SECRET LIBRARY OF EVERY BOOK IN THE WORLD

TRAPEZE

HIGHEST BED ON EARTH. YOU HAVE TO CLIMB A LADDER TO GET TO IT

INVISI-BLE DOOR TO THE OUTSIDE

MOVIE SCREEN WHERE YOU CAN SEE ANY MOVIE JUST BY THINKING OF IT

STACK OF MAGAZINES YOU CAN CUT UP

DRAWERS OF SISSORS, GLUE, PAINTS, COLORS, SPARKLE PAINTS CONSTRUCTION PAPER

HANGING TV THAT GOES UP + DOWN

SPECIAL PET ELEVATOR

BUILT-IN RECORD PLAYER PLUS 1,001 RECORDS

TRAMPOLINE

REVOLVING DOOR

SWIMMING POOL

3

DREAM BED ROOM OF MARLYS

"MARLYS" WALLPAPER

WHOLE WALL OF BUILT-IN WORLD OF BARBI'S AND ALSO: HER BEST FRIEND A NEW DOLL CALLED "MARLYS"

GOLD DIAMONDS SILVER RUBIES

CLOSET FULL OF BALLERINA DRESSES

THRONE WHERE I SIT WHEN I FEEL LIKE IT

THIS WHOLE WALL IS A BIG MIRROR

BARBI'S BEDROOM

BARBI'S BALCONY

MARLYS BEDROOM

BIG MIRROR

TOTAL STEPS MADE OF PEZ

MY STORE A PAINTING OF ME

BARBI'S DREAM KITCHEN

BARBI'S DREAM HALL

MARLYS' DREAM KITCHEN

MARLYS DREAM GARAGE

MICRO-PHONE

MARLYS PILLOWS

TV RISES OUT OF HERE

RECORD PLAYER RISES OUT OF HERE

PINK FUR BED IN THE SHAPE OF A HEART THAT SPINS AND PLAYS MUSIC. NO ONE EXCEPT ME IS ALLOWED ON IT!

A BUTLER HOLDING A BOWL OF M+M'S CONSTANTLY FULL AND HE ANNOUNCES WHO CAN COME IN.

YES YOUR HIGHNESS MARLYS

WHAT HE ALWAYS SAYS

RED VELVET COVERED STAGE FOR ME TO DO MY SINGING ON

PINK FUR RUG

THE SMELL OF PERFUME IS EVERYWHERE: OH! DE LONDON.

44

MOVING AWAY

By LYNDA SLAMMER DOOR BARRY © 1987

UP THE STREET, ON THE DIRT PART OF THE ROAD, WAS THE HOUSE OF LOUIS CHEEK AND HIS SISTER SANDRA CHEEK. NONE OF US EVER LIKED THEM BECAUSE THEY HAD BAD TEMPERS, SO "BIG DEAL" IS ALL WE THOUGHT WHEN LOUIS TOLD US THEY WERE MOVING AWAY.

AND YOU GUYS WANNA KNOW WHERE WE'RE MOVIN' TO?

HUH?

WE'RE MOVIN' OVER TO DISNEY-LAND.

I'M GONNA LIVE AT DISNEYLAND YOU GUYS.

HOW COME PAPER ALWAYS STICKS TO POPSICLES?

LOUIS YELLED AT US THAT WE WOULD NEVER EVER SEE HIM AGAIN FOR THE REST OF OUR LIVES. HE WAS STANDING ON HIS PORCH WHEN HE YELLED IT AND HE YELLED IT ABOUT NINE HUNDRED THOUSAND TIMES 'TIL HIS MOM'S ARM CAME OUT THE DOOR AND YANKED HIM INSIDE. WE WERE TOTALLY USED TO LOUIS'S YELLING ANYWAY.

WHO EVEN CARES 'CAUSE I HATE ALL YOUR GUTSES ANYWAY!

THE END!

YOU'LL BE SORRY!

I HATE YOU. I'M GLAD I'LL NEVER SEE YOU GUYS AGAIN!

K'MON ARNA MAN! YOUR TURN.

DANG.

ARE YOU PLAYING?

SHOVE OVER ARNA. WHAT A HOG.

I WANT TO TELL YOU THAT NONE OF US EVEN KNEW WHAT MOVING AWAY WAS UNTIL WE ALL WALKED OVER TO LOUIS'S HOUSE AND SEEN IT WAS TOTALLY EMPTY. MY BROTHER AND MARLYS BOOSTED ME UP THROUGH THE WINDOW SO I COULD GO INSIDE AND OPEN THE DOOR. MAINLY I NOTICED A SMELL. THE SMELL OF LOUIS AND HIS SISTER. AND SEEING STUFF ON THE FLOOR, LIKE A BLUE CURLER AND SOME MATCHES. IT GAVE ME THE SHIVERS.

AND EVEN THOUGH WE NEVER LIKED LOUIS WE DIDN'T THINK IT WAS ANY FAIR THAT WE WOULD NEVER, FOR THE REST OF OUR WHOLE ENTIRE LIVES, GET TO SEE HIM AGAIN. MY BROTHER MADE US A BET WE WOULD SEE HIM SOMEWHERE IF WE KEPT LOOKING AROUND BUT YOU KNOW WE NEVER DID.

AND EVEN THOUGH A BUNCH OF DIFFERENT FAMILIES LIVED IN THAT HOUSE LATER ON WE STILL CALLED IT LOUIS CHEEK'S HOUSE. THAT WAS THE REAL NAME OF IT AND SINCE WE WERE THERE THE LONGEST, WE MADE THE RULES.

YOU'RE THE ONE WHO LIVES OVER AT LOUIS CHEEK'S HOUSE NOW, RIGHT?

IT AIN'T NO LOUIS CHEEK'S HOUSE, SO QUIT CALLIN' IT THAT. IT'S MY DAD'S HOUSE.

THE RULES OF TV

LYNDA : LOVE CONNECTION : BARRY © 1987

EVERYBODY KNOWS THAT THERE CAN ONLY BE ONE MASTER OF THE TV AT A TIME, BUT HOW DO YOU DECIDE IT? AT MARLYS'S HOUSE YOU HAD TO ROTATE EVERY HOUR.

AT OUR OTHER COUSINS' HOUSE WHOEVER WAS SITTING IN UNCLE LOUIS'S CHAIR WAS THE AUTOMATIC CONTROLLER OF THE TV. THEN WHEN YOU GOT UP YOU HAD TO SAY "HOT SEAT" OR YOU WOULD LOSE IT. BUT IF UNCLE LOUIS CAME IN YOU HAD TO MOVE. HE WOULD SWITCH THE CHANNEL TO THE FIGHTS AND TAKE OUT HIS TEETH AND CHEW ON HIS FINGERS WHICH WAS ALWAYS INTERESTING TO WATCH.

AT OUR HOUSE WHAT YOU HAD TO DO WAS TURN THE TV TO YOUR FAVORITE CHANNEL THEN PULL THE CHANNEL SELECTOR OFF OF THE TV AND TAKE IT APART AND HIDE ALL THE PARTS IN DIFFERENT ROOMS OF THE HOUSE AND IF, SAY, YOUR BROTHER COULD FIND ALL THE PARTS THEN OK, IT WAS HIS TURN TO CHANGE THE CHANNEL.

EXCEPT FOR ONE TIME MY BROTHER GOT THE GENIUS IDEA TO HIDE ONE PART DOWN IN THE HEATING VENT AND WE COULD NEVER GET IT OUT SO THAT'S WHY WE USE PLIERS ON OUR TV.

46

UNDER the PORCH

BY LYNDA BARRY © 1988

UNDER THE PORCH, WAY IN THE CORNER UNDER SOME BOARDS, BY ACCIDENT I FOUND A DUG UP HOLE WHERE MY BROTHER HIDES THINGS. YOU KNOW THAT SHIVERY FEELING YOU GET FROM LOOKING AT SOMEONE'S PRIVACY?

THERE WAS LIGHTER FLUID, MATCHES, A PLASTIC BOX OF FISH HOOKS WITH A MINIATURE SCREWDRIVER MIXED IN, AND A TINY ASPIRIN BOX THAT INSIDE WAS A FOLDED SILVER GUM WRAPPER THAT WHEN YOU UNFOLDED IT, YOU SAW THE WORD "PUSSY" WRITTEN IN CURSIVE RED FLAIR AND UNDERLINED.

ALSO A BOOK CALLED WAY OF THE NUDIST, BY FLOYD GREEN. ON THE COVER WAS A PICTURE OF A LADY WITH NO CLOTHES ON LOOKING AT A PICTURE OF A LADY WITH NO CLOTHES ON LOOKING AT A PICTURE FROM A LADY WITH NO CLOTHES ON, THAT JUST KEEPS GOING UNTIL YOU THINK YOUR BRAINS WILL GO CRAZY FROM INFINITY.

I WAS READING SOME OF THE COMMENTS MY BROTHER WROTE ON THE PICTURES LIKE "HEY LADY GIVE ME BACK MY PANTS" WHEN I HEARD HIM COMING DOWN THE STEPS. I PUT EVERYTHING BACK IN ORDER FAST AND GOT THE BOARDS BACK ON TOP, AND WHEN HE MOVED THE PLYWOOD OVER TO COME IN, I TRIED TO SAY HI NORMALLY LIKE EVERYTHING WAS JUST NORMAL LIKE NORMAL.

47

DRACULA

LYNDA BARRY ©1988

ON WARM NIGHTS AFTER IT WAS TOO DARK TO PLAY KICKBALL, WE WOULD GO TO MRS. VIDRINE'S AND ASK COULD WE PLEASE PLAY "I'M DRACULA" IN HER YARD. SHE WAS HARD OF HEARING SO SHE ALWAYS SAID YES.

SHE HAD TALL TALL GRASS AND SEVEN PLUM TREES YOU COULD HIDE IN LIKE CRAZY WHILE WHOEVER WAS "IT" FOR DRACULA LAID ON THE BACK PORCH COFFIN COUNTING TO 50 AND THEN SCREAMED OUT IN THE DARK "I'M COMING ALIVE!" WHICH WOULD MAKE YOU FEEL LIKE SUDDENLY PEEING.

THE MOST REALISTIC DRACULA WAS MY BROTHER ARNOLD. HE WAS THE KING OF EVIL LAUGHTER AND PERFECT ACCENT ON "I VANT TO SUCK YOUR BLOOD." THE WORST WAS MARLYS WHO YELLED "YOU'RE CHEATING, YOU GUYS! I'M TELLING!" AS IF DRACULA EVER TALKED LIKE THAT.

YOU'RE SUPPOSED TO SAY "HAIL MARY 1-2-3" BEFORE YOU TOUCH THE BASE. YOU'RE OUT! AND QUIT MAKIN' THE SIGN OF THE CROSS AT ME, YA STUPE. IT'S TOO LATE. I SAID YOU ARE OUT! NOW GO TO MY COFFIN, I DON'T GOT ALL DAY.

ON THE NIGHT I HID THE LONGEST, THE TREES WERE COVERED WITH WHITE WHITE FLOWERS. I CLIMBED ONE BAREFOOT AND SAT WAY UP ON A HIGH BRANCH SMELLING THE AIR AND WATCHING THE SHAPE OF MY BROTHER WALKING SLOW THROUGH THE GRASS BELOW ME WITH HIS ARM ACROSS HIS FACE LIKE A CAPE, WONDERING WHERE IN THE WORLD I WAS.

T-POLE

Lynda Barry ©1988

IN MY COUSIN MARLYS'S BACKYARD WAS THE CLOTHESLINE T-POLE WHICH WE LOVED TO HANG UPSIDE DOWN ON. IN FACT, WE WERE BECOMING PURE EXPERTS AT IT.

IF YOU HOOK YOUR LEGS JUST RIGHT AND SWING, THERE'S THIS FEELING YOU CAN GET LIKE YOUR PANTS ARE ITCHING YOU IN THIS MOST PERFECTLY GORGEOUS WAY.

AND WHEN YOU LET YOUR ARMS HANG DOWN AND CLOSE YOUR EYELASHES SO THERE'S THE SPARKLING RAYS AND YOUR DOG COMES OVER AND LICKS YOUR HAND, WELL, HOW CAN YOU RESIST IT?

MY AUNT YELLS OUT THE WINDOW WATCH IT, THE BLOOD'S GONNA RUSH TO YOUR HEADS AND YOU'LL PASS OUT AND FALL OFF AND CRACK YOUR SKULLS, BUT ME AND MARLYS AGREE. IT WOULD STILL BE TOTALLY WORTH IT.

CAPS

Lynda Barry © 1988

WALK UP TO THE SCHOOL IN THE SUMMER AND YOU KNOW THAT GIRL THAT'S ALWAYS SITTING THERE ON THE TOP STEPS? WELL WATCH OUT FOR HER BECAUSE SHE SPITS. HER NAME IS TRACEY SOMETHING.

BY HER FEET THERE'S SO MUCH RED EXPLODED CAP PAPER AND AROUND A THOUSAND BURN MARKS ON THE CONCRETE. SHE POPS CAPS WITH ROCKS FOR THE SMELL. A <u>GIRL</u> LOVING THE SMELL OF CAPS.

SHE HAS A SCAR FROM HER LIP TO HER NOSE SO SHE DOESN'T LIKE ANYONE. I HAVE A COUSIN WITH THE SAME THING AND HE DOESN'T LIKE ANYONE EITHER BUT AT LEAST HE DOESN'T SPIT ON YOU TO PROVE IT.

SOMETIMES WHEN NO ONE'S AROUND, SHE UNPEELS A ROLL OF CAPS WITH HER FINGERNAIL AND THROWS IT DOWN TO ME. AND I POP THEM ALL FOR HER WHILE SHE WATCHES. EVERY ONE OF THOSE PERFECT BLACK BUMPS FOR HER.

BIG SISTER

L Y N N A B A R R Y © 1 9 8 8

MARLYS'S SISTER MAYBONNE HAD THE BIG SLUMBER PARTY OF HER LIFE LAST NIGHT. 12 TEENAGE GIRLS ASKING THE OUIJA BOARD DOES DONNY LIKE ME.

YOU PUSHED IT!

DIDN'T EITHER.

YOU DID.

E F G

AS IF I NEED TO!

DELORES ALWAYS PUSHES IT!

YES

SHE DOES!

DON'T EITHER! GOD!

FOR FOOD THEY HAD RUFFLES, DORITOS, FRITOS, CHEETOS. FOR POP, YOUR CHOICE OF GRAPE, ORANGE, OR REGULAR. ONE GIRL'S DAD WORKED FOR BEEF JERKY, SO TONS OF THAT. ALSO, MINIATURE MARSHMALLOWS, EVERY COLOR.

WHEN MAYBONNE CAME UPSTAIRS IN HER NEW BABY-DOLL PAJAMA SET TO SNEAK SOME CANDLES FOR THE SEANCE OUT OF THE KITCHEN DRAWER, WE HAD TO ADMIT SHE LOOKED GORGEOUS. SHE WAS SO HAPPY SHE EVEN SAID HI TO US.

WHAT IT IS.

AND SOMETHING HAS HAPPENED TO MARLYS BECAUSE WHEN THE BOYS CAME AROUND THE SIDE OF THE HOUSE IN A LINE TO THE BASEMENT DOOR SHE DIDN'T YELL FOR HER MOM LIKE LAST YEAR. SHE JUST LAID ON HER STOMACH AT THE TOP OF THE STEPS LISTENING TO THEM WHISPERING AND LAUGHING AND BEING SO PERFECT.

51

DON'T BUG ME

BY LYNDA BARRY ©1988

IT STARTED BY MY COUSIN MAYBONNE SAYING DON'T BUG HER BECAUSE HER BODY WAS GOING THROUGH SPECIAL CHANGES. THEN SHE CALLS UP HER FRIEND SHARON AND WHISPERS "GUESS WHAT, GEORGE IS VISITING."

WHO'S GEORGE?

DON'T BE SO RETARDED.

THEN SHE GOES INTO THE FRONT ROOM AND LIES DOWN ON HER STOMACH AND LISTENS TO THE SONG "COLOR MY WORLD" OVER AND OVER WHICH MARLYS SAYS MEANS SHE HAS CRAMPS.

AND WHEN MARLYS GOES TO TURN ON THE WONDERFUL WORLD OF DISNEY, MAYBONNE STARTS YELLING <u>NO WAY</u> BECAUSE SHE IS TOO SENSITIVE TO WATCH ANY PROGRAMS OF HELPLESS ANIMALS IN DANGER RIGHT NOW AND MARLYS SAYS THAT'S TOO BAD, TOUGH LUCK, I'M WATCHING IT.

SO THEN MAYBONNE STARTS SCREAMING "<u>MOM!</u> <u>MOM!</u>" AND MARLYS OPENS THE FRONT DOOR AND YELLS OUT "MY NAME IS MAYBONNE AND I CONTROL THE WORLD BECAUSE OF OH MY UTERUS!" AND I DON'T KNOW WHAT HAPPENED AFTER THAT BECAUSE THE FIRST THING MY AUNT SAID WHEN SHE CAME IN THE ROOM WAS FOR ME TO GO HOME.

GUM of MYSTERY

BY LYNDA BARRY WITH LISA JARRETT and BRENDA KIDDER © 1988

WE HAD AN EVIL MYSTERY GOING ON AT THE COATROOM. A SECRET JUVENILE DELINQUENT WAS PUTTING CHEWED UP GUM IN THE UNDERARMS OF EVERYONE'S COATS. WHAT A BAD CITIZEN.

AAUGH!

MISS MARTLES!

EEUH!

OH MAN!

BOTH ARMS!

DANG!

MRS. MARTLES! HE HAS STRUCK AGAIN!

THE THREE MAIN SUSPECTS WERE MY COUSIN MARLYS, KENNETH WATFORD, AND THAT NEW BOY, DEWEY-SOMETHING-IN-SPANISH.

MARLYS.
MAIN EVIDENCE: IN A GUM WRAPPER CHAIN CONTEST WITH ESTHER COX FROM ROOM 9. HAS TO DO SOMETHING WITH EXTRA GUM. SHE SAYS SHE'S THE QUEEN OF ALL GUM.

KENNETH WATFORD
MAIN EVIDENCE: ALWAYS TRYING TO GET ATTENTION, THROWS DIRT CLODS AT CARS, SPITS. PLAYS WITH HIS GUM. STRETCHES IT OUT OF HIS MOUTH, PUTS IT ON HIS FACE.

DEWEY M.
MAIN EVIDENCE HE'S NEW AND RUNS AROUND LIKE A WILD TIGER AND TALKS OUT OF TURN AND ALWAYS ACTS LIKE HE HAS TO PEE. ALWAYS HAS CHICLETS.

WE EVEN HAD TO HAVE A DISCUSSION GROUP ABOUT IT BY SITTING IN INDIAN STYLE ON THE FLOOR AND RAISING OUR HANDS ABOUT "DISRESPECTING OTHER PEOPLE'S PRIVATE PROPERTY" AND "WHY GUM IS INSULTING"

1. Rude
2. Makes a mess
3. Tooth Decay
4. Unsightly
5. Waste of time
6. Disturbing
7.

ANYONE ELSE?

COME ON, CLASS, MISS MARTLES DOESN'T HAVE ALL DAY TO SPEND ON THIS SUBJECT.

CAN YOU BELIEVE IT WAS PAMMY LYONS THE WHOLE TIME? OUR QUIETEST, MOST SMARTEST GIRL OF THE CLASS WITH GLASSES WHO NEVER TALKS? WELL IT TURNS OUT THAT JUST BECAUSE SOMEONE IS SHY AND GETS ALL STRAIGHT AS DOES NOT MEAN THEY WON'T PUT WADS OF GUM IN YOUR ARMPITS.

PAMMY, WE ARE ALL WAITING TO HEAR WHY YOU DID THIS, AREN'T WE CLASS?

PAMMY?

VALUABLE CLASS TIME IS BEING WASTED.

WOULD YOU RATHER TELL IT TO THE PRINCIPAL?

PAMMY?

WE CAN ARRANGE THAT.

EXTRA CREDIT

BY LYNDA BARRY ©1988

MY BROTHER ARNOLD HAD SOUTH AMERICA THIS YEAR AND HE THOUGHT UP THE EXTRA CREDIT IDEA TO MAKE A MODEL OF IT OUT OF CHEWED UP GUM. YOU MIGHT THINK THAT WOULD BE UGLY BUT IT CAME OUT BEAUTIFUL.

HE SAID GUM WAS PERFECT BECAUSE THERE'S 13 KINDS FOR THE 13 COUNTRIES AND GUM LASTS GOOD. WE HAVE SOME STUCK ON THE SIDE OF THE GARAGE FROM WAY LAST SUMMER AND IT'S STILL THERE. HE SPENT $2.49 ON GUM FOR THAT MODEL. WE ALL THOUGHT HE WAS GOING TO GET AN "A" FOR SURE.

PAT PAT PAT

HE SAID THE HARD PART WAS DRAWING THE COUNTRIES RIGHT ON THE CARDBOARD. AFTER THAT ALL HE HAD TO DO WAS REMEMBER WHICH GUM WAS WHICH COUNTRY. URUGUAY WAS CINCHY: TWO DENTYNES. BUT BRAZIL TOOK SO MUCH BAZOOKA, ARNOLD SAYS EVEN JUST THE <u>SMELL</u> OF THAT GUM STILL MAKES HIM ABOUT THROW UP.

WHEN HE PRESENTED IT TO MRS. BROGAN SHE TOLD HIM IT COULD SPREAD DISEASE. I HAD MRS. BROGAN LAST YEAR AND SHOULD HAVE KNOWN TO TELL HIM THE TOPIC OF HER WHOLE LIFE IS GERMS. ARNOLD SAID JUST SPRAY IT WITH LYSOL, KILLS GERMS ON CONTACT, DON'T THROW IT OUT! BUT NO.
    THAT'S WHY YOU SHOULD NEVER MENTION SOUTH AMERICA TO MY BROTHER.

CLASS, WHAT VALUABLE LESSON HAS ARNOLD HELPED US LEARN TODAY?

KINGDOMS

BY LYNDA BARRY ©1988

MY BROTHER FREDDIE IS GROWING MOLD IN JARS UNDER HIS BED. I DON'T KNOW IF I SHOULD TELL ON HIM NOW, OR JUST WAIT UNTIL MOM FINDS OUT ABOUT IT NATURALLY.

I KEPT WONDERING WHY ARE HIS LEGS ALWAYS STICKING OUT FROM UNDER HIS BED EVERY TIME I GO BY FOR ABOUT FIVE DAYS NOW? THE ANSWER IS TEN JARS OF MOLD, ALL KINDS. MILK MOLD, ORANGES MOLD, DOUGHNUT MOLD, MOLD GALORE. HOW CAN ANYONE GET SPECIAL FEELINGS FROM SOMETHING LIKE THAT?

LAST NIGHT I SAW HIM SNEAK THE FLASH-LIGHT UP FROM THE BASEMENT AND I SAID "I'M TELLING" AND HE SAID "OK BUT COME LOOK FIRST." WE LAID ON OUR STOMACHS UNDER HIS BED AS HE FEATURED EACH ONE OF THE MOLDS IN THE SPOTLIGHT. HE TOLD ME THERE WAS A WHOLE MIDGET KINGDOM IN EVERY ONE OF HIS JARS.

HE TOLD ME A POLICEMAN CUT HIS FACE SHAVING ONE MORNING AND HIS WIFE PUT SOME MOLDY BREAD ON IT AND HE GOT INSTANTLY HEALED. "WHAT A DISCOVERY!" MY BROTHER SAID.
SO THAT'S WHY I GOT THIS CORN IN THE BABY FOOD JAR SAVED FROM LUNCH TO GIVE TO HIM AS A SURPRISE. SOMETIMES IT JUST KILLS ME THE THINGS HE DOES.

YOO HOO FREDDIE.

NEW NEIGHBORS

BY LYNDA BARRY © 1988

WHO MOVED IN NEXT DOOR WHERE NOBODY LASTED WAS THE DAWSINS. A MIXED-UP COUPLE, BOTH OLD. MR. DAWSIN HAS A NAKED TATTOO ON ONE ARM AND TAKES OUT HIS TEETH WHENEVER WE SAY HI. HE'S FRIENDLY.

MRS. DAWSIN IS FROM ANOTHER COUNTRY WHERE IT'S NORMAL TO SIT DOWN AND SMOKE A CIGARETTE WITH THE LIGHTED END IN YOUR MOUTH. HER MAIN ENGLISH TO US IS "NO MY DARLING" EVERY TIME WE BEG HER PLEASE PLEASE PLEASE TEACH US HER GREAT SMOKING ABILITY.

AND DON'T FORGET ABOUT THE CATS. 14, I SWEAR ON THE BIBLE. THEY BUILT A PEN ON THE BACK OF THE HOUSE AND I CAN SEE FROM MY BEDROOM THE CATS COMING OUT THE LITTLE DOOR, WALKING IN A CIRCLE AND GOING BACK IN NONSTOP. MY AUNT SAYS MRS. DAWSIN'S PEOPLE EAT CATS BUT I COUNTED AND THERE'S STILL NONE MISSING.

I WAS OVER ENJOYING MR. DAWSIN SINGING TO HIS FAVORITE RECORD "COUNTING FLOWERS ON THE WALL" WITH HIS FACE ABOUT ONE INCH FROM THE SPEAKER, WHEN I NOTICED A LITTLE PICTURE OF A LADY, ALMOST A HULA, NEXT TO A SAILOR MAN. CAN YOU BELIEVE IT? IT'S THEM FROM ABOUT FIFTY THOUSAND YEARS AGO.

AUNT LESLIE

LYNDA BARRY © 1988

BOTH ME AND MARLYS HAVE A GORGEOUS AUNT, AUNT LESLIE WHO'S NOT MARRIED, WHO HAS ALL GOLD FILLINGS, WHO COMES TO VISIT. SHE WEARS BEAUTIFUL EYELINER.

SHE HAS SUCH LONG HAIR THAT WE DIVIDE IN HALF AND COMB WHILE SHE CLOSES HER EYES AND TELLS REAL STORIES OF VAMPIRES LIVING IN HOTELS WHERE THE CEILINGS DRIP BLOOD. SHE LETS ARNOLD AND FREDDIE RUB HER NYLONS.

SHE LETS HER HAIR DRY BY LYING THE WRONG WAY ON MY BED, BAREFOOT, READING OFF LIMITS LOVE MAGAZINES AND SMOKING FILTER TIPS. I ADORE THE SMELL OF SMOKE IN MY ROOM.

AND WHEN SHE DOES HER NAILS, SHE'LL DO ANY ONE'S NAILS, EVEN ARNOLD'S, WHO SPREAD HIS FINGERS OUT ON THE KITCHEN TABLE AND THEN CLIMBED UP ALONE ONTO THE ROOF OF THE GARAGE TO STARE AT THEM.

AFTER SCHOOL

BY LYNDA BARRY © 1988

MY COUSIN FREDDIE GOT BEAT UP BY THERESA WATFORD'S BROTHER DUANE, WHO KEPT CALLING HIM A GIRL AND FREDDIE WOULDN'T DO NOTHING ABOUT IT SO DUANE PUSHED HIM DOWN.

DELORES QUIM YELLED "FIGHT! FIGHT!" AND EVERYONE CAME RUNNING TO WATCH DUANE SLUGGING MY COUSIN AND SHOUTING "COME ON GIRL! HIT ME BACK, YOU GIRL!" BUT FREDDIE NEVER HITS ANYBODY.

THEN WE HEAR A WHISTLE BLOW AND IT'S MRS. BUCKHOLT COMING, SO EVERYBODY TAKES OFF RUNNING EXCEPT FOR ME AND FREDDIE AND MARLYS WHO IS CRYING AND TRYING TO MAKE FREDDIE STAND BACK UP.

MRS. BUCKHOLT SHOUTS AT US "WHO IS INVOLVED HERE?!!" AND FREDDIE WON'T SAY. —HE WON'T SAY AND HE WON'T SAY SO MRS. BUCKHOLT SHOUTS IT AGAIN AND WHEN MARLYS SAYS THE NAME OF DUANE WATFORD, FREDDIE TURNS AROUND AND SLUGS HER SO HARD HER GLASSES FLY OFF.

59

MOTION PICTURE

LYNDA BARRY ©1988

MY BROTHER FOUND A PICTURE OF OUR MOM AND DAD IN A BOX. IT'S OF THEM FROM BEFORE US. THEM STANDING BY SOME WATER, LAUGHING.

YOU CAN SEE HOW MY DAD'S BRAND IS LUCKY STRIKES AND BEHIND HIM THERE'S FLOWERS AND A BLUE CAR. YOU CAN SEE MY MOM IN A YELLOW DRESS AND HER PURSE IS OPEN AND SHE HAS HER MOUTH LIKE MY DAD JUST TOLD HER ANOTHER GREAT JOKE. YOU CAN SEE HOW IT'S A LONG TIME AGO.

MY BROTHER INVENTED THIS THING WHERE IF YOU PUT A MAGNIFYING GLASS ON THE PICTURE, IF YOU HOLD IT JUST RIGHT AND SHAKE IT, IT CAN LOOK LIKE THEY ARE MOVING. LIKE IT'S AN UNDERWATER TV SHOW WHERE TIME CAN SECRETLY COME BACK TO LIFE.

HE SAID THIS WAS OUR HOME MOVIES LIKE THEY SHOW OVER AT HIS NORMAL FRIEND'S HOUSE UP THE STREET, AND WE BOTH STARTED LAUGHING AT THAT, THEN OUR MOM WALKED IN AND ASKED WHAT ARE YOU DOING AND MY BROTHER COVERED THE PICTURE AND SAID NOTHING MOM, NOTHING.

MOVIE REVIEW OF:
SUPER KUNG FU DUDE

AS TOLD AND PART-DRAWN → BY DEWEY MUÑOZ TO: LYNDA BARRY © 19 89

OK. SO I WENT WITH OSCAR FUNG AND HIS MOM, MRS. FUNG TO THE CHINESE MOVIES, RIGHT? AND WE SAW THIS KUNG FU MOVIE IN TOTAL CHINESE THAT OSCAR SAID THE TITLE OF WAS "SUPER KUNG FU DUDE" BUT OBVIOUSLY THAT'S NOT THE REAL NAME OF IT.

SO THE SUPER KUNG FU GUY IS WALKING, THEN 3 BANK ROBBERS RUN OUT AND HE TRIES TO STOP THEM SO THE MAIN DIA-BOLICAL ROBBER HURLS A CHINESE COIN AT HIM AND IT GOES RIGHT INTO HIS STOMACH. LIKE ACTUALLY ENGRAVED ON HIS STOMACH, RIGHT? THE METAL PART.

SO THEN THE ROBBERS ESCAPE TO THEIR SWAMP HIDEAWAY AND THE KUNG FU MAN BUILDS HIS MUSCLES AND CAN SUD-DENLY FLY 50 FEET IN THE AIR AND HE KEEPS ASKING EVERYONE "TELL ME WHERE IS LONG-LOW-FUNKY-TONGUE-DOW!" AND THE PEOPLE SAY "I DON'T KNOW" SO HIS EYEBROWS GO UP IN FURY AND HE SHOUTS "LIAR!" AND KARATE CHOPS THEM.

THEN HE FINDS THEM AND OPENS THE DOOR AND THE GIRL PRISONERS IN BIKINIS RUN OUT AND HE GETS IN A MASSIVE SWORD FIGHT AND HE STABS THE DIABOLICAL GUY IN THE STOMACH BUT THEN HE GETS STABBED IN THE EYEBALL AND THEY BOTH DIE AND THEY PLAY CHINESE MUSIC AND THEN THE END.

JUMP SHOT

BY LYNDA BOLD SOUL SISTER BARRY © 1988

THE TEENAGER NAME OF RICHARD COMES OUT LATE SOME NIGHTS TO SHOOT BASKETS ON OUR CORNER. YOU CAN WATCH HIM FROM MY BEDROOM WINDOW.

YOU CAN LIE ON THE BED AND HEAR THE BALL, THE PING PING OF IT AGAINST THE STREET BOUNCING. YOU CAN HEAR HIM WALK IT, THEN RUN IT AND DO HIS PERFECT HOOK SHOT.

BOUNCE, BOUNCE, BOUNCE, STOP. THE FAST NO-SOUND OF HIS FEET IN THE AIR, THE BALL FLYING UP, PAUSE, THEN WHAM-WHAM AGAINST THE BACKBOARD, A HIGH BOUNCE OFF THE RIM, HIM WHISPERING SON OF A BITCH.

HIM JUMPING UP ON THE CORNER, HIM JUMPING HIGH AND TURNING IN THE AIR UNDER A STREETLIGHT WITH A THOUSAND MILLION BUGS FLYING AROUND IT GOING WILD, WILD, WILD,

SMOKING WORLD
BY LYNDA BARRY

with your host, Marlys!

ENJOY THE ELEGANT SMOKING PLEASURES OF RAW SPAGHETTI, BUT WATCH OUT BECAUSE IT BREAKS EASY AND IF YOU GET TOO MUCH SPIT ON THE END, IT TURNS WHITE AND BENDS.

RED AND BLACK LICORICE IS LOVELY BUT IT ALSO HAS THE BENDING PROBLEM.

WHITE CRAYONS ARE GOOD WHEN YOU PEEL OFF THE PAPER AND PUT THE POINTED END IN YOUR MOUTH. LOOKS GENUINE!

WHITE PAPER STRAWS ARE NICE AND YOU CAN ACTUALLY LIGHT THE ENDS TO MAKE IT REALISTIC. DON'T LIGHT THE PLASTIC ONES, THOUGH, BECAUSE A WAD CAN MELT OFF AND LAND ON YOUR LEG AND YOU WILL RUN SCREAMING.

2

CANDY CIGARETTES: THE HARD KIND WITH THE RED END. PERFECT NOT JUST FOR SMOKING, BUT YOU CAN SUCK ON THEM UNTIL THEY GET REALLY POINTED, THEN STAB PEOPLE WHO WON'T QUIT BUGGING YOU.

CANDY CIGARETTES: THE GUM KIND WITH PAPER. — THE MOST EXCELLENT FOR WHEN YOU BLOW ON THEM, ACTUAL POWDER SMOKE COMES OUT. AND IF YOU ACCIDENTALLY SUCK IN YOU WILL REALISTICALLY COUGH LIKE CRAZY. THIS KIND HAS THE MOST BEAUTIFUL BOXES, TOO.

A COLD HOT DOG CAN GIVE YOU THE LOOK OF A CIGAR FOR WHEN YOU'RE HAVING HOBO FEELINGS. THE PROBLEMS ARE IT CAN SMELL BAD IF YOU USE THE SAME ONE TOO LONG AND WATCH OUT FOR GERMAN SHEPHERDS.

3

IF YOU GOT MATCHES:

• PUNKS FROM 4TH OF JULY ARE GOOD, ESPECIALLY AT NIGHT IN THE BASEMENT WITH NO LIGHTS ON.

• GRAPE VINE STEMS ARE GOOD BUT WATCH OUT FOR THE SMELL IT GETS ON YOUR FINGERS! YOU CAN'T EVEN WASH IT OFF!

• WEEDS FROM UP BY THE CHURCH ARE GOOD BUT ONLY THE DRIED-UP ONES. YOU CAN REALLY SMOKE ON IT!

• CURLED UP SKIN FROM CERTAIN TREES IS OK, BUT DON'T STAY LIT DECENT.

#1! THE BEST! HAIR OFF OF CORN! LAY IT OUTSIDE UNTIL IT TURNS BROWN, THEN ROLL IT IN A GOOD PAPER AND GLUE IT SHUT. CAUTION: DON'T USE TOILET PAPER THOUGH FOR THAT'S HOW MY BANGS AND EYEBROWS GOT BURNED OFF.

x

SPELLING

LYNDA BARRY © 1987

SOME PEOPLE ARE JUST NATURALLY GOOD SPELLERS BUT IT DOES NOT MEAN THEIR LIFE IS PERFECT BECAUSE OF IT. MY COUSIN MARLYS FOR EXAMPLE CAN SPELL ANYTHING: SPATULA, DISQUALIFY, CHIHUA-HUA, MEDITERRANEAN.

BORIS. B-O-R-I-S. NATASHA. N-A-T-A-S-

SHUT UP FOR AT LEAST ONE SECOND OK MARLYS? I'M TRYING TO HEAR.

BOREES

WE MUST GET SQUIRREL

SQUIRREL. S-Q-U-I-R-R-E-L.

EVERY YEAR WHEN THEY HAND OUT THE SPELLING FOR WORD MASTERY BOOKS, MARLYS ALWAYS RAISES HER HAND TO TELL THE TEACHER GUESS WHAT, SHE KNOWS ALL THE WORDS AL-READY. YOU'D THINK THIS MIGHT MAKE A GOOD IMPRESSION BUT IT DOESN'T.

AND YOU ALREADY KNOW I'M A GIFTED CHILD, RIGHT MISS MARTLES?

SPELLING FOR WORD MASTERY

2

AND FOR AS GOOD OF A SPELLER AS MARLYS IS SHE CAN NEVER BE IN THE ALL-CITY SPEL-LING BEE AGAIN FOR HURLING ERASERS WHEN SHE MISSED ON "PHOSPHOROUS" AND FOR KICKING AT THE TEACHER WHO CAME TO GET HER WHEN MARLYS WOULD NOT GO SIT DOWN.

DO OVERS! DO OVERS! DO OVERS! DO OVERS! DO OVERS! DO OVERS!

COME NOW MARLYS. LET'S BE GOOD CITIZENS, SHALL WE?

OF COURSE THIS INCIDENT WENT ON HER PERMANENT RECORD WHICH WILL FOLLOW HER FOR THE REST OF HER LIFE.

FRANKLY, WE'D HIRE YOU IN A SECOND IF IT WEREN'T FOR THIS NASTY BIT OF BUSINESS ABOUT YOUR BEHAVIOR AT A CERTAIN SPELLING BEE.

I'M VERY SORRY, MISS.

3

X

64

MARLYS' LOVE

BY LYNDA BARRY ©1988

MY COUSIN MARLYS WAS BENDING OVER ONE DAY, LOOKING AT SOME ANTS, WHEN A TEENAGER NAMED RICHARD CAME THROUGH THE GATE WITH A TENNIS RACQUET LOOKING FOR MARLYS' SISTER, MAYBONNE.

WHEN HE WALKED BY MARLYS HE SAID "HI, SQUIRT" AND TAPPED THE TENNIS RACQUET ON HER BEHIND LIKE YOU DO WHEN ANYBODY'S BENT OVER, AND WHEN MARLYS STOOD UP, SHE WAS IN LOVE.

MAYBONNE'S VOICE CAME OUT THE FRONT DOOR SAYING JUST A SEC SO RICHARD SAT DOWN ON THE TOP STEP AND MARLYS STOOD ON THE BOTTOM ONE AND SAID WANT TO SEE ME DO THE MEXICAN HAT DANCE?

IT WAS HER SPECIALTY.

THE UPSTAIRS WINDOW SHOVED OPEN AND MAYBONNE'S HEAD CAME OUT YELLING BUG OFF MARLYS, WILL YOU? BUT NO, SHE COULDN'T. SHE COULDN'T, SHE COULDN'T, SHE JUST COULDN'T.

If you want to know teenagers by Marlys

BY LYNDA MARGY ROCHLIN BARRY © 1991

Poetry by Marlys. Made up.

teenagers teenagers sometimes they are nice. I can't think of nothing that ry rhymes with nice sometimes they are coldblooded they can hate you.

they can look beautiful. beautiful make up. clothes. handwriting.

When they are riding on bummers you must watch out. could be they want to talk to you. Could be they will yell in your face. But can you remember they are sad.

One main thing you got to know is they have secrets. you must not bust them on the secrets. Teenagers teenagers there's things that they do. And if you tell anyone they will cream you.

sorry for no picture.
I saw something I
can't even draw it.
Don't try to guess it.
Just forget it.

66

MAYBONNE'S DIARY

BY LYNDA BARRY ©1988

MY COUSIN MARLYS READ SOME DAYS IN HER SISTER MAYBONNE'S DIARY WHICH I SAID WAS SORT OF CRUDDY AND SHE SAID SHUT UP, I KNOW YOU'RE INTERESTED.

SHE SAID, OK, #1, LAST FRIDAY THE TEEN-AGER RICHARD HAD A HOOKEY PARTY AND MAYBONNE WENT. THEY HAD BOONE'S FARM APPLE WINE AND MAYBONNE HELD HER NOSE TO PREVENT THE TASTE AND DRANK A FULL FLINTSTONES GLASS IN ONE TRY.

OK, #2. THEN IT WAS A MAKE OUT PARTY. JOEL GOT SHARON, TONY GOT MARGY AND RICHARD GOT MAYBONNE. THEY FRENCHED 16 TIMES TO THE SONG "LA-LA MEANS I LOVE YOU." IT WAS BEAUTIFUL.

OK #3, RICHARD SAID FOR MAYBONNE TO PUT HER WHOLE HAND ON HIS PANTS BUT MAYBONNE HAD TO BARF AND THEN HER RETAINER WENT IN THE TOILET. NOW SHE DOESN'T KNOW IF RICHARD WAS JUST USING HER OR IF HE'S HER BOYFRIEND.

I SAID TO MARLYS, ARE YOU GOING TO TELL? AND MARLYS SAID TO ME, ARE YOU RETARDED?

67

ON TUESDAY

BY LYNDA BARRY ✿✿✿✿✿✿✿ ©1988

MY SISTER MARLYS ANSWERED THE PHONE AND THEN YELLED THROUGH MY DOOR "IT'S BRIAN BANO!" AND AT FIRST I ALMOST DIDN'T UNLOCK IT BECAUSE I THOUGHT SHE WAS LYING. YOU KNOW HIM? HE'S IN NINTH. A NINTH GRADER.

YOU SWEAR TO GOD?

WHY. IS HE SOME KIND OF BIG DEAL?

I SPENT MY WHOLE PHONE LIMIT ON HIM. ONE HOUR OF TALKING ON MY MOM'S BED WITH ALL THE LIGHTS OFF AND THE UNIVERSE FEELING PERFECT. THEN HE CALLED ME FOR AROUND 9 STRAIGHT NIGHTS AND I WAS WONDERING: DOES IT EQUAL HE IS MY BOYFRIEND?

OH, I DON'T KNOW. YEAH. SORT OF. WHY? DO YOU? REALLY? SERIOUSLY? UH-HUH. YEAH.

NO! NO WAY! YOU DO? SAME HERE. YEAH.

2

THEN HE SAID DID I WANT TO SKIP WITH HIM ON TUESDAY AND MEET UP AT CROFTON PARK. THERE'S SOME PLACES HE KNOWS OF WHERE YOU CAN GET YOUR PRIVACY. I DIDN'T KNOW IF IT WAS ONE OF THOSE THINGS WHERE IF YOU SAY NO, THEY QUIT LIKING YOU, SO EVEN THOUGH I FELT ONLY HALF AND HALF, I SAID OK.

HI.

HI.

3

AFTERWARDS, WALKING HOME, I KEPT FEELING LIKE WHOEVER EVEN LOOKED AT ME COULD TELL WHAT I JUST DID. I MADE A HOLY VOW 100 TIMES OF: NO WAY NEVER AGAIN. THEN FOR 11 DAYS HE DIDN'T CALL AND DIDN'T CALL, AND I KEPT THINKING ABOUT HIM MORE AND MORE AND NOW THE PHONE JUST RANG, HIM SAYING MEET ME UP AT CROFTON PARK IN ONE HOUR AND I DON'T KNOW. I GUESS I'M GOING.

X

68

ON·THURSDAY·

BY·LYNDA·BARRY· ©·1988·

This class sucks!!

I know. I am so bored

Look at Mrs. Lahaye's armpits

Aren't you glad you use dial?
Don't you wish everybody did?

Do you know whats for lunch?

I think chili

Is it true about you and Brian Bano?

what?

CROFTON PARK and all that.
No. Who said?
DEB BARTLETT who else?
What did she say?
YOU HAD A MAKE OUT SESSION
I'm sure! How should she know about my life?
HER LITTLE Sister KNOWS YOUR LITTLE Sister
I don't get it.
Your sister read your diary and told her.
Marlys?
Is it true?
I don't even have a diary.
Deb Bartlett told the story of it on the bus.
Shes such a liar!
It sounded realistic.
100% No way!!!!!!!!!!
Brian Banos cute. I wouldn't mind it.
Come off it!
Are you being for real? Please tell me!
As if I would even have to lie!
Then you better get Deb Bartlett for it at lunch
because she is spreading it to the
whole universe.

2

There is just no way!
better act cool or we are gonna get busted.

Its not true.
OK.

Do You know what you are doing
your report on yet?
No.
DO DESEASES OF PLANTS WITH me.
Maybe.

Are you mad at me?
no.

Do you even like Brian Bano?

no.

3

SLAM!

MAR-LYS!!

UH-OH.

HOW TO DRAW GIRLS

L Y N D A 12 STITCHES B A R R Y © 1988

WITH YOUR HOST MARLYS

"OK. THE FIRST NUMBER ONE THING IN DRAWING GIRLS IS PRACTICE YOUR EYES! GET THEM MATCHING OR YOUR DRAWING WILL LOOK LIKE THERE'S A MENTAL PROBLEM!"

EYEBALL GOES IN THE MIDDLE. OK NOW PUT ON THE LINES

EYEBROWS

DIN'T FORGET CURLY EYELASHES. IT MAKES THE EYES BEAUTIFUL!

KEEP ON DOING IT UNTIL YOU GET IT PERFECT BUT DON'T JUST WASTE PAPER!

NUMBER TWO: THE MOUTH AND NOSE IS EASY! FIRST DRAW THE SHAPE OF HER HEAD IN A "U". THEN YOU JUST ADD ON THE KIND OF MOUTH AND NOSE YOU WANT DEPENDING ON HER PERSONALITY!

SHY

SAD

MOVIE STAR

BEAUTIFUL VAMPIRE

FASHION MODEL

STEWARDESS

NUMBER THREE: WHAT ABOUT HER HAIR? THERE'S A LOT OF HAIRDOS FOR HER TO HAVE! THERE'S A LOT OF STYLES!

PEEK-A-BOO

A BEAUTY PAGEANT

INDIAN PRINCESS

A FRANCE LADY

A GORGEOUS FLIP

RATTED BUBBLE

NUMBER FOUR: THE HARDEST PART: YOU HAVE TO DRAW HER WHOLE BODY AND THIS IS WHERE YOU CAN WRECK EVERYTHING SO BE CAREFUL! MY SECRET IS: DRAW A LONG BEAUTIFUL DRESS AND HER HOLDING FLOWERS AND DON'T FORGET SOME ELEGANT ACCESSORIES!

A CROWN ALWAYS LOOKS LOVELY.

FLOWERS CAN HIDE HANDS THAT'S TOO HARD TO DRAW

PUT IN BIRDS

DRAW ON A WATCH

HER PURSE. ITS IMPORTANT

DECORATE THE DRESS PLEASE

DRAW A TREE HERE AND SHE CAN LOOK LIKE SHE'S IN THE FOREST

SHOES CAN STICK OUT

THE END BY MARLYS

PIXIE

BY LYNDA BARRY © 1987

IF YOU GO UP PAST THE SCHOOL, WAY UP PAST THE FIRE STATION, KEEP GOING, KEEP GOING, UNTIL YOU GET TO THAT YELLOW GAS STATION. IN THE PINK HOUSE NEXT TO IT, OUT IN THE YARD, IS A DOG WEARING CLOTHES.

OUR MOM SAYS MRS. SANTOS, THE LADY OF THE DOG, IS SO LONELY THAT THE DOG IS HER ONLY FAMILY. SHE TREATS PIXIE LIKE A REAL BABY FEEDING HIM SCRAMBLED EGGS WITH A TINY SPOON AND MAKING THE SAME FACES REGULAR MOMS MAKE WHEN THEY FEED REAL BABIES. ISN'T IT HEARTBREAKING, OUR MOM SAYS.

HERE COMES THE AIRPLANE!

"ISN'T IT HEARTBREAKING HOW SHE PUT A STATUE OF THE VIRGIN MARY AND A MILLION PLASTIC FLOWERS ON HIS DOGHOUSE? AND ALL THE PICTURES TAPED INSIDE, OF MOVIE STARS LIKE ROBERT MITCHUM? THAT DOG IS HER WHOLE LIFE, OUR MOM SAYS. SHE'D STARVE BEFORE SHE'D LET THAT DOG GO HUNGRY AND THAT DOG IS SO SPOILED. I'VE SEEN IT TRY TO BITE HER WHEN SHE GAVE IT A POWDER SUGAR DOUGHNUT. SHE WORSHIPS THAT DOG."

CHEF BOY-AR-DEE
Pixie
UH-OH SPAGETTI-O's!

"I FEEL SO SORRY FOR HER," SAID MOM. BUT WE FELT A LOT SORRIER FOR PIXIE WHO THREW UP ALL THE TIME AND WAS MRS. SANTOS'S THIRD DOG THIS YEAR.

YOO-HOO! ♫ PIXIE! ♫ HERE BOY! ♫ MOMMY HAS MORE CAKE AND ICE CREAM FOR HER LITTE BOO-BOO! ♫

TRIXIE   DIXIE

ZOOM

OUR FAVORITE THING

BY LYNDA BARRY · WITH · IRA GLASS © · 1 · 9 · 8 · 8 · + 0

YOU KNOW THAT ONE KIND OF JEWELERY BOX THAT WHEN YOU OPEN IT, THERE'S MUSIC AND A BALLERINA STARTS TWIRLING ON ONE LEG IN FRONT OF A MIRROR?

WELL, MY COUSIN MARLYS GOT ONE, ONLY WHOEVER MADE IT DID CRUMMY PAINTING ON THE BALLERINA LIPS, SO MARLYS TRIED TO FIX IT WITH NAIL POLISH REMOVER, AND THEN THE WHOLE FACE JUST SORT OF MELTED OFF.

THE TRAGEDY OF IT MADE MARLYS CRY, SO HER BROTHER FREDDIE TRIED TO FIX IT FOR HER, AND THEN THERE WAS ANOTHER TRAGEDY, WHICH WAS HE ACCIDENTALLY BROKE OFF THE REST OF THE HEAD.

OOPS.

SORRY, MAN.

IT WAS TOO PITIFUL, EVEN FOR MY BROTHER ARNOLD, TO WATCH THE BALLERINA TWIRLING WITH NO HEAD TO THE LOVELY MUSIC, SO HE TOOK THE GUM OUT OF HIS MOUTH AND STUCK IT ON HER NECK, AND THAT'S HOW MARLYS'S JEWELRY BOX BECAME OUR FAVORITE THING.

NOW TURN THE KEY THING AT THE BOTTOM SO SHE STARTS GOIN' REALLY FAST AGAIN!

WHOA!! SHE'S PSYCHIN' OUT, MAN! AAAAH!!!!

WAIT! WAIT! GO GET YOUR CREEPY CRAWLERS AND PUT THEM IN THE BOX TO BE THE AUDIENCE!

YEAH! THEY WORSHIP HER! SHE'S THE TOTAL GOD OF THEM!

FLY LAND

BY LYNDA SANDSKINK BARRY ©1988

YOU ALREADY KNOW, RIGHT? HOW MY COUSIN FREDDIE IS THE GENIUS OF PROJECTS? THAT'S WHY HE'S ALWAYS FIGHTING MARLYS FOR SHOE BOXES. HE MAKES REALISTIC LANDS IN THEM: THE CAVEMAN VOLCANO TOWN, THE CAVEMAN SEA HUNT, THE CAVEMAN WENT TO VENUS.

WHO STARS AS THE CAVEMAN ARE FLIES, THE WORLD'S HARDEST INSECT TO CATCH. JUST FORGET ABOUT TRYING TO CATCH A FLY OUTSIDE. IF THEY COME IN THE HOUSE, OK, YOU CAN TRAP THEM GOOD IN THE CURTAINS AND THAT'S WHY FREDDIE HAS TO ALWAYS LEAVE THE SCREEN DOORS OPEN WHICH HIS MOTHER SAYS HE DOES JUST TO TORMENT HER.

PSST.... FREDDIE! FLY! FLY!

YOU KNOW THAT SHOE TISSUE PAPER? HE TAPES THAT ON THE TOP AND THEN YOU GO HOLD IT BY THE LAMP FOR LIGHT AND STARE THROUGH THE SARAN WRAP PEEPHOLE AT THE CAVEMAN WALKING AROUND UPSIDE-DOWN EVERYWHERE. SOMETIMES YOU'LL LOOK IN AND NOTICE IT'S TIME FOR A NEW CAVEMAN.

UH-OH... FREDDIE...

THE FLY IN THE VENUS ONE IS DEAD AGAIN.

DID YOU KNOW THAT FLIES WIN FOR INSECT COVERED WITH MOST DEADLY GERMS? WHEN FREDDIE'S MOM CAUGHT HIM HOLDING ONE IN HIS BARE HAND TO GET IT THROUGH THE DOOR OF THE CAVEMAN'S MINIATURE CHRISTMAS, THAT'S WHEN HE HAD TO SWITCH TO SPIDERS WHICH MAY BE CLEANER BUT THEY ARE JUST NOT AS GOOD.

HE MOVE YET?

NOPE. HE'S STILL JUST SITTING THERE BY THE FIREPLACE.

MAN, SPIDERS ARE TOO LAZY FOR ME

SAME HERE.

73

MY BEAUTIFUL DRESS

BY LYNDA BARRY © 1988

IT CAME FROM MY COUSIN DEBBIE'S IN THE MAIL. HER MOM WROTE A LETTER THAT DEBBIE COULDN'T FIT IT NOW BECAUSE SHE WAS SO MATURE UPSTAIRS. I ABOUT HAD AN ATTACK WHEN I SAW IT, IT WAS SO BEAUTIFUL.

"PROBABLY DIDN'T EVEN WEAR IT TEN TIMES" MY MOTHER SAID. "THE WAY MY SISTER THROWS MONEY AWAY ON THOSE KIDS, I'M TELLING YOU. MY GOD, THE IRONING THAT HAS TO GO INTO IT! THE SKIRT MUST HAVE TEN YARDS OF FABRIC. TRY IT ON." SHE SAID.

THAT NIGHT WHEN EVERYONE WAS ASLEEP, I PULLED THE DRESS OFF THE HANGER AND PUT IT ON IN THE BATHROOM. I HAD TO BALANCE MYSELF UP ON THE EDGES OF THE TUB TO SEE IN THE MIRROR HOW GORGEOUS I LOOKED, AND EVERYTHING WOULD HAVE BEEN OK IF I DIDN'T SUDDENLY GET THE IDEA TO DO SOME OF MY MODERN DANCES.

AT THE HOSPITAL THEY SAID THERE WAS NO CHOICE ABOUT CUTTING THE DRESS OFF OF ME IN ORDER TO SET MY BROKEN COLLAR-BONE. I SAID TO MY MOTHER AT LEAST SAVE THE PIECES, MAYBE WE COULD SEW IT BACK TOGETHER. "THE HELL I WILL" MY MOTHER SAID.

THE TOTAL BOOK

BY LYNDA BARRY x o x x o o x © 1988

YOU KNOW HOW MY BROTHER ARNOLD'S LATEST BIG DEAL IS WRITING STAPLED TOGETHER BOOKS? NOW HE'S WRITING ONE CALLED THE TOTAL INFORMATION OF EVERYTHING. IT'S GOING TO BE HIS LONGEST BOOK YET.

MAINLY, THE IDEA OF IT IS LISTS OF KNOWLEDGE: KINDS OF DOGS, WHO ARE THE PRESIDENTS, FAKIEST MONSTERS, MOST INTERESTING THINGS TO CATCH ON FIRE, AND WHAT THINGS WOULD BE THE WEIRDEST IN YOUR BEDROOM AT NIGHT IF THEY SUDDENLY JUST STARTED COMING TO LIFE.

THERE'S ONE CHAPTER CALLED "WHICH IS THE WORST?" IT'S SORT OF A CONTEST OF AWFUL SITUATIONS.

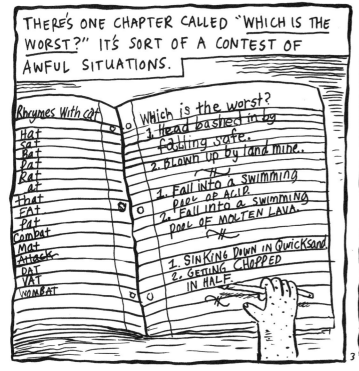

Rhymes With cat
Hat
Sat
Bat
Pat
Rat
at
that
EAT
Pat
Combat
Mat
Attack
DAT
VAT
WOMBAT

Which is the worst?
1. Head bashed in by falling safe.
2. Blown up by land mine.

1. Fall into a swimming pool of ACID.
2. Fall into a swimming pool of MOLTEN LAVA.

1. SINKING DOWN IN Quicksand.
2. GETTING CHOPPED IN HALF.

THE MOST EXCITING FEATURE OF THE BOOK, THOUGH, IS CALLED: THE EARTH'S MOST COMPLETELY LONGEST LIST IN THE GALAXY AND UNIVERSE, OF ALL TIME. IT TURNS OUT TO JUST BE THE LIST OF ANYTHING, ONLY NUMBERED, SO BY THE END YOU CAN TELL EXACTLY HOW MANY.

OK. NAME SOMETHING ELSE.
UM, PING-PONG BALLS?
GOT IT ALREADY. SOMETHING ELSE.
ALFRED ON BATMAN.
ALREADY GOT IT. SOMETHING ELSE.
A WATER WIGGLE.
OH YEAH!

GOOD DOG

TOLD BY GAIL F. • MAJOR EMBELLISHMENTS BY LYNDA BARRY ©87

ONE TIME IN THE SUMMER I HAD THIS DREAM OF MAKING FRIENDS WITH THIS ONE DOG IN OUR ALLEY NAMED TIMMY WHO EVERYONE WAS TOTALLY SCARED OF BECAUSE HE WAS A WILD TIED UP KIND OF DOG WHO SOMETIMES GOT LOOSE AND WOULD RIP GIANT HOLES IN YOUR PANTS AND ALSO TRY TO DANCE WITH YOU.

IT TOOK ABOUT TWO HOURS BUT HOW I DID IT WAS BY TALKING TO HIM AS SWEET AS IF HE WERE THE BABY JESUS AND GIVING HIM BOLOGNA AND MOVING TOWARD HIM IN PERFECT SLOW MOTION. WHEN HE FINALLY LET ME PET HIM I FELT LIKE I WAS THE WINNER OF THE WHOLE WORLD.

I JUST KEPT PETTING HIM AND PETTING HIM AND SINGING HIM A MILLION SONGS LIKE "THE HILLS ARE ALIVE" AND "RICE-A-RONI THE SAN FRANCISCO TREAT." MY MAIN PROBLEM CAME WHEN I TRIED TO GET UP, TIMMY TRIED TO BITE ME. IF I TRIED TO MOVE HE'D START GROWLING. HE WOULDN'T LET ME LEAVE. I STARTED YELLING FOR HELP. I YELLED ABOUT SIX HUNDRED TIMES BEFORE MY COUSIN MARLYS CAME.

MARLYS GOT THE PLAN OF GETTING A HOT DOG AND FLINGING IT TO THE SIDE SO WHEN TIMMY WENT TO GET IT I COULD ESCAPE, AND HER PLAN WORKED. WHEN I GOT BACK TO THE YARD I STARTED SHAKING AND SHAKING AND I COULDN'T STOP. WHEN I TRIED TO TALK I STARTED CRYING FOR NO REASON. AND THEN OF ALL THINGS, MARLYS, MY DREADED COUSIN, PUT HER ARM AROUND ME.

76

UGLIFUL
BY LYNDA BARRY ©1989

THE FIRST THING ABOUT MY MOM IS THAT SHE WAS VERY BEAUTIFUL WHEN SHE WAS YOUNG. IN FACT, GORGEOUS. THE GORGEOUS TWIN OF AVA GARDNER, EVERYBODY SAID IT. MY MOM HAS TOLD US THIS 10,000 TIMES.

AND DID YOU KNOW I HAD WHAT THEY CONSIDERED PERFECT EYEBROWS?

WELL, IT'S ALL GONE TO HELL NOW. WASTED. SHOWS YOU WHAT HAVING KIDS CAN DO TO YOU.

SHE WAS SO BEAUTIFUL, FIVE GUYS ASKED HER TO MARRY THEM BEFORE SHE PICKED MY FATHER, THE WORST MISTAKE OF HER LIFE. I ALWAYS WONDER WHAT I COULD HAVE LOOKED LIKE INSTEAD, IF SHE HAD PICKED ONE OF THEM.

HERMAN KOSARSKI LOOKED LIKE PERRY COMO

DAVID R. GAVLAK NOW OWNS "GAVLAK SANITATION"

PETER FERRARA BOY COULD HE DANCE.

WAYNE SHIPLEY LOOKED LIKE "MAVERICK"

WILBERT BRUTOUT NOW OWNS "BRUTOUT TEXACO"

WHEN I WAS LITTLE, I LOOKED JUST LIKE HER. WE HAD THOSE DRESSES THAT MATCH AND ACCORDING TO MY MOTHER, THE PEOPLE WHO SAW US SAID WE WERE WONDERFUL. THEN I HAD TO GET GLASSES WHICH MY MOTHER HATED BECAUSE IT SPOILED MY LOOKS. THIS WAS A LONG TIME AGO WHEN MY MOM'S EYES WERE PERFECT AND MY DAD WAS STILL WITH US.

MY BABY SISTER MARLYS WHO MY MOM SAYS WAS BORN WEARING GLASSES. AND ALSO "CHUBBY"

"YOU GOT YOUR FATHER'S LOOKS. THE BOTH OF YOU." SHE SAYS TO ME AND MY SISTER WHEN SHE GETS IN THAT ONE TALKING MOOD ABOUT HER MISTAKES IN LIFE. AND SHE TELLS ME I HAD BETTER GET BUSY WORKING ON MY CHARM. "WELL, BE GRATEFUL YOU DON'T HAVE A WEIGHT PROBLEM." SHE SAYS, THEN LOOKS STRAIGHT AT MY SISTER.

The WRONG candy

BY LYNDA GOOFBALL BARRY © 1988

MY COUSIN MARLYS STARTED LIKING A BOY SHE NEVER EVEN THOUGHT OF UNTIL HE STARTED LIKING HER SO THEN SHE STARTED LIKING HIM SO THEN HE QUIT LIKING HER SO NOW SHE IS SAD.

COME ON HE SAID LET'S GO TO THE STORE I HAVE MY 25¢ I'LL SPEND IT ALL ON YOU WHICH TO MARLYS WAS THE BIGGEST WORDS A BOY EVER SAID TO HER IN HER LIFE AND THEN SO SHE BELIEVED IN IT.

SHE PICKED ALL HER FAVORITES OF RED HOTS, JOLLY ROGERS, JAW BREAKERS AND M+Ms AND THE NEXT DAY HE AUTO-MATICALLY QUIT LIKING HER AND SO NOW SHE THINKS IT'S BECAUSE SHE PICKED ALL THE WRONG CANDY.

AS IF THERE EVEN IS SUCH A THING.

WADING MARLYS

O·NE· NIGHT

BY LYNDA BARRY © 1988

IT WAS THE HOTTEST NIGHT OF THE SUMMER AND ME AND MY COUSIN MARLYS WERE STANDING IN OUR UNDERPANTS IN FRONT OF THE FAN IN THE KITCHEN WATCHING MY MOM PUT HER MOM'S HAIR UP. WE COULD HEAR THE BOYS YELLING IN THE YARD AND THE NIGHT MOTHS KEPT LANDING ON THE SCREEN DOOR. THE RADIO WAS ON.

WE HEARD "YOU DID <u>NOT</u>, I DID <u>SO</u>, YOU DIDN'T <u>EITHER</u> YOU LIAR, I DID <u>TOO</u>, YOU PUNK!" THEN MY AUNT STUCK HER HEAD OUT THE WINDOW AND YELLED "JESUS CHRIST ALREADY!" AND MY MOTHER TOLD ME AND MARLYS TO GO GET THE LAUNDRY OFF THE LINE AND WE WALKED OUT INTO THE DARK FEELING DIFFERENT IN OUR UNDERPANTS.

MARLYS YELLED AT FREDDIE AND ARNOLD TO COME HELP AND WE WERE ALL ON OUR TOES TAKING OFF CLOTHESPINS, THEN A SONG COMES ON THE RADIO FROM INSIDE THE HOUSE AND MY MOTHER TURNS IT UP. — IT WAS "CAN'T GET USED TO LOSING YOU" BY I THINK ANDY WILLIAMS. THROUGH THE DOORWAY WE SEE MY MOM AND MY AUNT GET UP AND START DANCING.

WE STAND BEHIND THE CLOTHES AND WATCH THEM AND ARNOLD GRABS DOWN A BRA AND HOLDS IT UP LIKE HE'S A LADY AND STARTS DOING A CHA-CHA AT US WITH HIS REAR-END STUCK OUT AND THEN WE HEAR A ZOOMING NOISE AND LOOK UP TO SEE A BOTTLE ROCKET SHOOT SUDDENLY OVER THE ROOF OF THE HOUSE FREEZING EVERYTHING STILL WITH PERFECT LIGHT.

KNOWING THINGS

· L Y N D A · B A R R Y · © 1989

MY SISTER MARLYS IS DOING A PROJECT OUT ON THE BACK PORCH ABOUT PLANTS. SHE'S ONLY 8 SO SHE'S STILL NOT SICK OF KNOWING THINGS. I DID THAT SAME PROJECT ABOUT A MILLION YEARS AGO. YOU PLANT BEANS IN A MILK CARTON. BIG DEAL.

I TOLD HER SHE ONLY NEEDS THREE TO DO THE EXPERIMENT OF ① NO WATER. ② SOME WATER. ③ FLOODING. SHE PLANTED 30. SHE'S TRYING KOOLAID, MILK, AND CRAGMONT ROOT BEER. SHE RUBBED ONE WITH VICKS. SHE PUT MILK DUDS IN THE DIRT OF ONE. SHE SAYS SHE'S LOOKING FOR THE SECRET FORMULA.

WHEN I TRY TO TELL HER THERE'S NO WAY, SHE GOES: "THAT'S WHAT THEY ALL SAY." I DON'T KNOW WHERE SHE EVEN GOT THAT! IT'S FROM THE BOOKS YOU KEEP READING WITH NO REALITY IN THEM. A MAGIC TREE STARTS TALKING OR A MAGIC DOG STARTS TALKING AND EVERYTHING IN THE WORLD CAN BE MAGIC. EVEN YOUR SPIT CAN BE MAGIC. AND NOW THAT'S WHAT SHE THINKS. THERE'S ONE PLANT SHE SPITS ON.

I TRIED TO EXPLAIN TO HER THE CONCEPT OF REALITY AND THAT REALITY IS BEAUTIFUL AND SHE SAID HER PLANTS WERE REALITY AND SHE WAS REALITY AND HER EXPERIMENTS WERE REALITY AND I SAID THE REAL REALITY WAS SHE WAS THE TORTURER OF PLANTS AND ALL THE PLANTS WERE GOING TO DIE BECAUSE OF HER AND WHAT I SAID CAME TRUE. IT CAME TRUE. IT CAME TRUE. MARLYS, I'M SORRY IT CAME TRUE.

MARLYS the STAR

BY LYNDA 8-TRACK TAPE BARRY ©1987

WHO KNOWS HOW IT HAPPENED BUT MARLYS GOT PICKED TO RIDE ON THE UNDERLINE FLOAT IN THE PARADE WEARING A UNIFORM. WHEN MOM DROPPED US OFF, SHE HAD IT ON AND SHOUTED "ATTEN-HUT!", "ABOUT FACE!", AND "YOU HAVE THE RIGHT TO REMAIN SILENT!" MY BROTHER SECRETLY GAVE HER THE FINGER AND SO DID I BECAUSE THE FACT IS WE WERE SO JEALOUS WE COULD DIE.

DANG MARLYS, THE STUPID PARADE'S NOT 'TIL TONIGHT. WHADDAYA GOT YOUR DUMB UNIFORM ON ALREADY FOR?

AT EASE PRIVATE ARNOLD.

I'M NOT SALUTIN' YOU MAN. I'M JUST ITCHIN' MY NOSE.

AFTER ABOUT A ZILLION YEARS OF WAITING, RIGHT WHEN YOUR BUTT IS DEAD FROM SITTING ON THE CURB, THE PARADE MEN COME RUNNING BY POINTING TO YOUR SHOES AND YELLING "MOVE THEM BACK! MOVE THEM OUT OF THE WAY!" AND BEFORE YOU KNOW IT A MILLION THINGS ARE GOING BY. THE BANDS ARE SO LOUD IT'S LIKE THEY'RE MARCHING ALL OVER YOU AND IF YOU SQUAT DOWN IT CAN BE PRETTY INTERESTING TO WATCH THEIR FEET.

THE HORSE RIDERS GO BY, MORE BANDS GO BY, OUR PRINCIPAL AND ONE TEACHER FROM OUR SCHOOL AND THE JANITOR GO BY IN A GROUP OF DADS WEARING THEIR OLD ARMY UNIFORMS AND HATS AND MEDALS, THE BEAUTY CONTESTS GO BY SITTING ON THE BACKS OF CONVERTIBLES WAVING THEIR GLOVES AT YOU AND THE ONE CAR WITH THE QUEEN AND TWO PRINCESSES, HAS A GUY DRIVING IT WHO MY BROTHER BET ME A MILLION DOLLARS WAS DEAN MARTIN.

THE CLOWNS THREW THE WORST CANDY IN THE WORLD AT US AND WHEN THEY CAME UP TO GRAB YOU, YOU COULD SEE THEIR MAKEUP AND THEY SMELLED DRUNK. THEN ALL OF A SUDDEN, HERE COMES THE FLOAT WITH MARLYS ON IT— AND BEFORE ME AND MY BROTHER KNEW WHAT WE WERE DOING WE STARTED YELLING "YAY MARLYS! YAY MARLYS!" AND SCREAMING, AND MARLYS DID THAT GLOVE WAVE JUST PERFECT AT US AND SHE STARTED LAUGHING AND WE STARTED LAUGHING AND I GUESS I'LL JUST NEVER FORGET THAT FOREVER.

THE LAST UP

LYNDA BARRY © 1988

IT WAS AFTER DINNER ON THE LAST SUNDAY BEFORE THE FIRST DAY OF SCHOOL. WE WERE PLAYING OUR REGULAR KICKBALL GAME IN THE STREET AND IT WAS STARTING TO GET DARK. EVERYBODY WAS THERE.

EVEN THE TEENAGERS WHO COULD DRIVE WERE THERE. THE TEAMS GOT SO BIG, YOU HAD TO WAIT FOREVER JUST TO GET YOUR UPS. IT KEPT GETTING DARKER AND DARKER. PRETTY SOON THE MOMS STARTED TO COME OUT ON THE PORCHES TO CALL THE DIFFERENT NAMES OF US TO COME HOME.

YOUR MOM'S CALLING YA

THAT'S YOUR MOM

CAN I TAKE YOUR UPS, MAN?

EVERYONE KEPT SHOUTING JUST A SEC MOM, IN A MINUTE MOM, I'M COMING MOM, BUT NO ONE COULD STAND TO LEAVE BEFORE THEY GOT THEIR TURN. NOW IT WAS SO DARK YOU COULD HARDLY SEE THE BALL. FINALLY, IT WAS MY UPS. I WAS THE LAST ONE.

WHEN THE TEENAGER RICHARD ROLLED THE BALL TO ME, I COULD HEAR MY MOM START TO CALL MY NAME. I BACKED UP TO MAKE THE HARDEST KICK OF MY LIFE. WHEN MY FOOT TOUCHED THE BALL EVERY STREETLIGHT ON THE BLOCK SUDDENLY CAME ON AT ONCE AND MY BROTHER YELLED I GOT IT! I GOT IT! AND WE ALL STOOD STILL WATCHING HIM WITH HIS ARMS UP IN THE AIR WAITING TO MAKE THE LAST BIG CATCH.

86

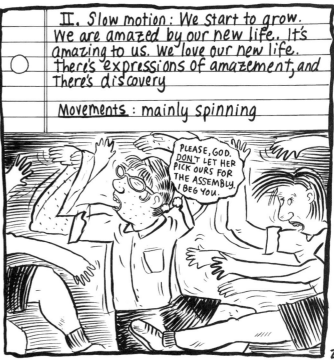

STAYING OVER

BY LYNDA BARRY © 1989

LAST NIGHT I STAYED OVER AT BRENDA'S. OUR GOAL WAS TO STAY UP ALL NIGHT. THE OUIJA BOARD TOLD US TO WATCH NIGHTMARE THEATER. THE MOVIE WASN'T THAT GOOD. IT WAS GIANT ANTS THAT WRECKED A TRAILER.

HOW COME THEY DON'T JUST DO A FIRE HOSE FULL OF RAID ON THEM?

IT'S OBVIOUS.

THEY'D BE DEAD IN AROUND ONE SECOND IF YOU FLOODED THEIR LIFE WITH RAID

EVEN CLOROX.

AROUND 2AM WE WENT TO MAKE PILLSBURY BISCUITS BUT WE COULDN'T GET THE BISCUIT THING TO POP OPEN. WE HIT IT ON THE COUNTER 500 TIMES THEN BRENDA HIT IT WITH A HAMMER AND IT FLEW ACROSS THE ROOM AND CRASHED INTO THE DOG DISH AND BRENDA'S MOM WOKE UP AND TOLD US TO GET TO BED.

THEN THE GUY ON KOL SAID CALL IN YOUR REQUEST SO WE SNUCK BACK IN THE KITCHEN AND BRENDA REQUESTED A SONG BY CREAM THAT SHE DIDN'T KNOW THE NAME OF ABOUT THE LOVE THAT YOU LAID ON MY TABLE. "IT'S FOR DONNY." SHE SAID. "MAKE IT FROM BRENDA TO DONNY." THE GUY SAID HE'D PLAY IT.

YOUR NAME'S GARY, RIGHT?

ONE SEC! ONE SEC MORE!

MY FRIEND'S IN LOVE WITH YOU.

SHUT UP!

SERIOUSLY!

SHE WANTS TO KNOW YOUR ASTROLOGY.

FOR AROUND 3 HOURS HE DIDN'T PLAY THE SONG. WHEN FINALLY IT CAME ON, HE LEFT OUT THE DONNY PART. BRENDA GAVE THE FINGER TO THE RADIO FOR AROUND ONE HALF HOUR AFTER THAT. THEN SHE ASKED ME IF I DARED HER TO CALL HIM UP AND SAY "YOU SUCK" AND ALSO DID I WANT TO MAKE SOME PANCAKES. AND THEN WE STARTED TO HEAR THE BIRDS, 10,000 BIRDS. AND THE LIGHT IN HER ROOM TURNED PALE PALE BLUE.

TOPIC: HAIR

BY LYNDA BARRY, © 1989 CHICAGO, ILL.

HAIR

Maybonne
Home Ec. Period 3

Topic: Hair

1. What is hair?

Hair is a projection growing off of a mammel. A certain kind of projection. It has many uses. It grows on every Mammel.

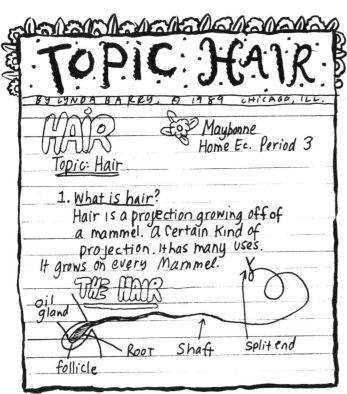

THE HAIR

oil gland

follicle

Root   Shaft   Split end

2. What is the best hairstyle for you?
It depends on your ~~face~~ head. face head

3. Give some examples of hairstyles for the different shapes of heads.

1. Long

DO try to get fullness. Bangs are good. Curl for fullness.

YES

DON'T Just let it hang straight Your head will look worse.

NO

2. Round

YES

DO Let it hang down pretty straight to cover sides of head. Curl the ends.

DON'T CURL it on top of your head unless you want to be a bowling ball head!!

NO

3. Pearshaped.

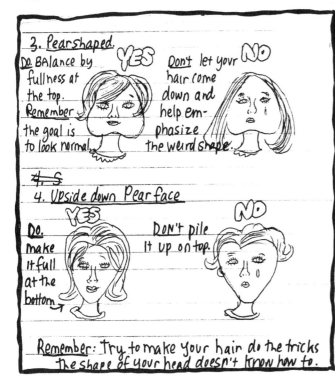

Do Balance by fullness at the top. Remember the goal is to look normal.

YES

Don't let your hair come down and help emphasize the weird shape.

NO

4. Upside down Pearface

YES

Do. make It full at the bottom.

Don't pile It up on top.

NO

Remember: Try to make your hair do the tricks the shape of your head doesn't know how to.

5. What is good for your hair?
Foods: milk, egg yolks, animal livers, oils
eating

6. Fact or Myth? jello will make your hair grow.
Myth

7. What are good things to do to your hair?
brushing, shampoo, creme rinse, a sensible hairstyle that does not look rediculous

8. What are bad things to do to your hair?
ratting.   Too much sun in. Ironing it. wearing a fall that doesn't match. letting your friend cut it. ~~think~~ you are cool because it looks good. thinking

9. What have you learned from this chapter?
I have a weird shaped head but I can correct it with hair. Also hair is dead.

STRING HEADS

·L·y·N·D·A·B·A·R·R·Y·©89

DEAR BRENDA, REMEMBER I TOLD YOU ABOUT MISS RAYBURN? I HATE HER. SHE PUT ME AND THIS GIRL NANCY NEWBY ON LUNCHROOM DUTY. I GOT IT BECAUSE I ACCIDENTALLY SLAMMED MY BOOK DOWN. NANCY GOT IT BECAUSE SHE ACCIDENTALLY SAID "HOME EC SUCKS" AND MISS RAYBURN WAS BY HER.

IF THEY GIVE YOU ANY TROUBLE...

CALL ME.

I SURELY WILL!

YOU HAVE TO WEAR A DORKED OUT APRON. ALSO, A HAIRNET. I SAID NO WAY AM I WEARING A HAIRNET. THEN THEY SAID OK GO TO THE VICE PRINCIPAL. NANCY NEWBY IS COOL. SHE SAID SHE WASN'T WEARING A HAIRNET EITHER SO THEN WE BOTH GOT SENT UP TO MR. VALOTTOS WHO SAID DID WE WANT TO GET SUSPENDED.

(THINKS HE'S HIP)

(SIDEBURNS)

(TURTLE-NECK DICKEY)

YOU GIRLS BETTER GET WITH WHAT'S GOING DOWN! . I AM NOT A JIVE TURKEY AND THIS SCHOOL IS NOT A JIVE TURKEY! ANY QUESTIONS?

(COMMUNICATION)

SO WE PUT ON THE HAIRNETS THEN NANCY NEWBY STARTS GOING "WE ARE THE STRING HEADS WE ARE THE STRING HEADS" IN THIS VOICE OF A ROBOT AND I WAS PEEING MY PANTS FROM IT. WE WERE CARRYING TRAYS AND THEN I DROPPED MY TRAYS THEN SHE DROPPED HER TRAYS THEN NO WAY COULD WE STOP LAUGHING. YOU KNOW THAT THING WHEN YOU CAN'T STOP LAUGHING?

GIRLS!

GIRLS!

GIRLS!

STOP I'M GONNA BARF.

SO THEN WE GOT SENT TO MR. VALOTTOS WHO ASKED US DID WE THINK WE COULD CONTROL OUR BEHAVIOR, BECAUSE ONE MORE PINK SLIP AND SUSPENSION. AFTER SCHOOL NANCY NEWBY CAME OVER. SHE SMOKES NEWPORTS. SHE SHOWED ME HOW SHE STOLE THE HAIRNET, IT WAS IN HER PURSE. I THINK SHE'S GOING TO BE ALL RIGHT AS A FRIEND. PLEASE WRITE BACK SOON. S4S4S4 ☺ LUV YA, maybonne ☺

YOU'RE SMOKIN!

DUH.

BUG OFF MARLYS.

YOU'RE SMOKERS.

MARLYS VOCABULARYS

BY LYNDA LING TING TONG BARRY HI SEAN C. ©1990

Can you say the word ~~element~~ *groovy?* Do you know what it means? You can easily find out. *By The Great Marlys!*

B−

My Word of Vocabulary by Marlys

My word of vocabulary is Groovy. It is the word for when somethings great! Use it in a sentence! It is also a song Feeling Groovy!

Hi Marlys your groovy

thank you its groovy of you to even say that because your a movie star right

yes I am will you be in my groovy movie made in england yes

Where did the word come from It came over from England which I love England! Theres a girl Christina going around saying it was her cousin from Indiana invented it what a lie! If I could have one wish it would be a british accent! Talking In British is #1!

here I got you a present english leather my favorite

it has a groovy odor

please go in my movie with me your perfect

Thats so groovy of a compliment But no ones perfect only god!

I saw some England movies one with the mummy and one that gots Julie Andrews you never saw a more beautiful lady also another english movie is the gorgon have you seen it where if you look at her you get turned into cement then they chop her head off! It goes rolling on the floor but the snakes stay alive because she gots snakes for hair. They got the best of monsters in england!

HEY you EXCUSE me

OH no I looked at you

HA ha Jolly good fellow you fell for my evil plan!

Help I cant move myself

Marlys, Please try to stay on the subject!

PIP PIP cherrio

I'm doomed

Groovy. Groo-vy. The accent is on the ~~sec~~ first syllable. The grooviest thing of my life would be to star in an English movie my title: The Sound of Marlys! of me singing with guest stars Peter and Gordon Hermans Hermits all people of England! It would be the groovy movie of all time! I will be a musical babysitter who wins versus the Nazis! Coming soon to your most groovy theater! Starring Marlys!

Hers my autograph for you

Thank you I love your handwriting

well its nothing

your accent is very fantastic

Thanks President Johnson your movie was worth the money

MY GROOVY life of the Future!

BEYOND the EARTH

BY·L·Y·N·D·A·B·A·R·R·Y·©89

If you could visit another planet, where would you like to go? Let us pretend to take a long, long trip through space.

VISIT! THE! PLANET! OF! MARLYS!!!!!!

The planet of marlys

mercury! venus! EARTH! Sun!

Facts about the Planet of Marlys!
- It has Oxygen!
- How many moons? 58!
- Hardly no Gravity!
- Free CANDY FOR MY FRIENDS!

NEWS SPECIAL BULLETIN! Astronauts have discovered the gorgeous planet of MARLYS! They thought that Earth was #1 now theres a tie of which is the best planet! Now they're Voting on Marlys!

Here YE HERE YE!

STOP TALKING!

Please raise your hand who votes MARLYS.

THAT'S 1,000,000,000,000 Votes.

now who is voting earth?

2 votes.

Planet marlys is obviously the winner

yea! yea!

The planet Marlys has incredible decorations and rides. It rotates quickly and the people of Marlys are good, they only want peace. Everythings free. For energy they use special dirt. The cars can run on dirt and you can cook with dirt. Also you feel like you are floating.

Welcome earthling

Take me to your leader

This place is Great!

On the planet Marlys anyone named Marlys is #1 But no Marlys starts acting all conceited Because of it. They have the Marlys parade and the main marlys rides a float. If you want to go to planet Marlys you will just have to wait for the future! In the future you can come to planet Marlys!!! It will be great!!!

OK, CLASS. PAPERS FORWARD

92

THANKS MARLYS

BY L. BARRY WITH RESEARCH ASSISTANCE FROM S. COLLINS & S. NEWMAN @ 90

OK everybody !!!!!!! Here comes my story of thanksgiving by the great Marlys! Ones upon a time there was Squanto the Indian spying on the starvation of the Pilgrims! This was in real! life! Not made up!

I must help them they are too stupid to grow corn!

OH NO!

HEY

we Have no FOOD!

SHUT UP IT WAS YOUR idea to come here!

BUT YOU SAID OK TO IT. AND IT WAS YOUR STUPID BOAT THE MAYFLOWER

Help we are doomed

Lets go back home

Squanto asked cheif Massassoit.

EXCUSE ME BUT can we help them

I Dont know what if they get very powerful from the corn and Go demolishing us

There is no way because they will be thankful

OH OK

Then Squanto showed them plant one corn plus one dead fish in each hole. Also shoot that turkey

ready aim fire!

Hold still you stupid idiot!

I hate you Squanto

corn grows plentiful now →

Then came the day that suddenly all the food was ready.

hey Squanto that thing with the fish worked great! sorry for thinking you were BAZURK when you first said it.

thats ok now lets harvest it

turkey   Corn   pumkins   green jello

The pilgrims had a great idea.

I got it! Lets have a party!

you said it!

OK and we will have Squanto and them over!

I'll make the incredible decorations

what shall we call our party how about thanksGIVING

Thats a great name!

The party was so great and everyone enjoyed it. Everyone was there just having the greatest time. They told jokes and were dancing. Then they got the idea to keep on doing it! Now we do it today in the future! Only difference now is you can't Hardly find indians to invite to the party. The end by Marlys. Happy Thanksgiving from the great marlys!

Squanto can I try on your hat

I am so full

same here

If I can try on yours

Turkey in the straw turkey in the hay

Squanto you are a great dancer

same goes for you

MORE BEAUTIFUL

BY LYNDA "WATCH THAT MONKEY" BARRY © 1991

WHEN YOU'RE CLOSE TO ME I CAN FEEL YOUR HEARTBEAT I CAN HEAR YOU BREATHING IN MY EAR. MY SISTER SINGS IT WITH THE RADIO. THE SONG "GROOVY KIND OF LOVE." SHE SAYS SHE NEVER HEARD A SONG MORE BEAUTIFUL.

SHE SAYS SHE WANTS GROOVY LOVE IN HER LIFE. I SAY "SAME HERE." THE SUN IS COMING THROUGH THE KITCHEN WINDOW AND SHE LAYS HER HEAD IN THE LIT UP SQUARE ON THE TABLE AND CLOSES HER EYES. HER MOUTH MOVES ON THE SONG WORDS THEN SHE TELLS ME THE SECRET OF THERE'S SOMEONE SHE LIKES. I SAY WHAT'S HIS NAME. SHE SAYS KEVIN TURNER.

HE SITS IN ROW THREE AND SHE KNOWS THE BACK OF HIS HEAD BY HEART. SHE ASKED THE MAGIC EIGHT BALL DID HE LIKE HER ALSO AND IT SAID ASK AGAIN LATER. SHE SAID SHE SPIT ON A GUY FOR CALLING HIM KEVIN TURKEY AND THE GUY SLUGGED HER BUT THE SLUG WAS WORTH IT. SHE SAYS KEVIN SMELLS LIKE MOTHBALLS AND NOW MOTHBALLS SMELL LIKE FLOWERS.

OUTSIDE IN THE GARDEN THERE'S PLANTS COMING UP AND MORE BIRDS SITTING ON THE CLOTHES POLE. "KEVIN RAN THE 100-YARD DASH THE FASTEST OF ANYONE AND HE DIDN'T ACT CONCEITED. WOULDN'T YOU AGREE BABY YOU AND ME GOT A GROOVY KIND OF LOVE." SHE SINGS IT TO HIM WITH HER EYES SHUT TIGHT. KEVIN TURNER CAN YOU HEAR IT?

ALL DIFFERENT

BY LYNDA "HONESTYVILLE" BARRY © 1991

HAVE YOU EVER WATCHED SOMEONE FALL IN LOVE? HOW THEY TURN ALL DIFFERENT? THAT'S MY SISTER MARLYS. RIGHT NOW SHE'S MAKING KISSING NOISES TO MR. LUDERMYER'S DOG.

YOU NOTICE HOW NO MATTER WHAT YOU SAY TO THEM THEY KEEP BEING HAPPY? THIS MORNING I BURNED THE PANCAKES. MARLYS SAID THEY NEVER TASTED BETTER. I SUCKED THE HEAD OF HER BARBIE UP THE VACUUM CLEANER. SHE SAID SHE ALWAYS HATED THAT DOLL.

RIGHT NOW SHE IS LOVING ALL MUSIC. EVEN THE SONGS ABOUT STOMACH RELIEF. AND ALL THINGS LOOK BEAUTIFUL TO HER INCLUDING LINT BALLS AND MEATBALLS AND OLD GUM IN THE STREET.

OUR FATHER WHO ART IN HEAVEN IT'S HER FIRST TIME AND SHE DOESN'T KNOW THAT FEELING GOES AWAY, SO PLEASE FATHER, IN ALL YOUR MERCIFUL WISDOM, COULD YOU PLEASE JUST KEEP YOUR MOUTH SHUT A LITTLE LONGER?

WHY DID HE?

BY LYNDA BARRY WITH LAUREN GAFFNEY © 1991

THE BOY NAMED KEVIN TURNER WHO MARLYS LOVES, LOVES HER BACK. MARLYS SAYS SHE KNOWS HE LOVES HER BACK OR ELSE WHY DID HE WAIT FOR HER EVERY DAY BY ROOM 4 SAYING "HI MARLYS. HI TWINKIE."

TWINKIE BECAUSE MARLYS ALWAYS SPLIT HER PACKAGE WITH HIM. SHE HAS WIPED OUT ALL THE MONEY IN HER ABRAHAM LINCOLN HEAD BANK BUYING TWINKIES TO SPLIT WITH KEVIN TURNER. KEVIN TURNER, KEVIN TURNER. SHE HAS SAID HIS NAME 100 TIMES FAST WITH HER EYES CLOSED TIGHT.

MARLYS SAYS SHE KNOWS HE LOVES HER BACK EVEN THOUGH AROUND HIS FRIENDS HE ACTED DIFFERENT. TODAY AROUND HIS FRIENDS HE SAID THE SAME NAME FOR HER, TWINKIE, ONLY SHOUTING IT NOW AND LAUGHING. TWINKIE AND SOME OTHER WORDS AND MARLYS SAYS IT'S NO BIG DEAL.

NO BIG DEAL, SHE SAYS, THEN LOOKS DOWN AND STOPS TALKING. AND FOR THE FIRST TIME I EVER SAW, SHE'S QUIET. JUST QUIET AND STARING DOWN WITHOUT MOVING.

IF YOU CAN BELIEVE IT

© by LYNDA "EL HOSEMASTER" BARRY ©1991

DON'T EVER ASK A GUY IF HE LIKES YOU, THAT'S THE NUMBER ONE THING YOU CAN DO TO WRECK YOUR CHANCES, I TRIED TO TELL MARLYS BUT SHE JUST LOOKED AT ME AND KEPT WRITING: "DEAR KEVIN, TRUTH OR DARE"

"TRUTH IS: TELL ME DO YOU LIKE ME. DARE IS: I DARE YOU TO TELL ME DO YOU LIKE ME." YOU DON'T KNOW BOYS I TELL HER BUT SHE GIVES HIM THE LETTER ANYWAY WITH A PERFECT DRAWING ON IT OF A DADDY ROTH RACE CAR. KEVIN'S FAVORITE. "ART IS GOOD FOR THINGS" SHE SAYS.

IF YOU CAN BELIEVE IT THE ANSWER OF KEVIN IS YES. YES HE LIKES MARLYS BUT IT'S A LET'S MAKE A DEAL. DOOR NUMBER ONE IS SHE HAS TO KEEP IT SECRET. DOOR NUMBER TWO IS SHE HAS TO KEEP MAKING HIM DRAWINGS. AND DOOR NUMBER THREE IS HE GETS TO TELL PEOPLE IT WAS HIM WHO MADE THE DRAWINGS.

WORTH IT! SHOUTS MARLYS. WORTH IT WORTH IT WORTH IT TO THE MILLIONTH POWER! YOU CAN SEE HER RIGHT NOW BENDING OVER THE PAPER AND DRAWING. SNEAKING OUT OF BED AT NIGHT AND DRAWING THE PICTURES FOR KEVIN TURNER ALWAYS LEAVING THE PERFECT SPOT EMPTY FOR WHERE HE CAN SIGN HIS NAME.

SO THEY TRADE

by LYNDA "NOT THE MONEY" BARRY ©1991

I SAID TO MARLYS IF KEVIN REALLY LIKES YOU THEN WHY DOES HE SAY YOU CAN'T TELL, WHY DOES HE MAKE YOU KEEP DRAWING HIM DRAGSTERS, AND WHY DOES HE KEEP SAYING IT WAS HIM WHO MADE THOSE DRAWINGS? I TOLD HER THAT'S NOT LIKING, THAT'S USING.

I TOLD HER I KNOW GUYS AND I KNOW THEIR SPAZZY ACTIONS AND SHE SAID IF I DIDN'T MIND IT COULD I PLEASE JUST SHUT UP? I SAID DON'T YOU GET IT? THIS IS ADVICE, AND SHE SAID NO YOU'RE THE ONE WHO'S NOT GETTING IT. OH YEAH? I SAY. OH YEAH? THEN SHE TELLS ME.

NUMBER ONE: KEVIN SAYS DON'T TELL BECAUSE OF THE GIRL ALICE BULZOMI WHO ALSO LOVES HIM AND ALICE IS BIG AND WILL KICK MARLYS WITH HER POINTED SHOES AND ALSO KEVIN IF SHE EVER FINDS OUT. NUMBER TWO: MARLYS DRAWS HIM DRAGSTERS BECAUSE KEVIN LOVES DRAGSTERS BUT TRAGICALLY HE IS A CRUDDY DRAWER OF DRAGSTERS. THAT IS JUST LIFE MARLYS SAYS.

WHAT HE'S GOOD AT DRAWING IS NATURE AND FLOWERS. SO THEY TRADE. THEN MARLYS SHOWS ME THE STACK OF SECRET DRAWINGS HE MADE HER. TWENTY-SEVEN DRAWINGS IN A PAY 'N' SAVE BAG WITH THE PENCIL HANDWRITING ON THE TOP:

To Marlys your the greatest girl artist of dragsters from Kevin.

PENCIL HANDWRITING SHE TRACES WITH HER FINGER, THEN SHE LOOKS AT ME AND SMILES.

The MARLYS NEWSPAPER!!!

by LYNDA "GOODBYE SEAN COLLINS" BARRY © 1991

the #1 reporter.

Please read Marlys newspaper! It is a great newspaper for all your information!

Price? It is free for my friends

Weather today. It will be great!!

Table of contents

other things are everywhere else

KEVIN TURNER LOSES HIS OTHER TOOTH!!

IT WAS here
THIS DOES NOT LOOK LIKE HIM THAT MUCH.

Last night he was eating a sucker called Black Cow and it came out. The first tooth he lost still has not grown in. Kevin is in stable condition he got 25¢ under his pillow

Marlys SETS RECORD on eating MARISHINO CHERRIES!

On monday Marlys bought a full jar of marishino cherries from A+P with her own money. One by one she ate them. 47 cherries!! She had a comment: They are so delicious!! She drank grape pop to go with it!

ADVICE OF MARLYS by Marlys!

Dear Marlys, I think you are incredible on advice. Here's my problem. A person whose name I won't say is looking inside peoples lunch boxes every day but he just tells the teacher I have to get something in my coat. She always lets him in the coat room. Then he goes all in your lunch box and moves around your sandwhich what should I do? signed "Mysterious."

Dear Mysterious know what I would do is write a note in my lunch box with that guys name on it. Write "I know You are doing This! So quit it!

COMICS

NORMAN the CAT
by Kevin turner

(1) how many times I tell you norman don't play with matches!

(2) norman thats real dynamite not a toy oh No!

(3) KABLOOOEY

(4) oh Good it was just a dream
THE END??

SPORTS

Tumbeling Class after school in Mrs. Allen's. Rm 9.

Please join our tumbeling class in Mrs. Allen's room, room 9. We use mats and music you can bring your own records. You will learn gracefullness. Its not just for girls!! Come on to tumbeling! Marlys did the record on backwards summer saulting. 27 could have done more except she hit a desk and had to relax.

4th Graders Clobber 5th Graders in Lunch Kickball Game!!! IT WAS SO Great!!!

WE WON IT!
yay
yay
your cheated
sore loser

The 4th graders won at lunch Kickball. Theres people saying we cheated because they're sore losers. Just ignore them! Victory is ours!!!

MOVIES

In mrs. allens we saw a filmstrip from Larva to butterfly. It was incredible!! Only one person fell asleep during the show!!!!!!!!!!!

Pets

HAMPSTER CROAKS IN MRS. BRYANTS!!! BY Anonomys!!

mona
Look shes dead
oh my
People crying
GO BACK to your seats!
mrs. Bryant
MONA
our grave for Mona

Mona the hampster in Mrs. Bryants is dead. One guy in the class said the name of the desease that killed mona is a famous desease of hampsters called The Big Butt Desease. (Please don't laugh its tragic) People said lets bury her at least but Mrs Bryant said I'll take care of it and later someone saw her put Mona in the janitors garbage! Cold blooded Award #1 Goes to Mrs Bryant but lucky thing we got Mona out + Buried Her!

OUR·DOMESTIC·POULTRY

BY LYNDA "TAKE A LETTER MARIA" BARRY ✿ ©1991

Workbook p. 36 chap. 6
Marlys Mullen

Our Domestic Poultry.
by Marlys Mullen

Chickens are old. In china there was chickens 3,000 years ago. In India. In the Indies. In Columbus He ate them. They came to the USA on boats.

here Col. Sanders! a present

Pilgrim

What is it?

The name OF It is a chicken

oh thank you now I got a job!

I will call it finger licking good!

Theres 2 kinds of chickens. Useful and Fancy Fancy ones are just for looks. To run in your yard to make it look beautiful.

Come Back!

NO ONE RUNS FROM COL. SANDERS!

Fancy   USEFUL

The useful ones make eggs and also you eat them. Theres lots of varieties But they ALL hate Col. Sanders. (Thats a joke, Son!) People have fixed It so useful chickens Cannot Fly. That can be called coldblooded. They have 3 stomachs. They eat chicken-feed but they will eat Fritos.

2. proventriculus

1. crop

3. gizzard

Food in a chicken will not Get chewed! So Don't give them Gum not even Dentene. It goes down to the first stomach called Crop. Then into proventriculus. then Gizzard where theres rocks (actual) grinding it. The rest is usual. A certain chicken can lay 300 Eggs a year! It is done by breeding.

I can tay 300 eggs a year

So could my mom!

please fall in love

GIRL   BOY   farmer

The little egg grows in the chicken then goes down a tUBE.
Then a shell Goes around it. But the workbook didn't say how. or how The chicken can lay it without Breaking it. Thats the part I don't Get.

IT TAKES ABOUT 21 DAYS For The chick TO Grow in the EGG then They Poke a hole in the Shell with the BEAK. Some chicks WILL Grow up TO LAY EGGS. OTHER CHICKS WILL grow up TO BE Meat or Fried chicken. Except very smart Fast runners.

hey you

The end?

EXTRA credit: Do chicken pox come from chickens?
   A. NO. It comes From Smelling some ones breath or the scabs of the chicken pox. Chicken pox makes you feel terrible. Chickens Do not.

MARLYS NEW YEAR

BY LYNDA KING KONG DING DONG BARRY ⊛ ©1990

HOW TO HAVE A PERFECT NEW YEARS!!
FOR THE WHOLE WORLD!!!!!!!!
Written by Marlys! For the whole world!!!

#1. Practice your shout of <u>HAPPY</u> <u>NEW</u> <u>YEARS</u>!

Q. wheres the good places to practice at?

  A. in the bathtub

Q. wheres the bad places to practice at?

  A. by your grandma.

#2. Go to your Uncles where all the people are at the Party and they KEEP YELLING "You KIDS STAY UPstairs!" Go Ahead and put on your aunt Wildas WiG IF you want and heres how to Get the feeling OF Drunk: Spin 100 times then make your cousin sit on your Stomach but watch out For sudden barfing!!!

oh no look out

help you must save me

I am sorry everybody but I have to throw up

Doritos and creamed corn mixed in

#3. Make your promises for the new year like Quit acting all cruddy to people, no man from U.N.C.L.E. spys on your sister, don't write smart pants word ballons on the library books and stop acting all superior.

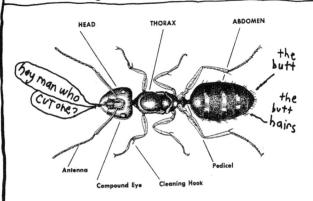

hey man who cut one?

HEAD   THORAX   ABDOMEN

the butt

the butt hairs

Antenna

Compound Eye   Cleaning Hook   Pedicel

#4. Dial the time lady to hear the EXACT at the tone the time will BE 12:00 EXACTLY! then Shout It! run in the street and shout it! BAng on pots and pans And make your shout FLy into Infinity!!!!
You're welcome for my great information! Happy new years From the great incredible #1 marlys!

HAPPY NEW YEAR!

our sun   mercury   venus   marlys the earth

DANCING MARLYS

MARLYS GOOD MANNERS

BY Lynda "HELLO BROTHER" Barry © 1991

number one on how to act decent: Don't go chewing with your mouth all open! It looks like a whole washing machine of food!

2 Don't grab other peoples food even if They are not looking and you want it really bad!

3 Don't go interrupting people even if their story is boring.

4 Don't stand in front of the TV when someones show is on

5 Don't stare at people too long even if they are BLOWING your mind with how they look

6 Don't listen in on the downstairs phone! if you don't know the conversation is private!

7 Don't chew your nails in front of people or behind people.

8 Don't ever shove people even if they are getting on your nerves.

MARLYS' GUIDE to QUEERS

by LYNDA "SEAN COLLINS" BARRY ©1991

EXCUSE ME BUT RIGHT ON AND WELCOME TO MY GUIDE TO QUEERS.

THIS IS FOR YOU TO READ SO YOU DON'T KEEP BLOWING YOUR MIND ON THE GREAT SUBJECT.

LIKE IF YOU GOT QUESTIONS FOR EXAMPLE WHAT DOES A QUEER DO WHEN HE SEES A DOG. ANSWER IT DEPENDS ON THE DOG. MAYBE PETS IT.

ALSO DEPENDS ON WHOSE DOG. IF IT'S A NICE DOG WITH A MEAN MAN? ANSWER FEELS SORRY FOR THE DOG. IF IT'S A MEAN DOG WITH A NICE MAN. ANSWER FEELS SORRY FOR THE MAN. IF IT'S A NICE DOG WITH A NICE MAN. ANSWER MAKE FRIENDS!

HI

Hi Your dog is nice also you are

THANKS

Hi what's his name

LOOK OUT HE'S A QUEER

Pooky do you think that's a dumb name

noway its great

RUN FOR IT.

ALSO THERE'S PEOPLE WHO DON'T LIKE QUEERS. ONE THING THEY'RE THINKING IS THE QUEER'S GOING TO KISS THEM

hey you! Don't come near me

LIKE I WOULD EVER WANT TO

YOU DO SO WANT TO!

AS IF.

WHY NOT?

YOU GET ON MY NERVES

ANOTHER THING IS WHO IS A QUEER? ANSWER MY UNCLE JOHN. ANOTHER ONE IS BILL. THEY TOOK ME AND MY SISTER TO THE DRIVE-IN AND MY FRIEND KEVIN TURNER. IT WAS SO GREAT BUT NOW THAT THEY ARE KNOWN QUEERS YOU CAN FORGET THAT WILL HAPPEN AGAIN UNTIL THE MIRACLE DAY OF PEOPLE QUIT BEING SO STUPID. WILL IT COME? I DON'T KNOW.

can kevin come to the movies

not if queers will be there

There's usually queers at movies though.

Then forget it

ok Bye Kevin

Sorry your moms BERSURK.

I AM DOOMED

THERE'S PEOPLE WHO WILL HIT YOU IF THEY FIND OUT YOU ARE QUEER

MY UNCLE JOHN HAS A SCAR ON HIS FOREHEAD FROM IT. THE POLICE SAID "FORGET IT."

PERSONALLY I LIKE QUEERS !!! SO FAR I ONLY KNOW TWO QUEERS AND I AM LOOKING FOR MORE QUEERS!!! SO IF YOU SEE ME PLEASE SAY HI DON'T BE ALL SNOBBISH!!! ALSO IF YOU KNOW OTHER QUEERS TELL THEM "MARLYS SAYS HI." SAY "RIGHT ON FROM MARLYS" AND DO THE POWER SIGN. AND IF YOU SEE MY UNCLE JOHN AND BILL PLEASE SAY I MISS THEM AND COME BACK SOON.

Love truly, * Marlys *

P.S. here's my school picture if you want to stick it in your billfold!!! It would be an honor!!!

MARLYS SPRING

BY LYNDA BARRY 🌸 FOR GARY COVINO 🌸© 1990

I SHARE THE BED WITH MY LITTLE SISTER MARLYS WHO SOMETIMES JUST KILLS ME. LIKE THIS MORNING SHE WAS SINGING "JEREMIAH WAS A BULLFROG" OUT THE OPEN WINDOW OF OUR BEDROOM.

IT WAS THE FIRST WARM DAY OF THE YEAR. IN THE FRONT YARD THERE WERE FLOWERS. SHE SAID DID I DARE HER TO GO OUT ON THE ROOF AND DO THE BUTT DANCE IN HER PAJAMAS. THIS IS THE DANCE WHERE YOU STICK YOUR BUTT OUT AS MUCH AS POSSIBLE. SHE INVENTED IT.

SHE CLIMBS OUT THE WINDOW AND STARTS SINGING "LA CUCARACHA" THEN SHE BENDS OVER AND SINGS "SOMEONE LEFT THE CAKE OUT IN THE RAIN." A CAR HONKS AT HER AND SHE STICKS HER ARM IN THE AIR AND SHOUTS "BLACK POWER!" THEN THE DOOR FLIES OPEN AND IT'S MY GRANDMA YELLING IS MARLYS TRYING TO KILL HER?

AT BREAKFAST MY GRANDMA WON'T SHUT UP ABOUT HOW I HAVE NO RESPONSIBILITY. HOW COULD I LET MY SISTER BEHAVE THAT WAY, SHE COULD HAVE FALLEN OFF THE ROOF AND WHAT ABOUT THE NEIGHBORS. THEN SHE TURNS HER HEAD TO GET THE TOAST, AND MARLYS LOOKS AT ME AND SMILES. MAN. I NEVER KNEW I LOVED HER SO MUCH.

109

CALLING OUT FOR LOVE

story idea By Susie Esbejornson. Draws by LYNDA BARRY © 1991

Where do dreams come from? <u>Number one</u>: your imaginations. <u>Number two</u>: Could Be a secret power of e.s.p. trying to tell you something! This is my dream I was playing with some friends by the Black Lagoon.

The Creature of the BLACK LAGOON!

For a long time the creature made noises and I tried to understand what was The problem. Finally I guessed it right!

Turns out the best thing to clean the creature with is school Paper towels. I GOT A Bunch.

I wiped off the creature until he was clean. He felt so beautiful and happy.

I tried to see if my sister would be the creatures girl friend but she was too stuck up for him. Then I woke up. What was the message of my dream? Sometimes A monster can be Great! Sometimes A monster can be doing a love call to you. The End? by Marlys

SUPER RIGHT ON!

BY LYNDA "CHECK OUT JOHN MOONEY ON ROUNDER" BARRY ©92

Here's a incredible list of RightOns by my family! You should also ask your family for a list of their RIGHT ons! Everyone should tell their RightOns! What's your right ons? Oh yeah say RIGHT ON !!! by *Marlys* *Right on* *right on hand*

My Mom's Right Ons:

Lysol liquid + spray!

Chances Are!

Johnny Mathis!

WOOLITE

SALVO

MR CLEAN

Formula 409

Shell no pest strips

SLUG BAIT

WINSTONS

PINESOL

The WHITE Tornado AJAX

rubber gloves

Freddie's RIGHT ONS:

* His pet fly name of JEFF!

The Parts of a insect leg! (he said I had to put it in)

trochanter   Femer   tibia   tarsus

tweezers!

please Don't BUG me I just croaked (my joke! Haha)

The song called psychotic reaction BY THE COUNT FIVE

Giant Water BUG Because it can pretend its dead for around 15 minutes.

His SECRET UNDERWEAR DANCING TO THAT SONG

Pulvilli. he said thats What insects use to walk on glass + the ceiling. He said he wants it on his feet. RIGHT ON PULVILLI!

SLUG BAIT

THROWING AWAY THE SLUG BAIT + no pest strip

Jars with holes in the lid + dirt in the bottom

LUCKY Glow in the dark Light Bulb 1¢ & PRIZES from Gum machines

GOING into OUTER Space to investigate if theres insects IN OUTER SPACE

Maybonne's RIGHT ONS:

nair!

Donovan!

peace!

Her diary!

FROSTED CHERRY LIPSTICK!

ecology

EQUALITY!

Astrology + ESP

Once she asked our mom the names of The Beatles and mom said
1. CURLEY
2. MOE
3. ROGER
4. SWIRLEY.

the song, Groovin By Tommy James and the Shondells

Incredible Flower power Bell bottoms that mom won't Let her wear. But she sneaks them sometimes.

Maybonne says that's her FUNNY RIGHT ON!

Theres more But now she says for me to QUIT BUGGING HER SO FORGET HER THEN! FINE!!

The Great RIGHT ons of Marlys:

sweet tarts!

KevIn Turner!

THE FUNKY CHICKEN!

SOUR GRAPE
SOUR APPLE

ALL SOUR GUM FLAVORS!

People with Giant hind ends

Peace!

BIG EYE Pictures OF SAD DOGS!

hi marlys

the song IF YOU'RE GOING to San Francisco

the gorgeous smell of Gasoline

This nice Baby named Henry

Ballerina outFits!

my Glow in the dark Jesus

Eyelashes OF A COW

RIGHT ON PEOPLE WHO SAY RIGHT ON!

SORRY STORY

BY LYNDA · LOVE TO THE CAST AT THE REP!!! BARRY © 1992

the worlds lonliest outpost of the atlantic adventure report by Freddie

In the middle of the atlantic Ocean is a little island made of rocks where only 200 people live. theres more people at our school than the whole island called TristanDaCunha. Its an ugly island.

One great thing about it is a 8,000 Foot high VOLCANO

One BAD thing is the volcano is ice cold

It got its name from the man who discovered it. A explorer. the people told him it Already Had a name. He told them BIG DEAL

First came people from PORTUGAL then Scotland. they brought animals for the natives.

Then they showed the people their GODS were FAKE Outs.

Then the people came over from Holland, ITALY, America And A LOT OF ships crashed And sank when they got there

Then the brother of the guy that wrote Ala Alice In wonderland came. He was a missionary. He Brought A Lot of his friends And they got their WAY.

After awhile people from other lands got sick of this lonely Island And went back home. they didn't invite their new buddys who they taught to eat potatoes.

Now everyone lives in a little town around a BIG church. Now everyone is SICK OF potatoes. Now everyone is hoping a ship will come that they can sneak on And go to california. Until then the 200 people just FEEL sad And lonely.

In my opinion there are some people who should should go Back to the place called Tristan DaCunha And say they are sorry. IF I could go there I know I would say it.

ARTISTIC PROJECTS

BY LYNDA "EATING BANANAS IN HOUSTON" BARRY © 1992

have you ever thought of this one? You can carve _gorgeous_ in SOAP!! ★ ★ ★ by The Great Marlys!!! ALSO and some ideas by the great Freddie!!

WHAT YOU NEED

SOAP
• IVORY
• SAFEGUARD
• DON'T you WISH you use DIAL
• CAMAY
• DOVE ONE QUarter cleansing cream • DON'T TRY DiShwashing LiQUID

KNIFE
Sharp is GOOD But your mom WILL SAY NO. SO WAIT UNTIL She is at work or use

BUTTER KNIFE

YOUR GREAT BRAINS
OF IMAGINATION!

OR ASK Freddie iF you ARE STUCK.

DIRECTIONS:

① Get your SOAP. HARD SOAP IS the best DON'T TRY the SOAP THAT WAS LAYING IN THE TUB WITH YOU.

EXCUSE ME CAN I Have the SOAP

I am Shy if you DON'T NOTICE!

hey you GET OUT DO you THINK this is A NUDIST COLONY.

Hints on SOAP: ASK your mom first UNLESS She has A TON she got ON SALE AND then forgot it Then Just Sneak ONE ONLY!!! See iF you can USE COLORS!!!
CAMAY = PINK! DIAL:ORANGE! IRISH Psychadelic SPRING: Green!

② FIND A GOOD PLACE TO CARVE
IN THE KITCHEN if your mom already knows.   UNDER the porch if She doesn't

---

③ Figure OUT WHAT to CARVE.
Try _not_ to pick something skinny like:
• A Skinny man or lady, or their skinny children and pets. ITS TOO hard EVEN FOR ME. especially THE FINGERS.

EASY PROJECTS ARE

A Tiki Head IS GOOD !!!!
SIDE 1   SIDE 2
SAD TIKI   JOYFUL TIKI
YOU CAN TIE a rope on it and WEAR IT AS A NECKLACE! IT HAS MOODS!!

A HOUSE ← hard part

a pack OF Cigarettes.
a cigarette. (Don't smoke it! ha ha!!)

THE BIBLE

A BOOK

a Blockhead, or ABRAHAM LINCOLN OR ANY PRESIDENT

---

④ PRETTY Soon when you're advanced TRY:

EIFFEL TOWER   The SPACE needle   Johnny mathis   an award (1st)   RATFINK   your Sister

⑤ How to Keep your Soap sculpture from rotting
1. Don't Get it wet with ANYTHING not water. cake. milk. spit. KooLaid. hawaiian punch
2. Don't Let it get DUSTY OR DROP it on dirt UNLESS you WANT it to Look CRUDDED OUT WHICH to some people is interesting on art.
3. Donate it to the MUSEUM where DonAtions are welcome

heres some Great art!   we LOVE it!

⑥ A GOOD TRICK
PUT it in the FREEZER AND TELL Some one it is expensive ICE cream!! Say have Some to people who say constant SWEARS !!

BATS OF INTREST.

BY LYNDA "Winter Carnival in St. Paul!" BARRY © 1992

Title: Bats Bats Bats
Author Timothy Latta Pages 64
How did you hear about the book my library

Freddie
extra credit report. (Book)

Bats Bats Bats

Bats Bats Bats is a incredible book. It is mostly about Bats who are our only mammals with wings. Where did Bats come from? Even scientists don't know!

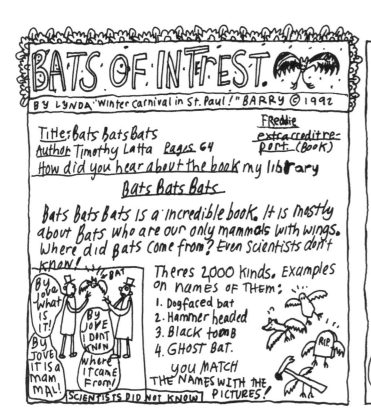

Theres 2,000 kinds. Examples on names of them:
1. Dogfaced bat
2. Hammer headed
3. Black tomb
4. GHOST BAT.

YOU MATCH THE NAMES WITH THE PICTURES!

Facts on Bats; They Fly with their mouths open and their noise bounces on things so they never crash. They believe in free love. The babies ride around on the moms, and the moms love them. If you STEAL a Baby Bat the mom will try to LOCATE you. They can Live to be 20 years OLD.

← Baby

← mother

One kind called Noctilio or Bulldog Bat smells horrible. The author says it is a Bad odor. said he picked up a Bulldog Bat and the smell stayed on his hands for around a WEEK even though he washed his hands

may I have this dance

Did you hold that same bat again?

I will dance with you next week

Vampire Bats are real. They have a special stomach for digesting blood. First seen by Charles Darwin who also invented our thing with the monkeys. They're only around as long as your long finger and they can run on walls. They slit the veins of victims with sharp front teeth but they are so good at it you can't hardly feel it. Then they lick the blood. Not really a big deal except they have major germs on their tongues.'

oh no!

what is it my dear

a bat is sucking your fore head!

and yet I feel nothing!

Oh honey theres one on you too

Bat Guano comes out of bats and people buy it. In the civil war part of it made gunpowder and soldiers guarded it with guns.

hey buster I will blow your head OFF!

←Bat

get away from it!

↓guano

Soon the guano will be mine!

robber

The Saddest Bats.
In world war two the U.S.A. tied bombs on free TAILED bats. Time Bombs that were even bigger then the bat! When it blew up the flame went 22 inches and burned for eight minutes. The plan was to blow up Japan and other enemies with Bats that would Fly the bombs into houses and buildings but then scientists finished the A-Bomb. Lucky for the bats. Unlucky for everyone else. I enjoyed Bats Bats Bats it is a great book for understanding Bats! by Freddie!

the end?

Tick Tick Tick

116

BY LYNDA • WHY DID WBEZ TAKE STUART OFF THE AIR?? ~ BARRY

GOT A LETTER FROM MY COUSIN MARLYS. IT SAID "DEAR ARNA HOW ARE YOU I AM FINE MAYBONNE IS FINE ALSO FREDDIE IS FINE EXCEPT FOR HE STILL KEEPS SEEING THE VIRGIN MARY PLAYING KICKBALL I GUESS THAT'S HER FAVORITE GAME WHAT'S YOUR FAVORITE SONG NOW?

I AM WRITING YOU FOR EXTRA CREDIT FOR MY CLASS MRS. ROSE IF YOU CAN WRITE BACK I GET TWO POINTS EXTRA CREDIT PLEASE WRITE BACK I NEED THE POINTS BECAUSE I SOCKED THIS ONE KID DICKIE IN THE BACK AND I DID NOT KNOW HE HAD A LUDENS CHERRY COUGH DROP IN HIS MOUTH IT STUCK IN HIS WINDPIPE BUT MRS. ROSE GOT IT OUT I GOT MINUS 25 POINTS.

WHO YA WRITING?

MARLYS

TELL HER SHE STILL OWES ME THAT 37¢ SHE OWES ME

DEAR MARLYS HI HOW ARE YOU I AM FINE I GOT YOUR LETTER BLAH BLAH BLAH

HEY! GIVE IT!

BORING BORING BORING

I AM DOWN MANY POINTS I WILL NOT GET TO GO ON OUR FIELD TRIP TO THE POST OFFICE. A TRAGEDY. HOW IS YOUR WEATHER. THERE IS ICE HERE. IN THE FREEZER THAT IS. HAR HAR LOVE YOUR EVERLOVING COUSIN OF YOURS Marlys. P.S. MRS. ROSE LOOKED AT THIS BEFORE I SENT IT SO I COULD GET TWO POINTS EXTRA CREDIT SO I COULDN'T WRITE THAT SHE IS VERY CHEAP WITH HER EXTRA CREDIT POINTS AND SO WHAT IF

I DON'T GO TO THE POST OFFICE IT WAS WORTH IT SOCKING DICKIE HE CALLED MAYBONNE A PROSTITUTE AND FREDDIE A QUEER AND ME A FATSO HE IS JUST JEALOUS OF MY MIND. BUT SERIOUSLY WRITE ME OK I DON'T CARE ABOUT THE EXTRA CREDITS JUST YOU ALSO HOW IS YOUR IDIOT BROTHER ARNOLD I AM STILL MAD AT HIM FOR HURLING HIS TONKA AT ME I STILL GOT THE SCAR ON MY LEG THE USED TO BE PERFECT LEG TELL HIM. LOVE M.M.M."

WRITE DOWN DEAR MARLYS YOU ARE WEIRD. ALSO YOUR SISTER'S WEIRD AND ALSO YOUR BROTHER IS MENTALLY ILL.

IT'S TRUE, RIGHT?

WELL WHAT ABOUT YOU ARNOLD?

I'M THE ONLY NORMAL ONE OF EVERYBODY.

TELL HER "SEND 37¢"

·ARNOLD·

BY LYNDA "I LOVE MR. ROGERS" BARRY © 1993

PRIVATE SERGEANT LIEUTENANT CAPTAIN CORPORAL LEADER OF THE COUNTRY THE WORLD THE SOLAR SYSTEM THE UNIVERSE ARNOLD A. ARNESON REPORTING FOR DUTY SIR. DON'T EVER SAY WHAT'S MY MIDDLE NAME SIR. IT HAS THE SOUND OF A QUEER SIR. <u>OVER</u>.

YES, ARNOLD A. ARNESON? <u>OVER</u>. DO YOU READ ME. <u>OVER</u>. YES SIR I READ YOU JUST WANTED TO SAY THE MISSION IS COMPLETE SIR I ELIMINATED ALL THE SPASTICS ON MARS VENUS JUPITER SATURN AND URANUS SIR ONLY GOT MERCURY AND PLUTO TO GO SIR. <u>OVER</u>. A-HEM ARNOLD A. ARNESON AREN'T YOU FORGETTING ONE CERTAIN PLANET? <u>OVER</u>. YOU MEAN PLANET EARTH, SIR? <u>OVER</u>.

OF COURSE YOU NINCOMPOOP ARNOLD A. ARNESON. YOUR MISSION IS TO ELIMINATE ALL THE SPASTICS IN THE SOLAR SYSTEM. YOU'RE <u>YELLOW</u> ARNESON. <u>OVER</u>. AM NOT EITHER SIR LET ME EXPLAIN. <u>OVER</u>. OK. THEN EXPLAIN. OVER. WAIT. TAKE BACKS ON THAT OVER ARNOLD A. ARNESON. SOURCES SAY THAT IT IS BECAUSE OF A GIRL. REPORT TO YOUR SENIOR OFFICER AT ONCE DO YOU READ ME. <u>OVER</u>. DO YOU READ ME. COME IN ARNOLD A. ARNESON!

JEANETTE! SIT UP STRAIGHT!

YES SIR I READ YOU. <u>OVER</u>. ARNESON OUR SOURCES SAY YOU LIKE A CERTAIN GIRL IN YOUR CLASS WHO IS <u>A KNOWN</u> SPAZ + <u>A KNOWN</u> WEIRDO. YOU MUST DESTROY HER ARNESON DO YOU READ ME? <u>OVER</u>. YES SIR I READ YOU. <u>OVER</u>. ARNESON COMPLETE YOUR MISSION THEN REPORT TO ME AT ONCE. <u>OVER AND OUT</u>. WHAT WILL ARNOLD ARNESON DO? FOR THE LOVE IS FORBIDDEN! PLUS SHE DOESN'T EVEN KNOW I LOVE HER! ARNOLD IS DOOMED!

JEANETTE.

·O·P·E·N·E·YE·D·

BY LYNDA "LA VALSE DE PONT D'AMOUR" BARRY © 1993

JEANETTE. JEANETTE. I AM CRAZY WITH LOVE FOR YOU JEANETTE. I LOVE THE WEIRD SHOES ON YOUR FEET, I LOVE THE SCAR ABOVE YOUR LIP, I LOVE THE WART ON YOUR THUMB JEANETTE OH JEANETTE MY JEANETTE.

CLEFT: PARTIALLY SPLIT OR DIVIDED. PALATE: THE ROOF OF THE MOUTH. HARE: ANY OF VARIOUS SWIFT TIMID LONG EARED MAMMALS HAVING A DIVIDED UPPER LIP, LONG HIND LEGS, A SHORT COCKED TAIL, AND THE YOUNG FURRED AND OPEN-EYED AT BIRTH. I HAVE SEEN YOU RUNNING JEANETTE. FIRST PLACE IN THE 100 YARD DASH.

HARE LIP: A CONGENITAL DEFORMITY IN WHICH THE UPPER LIP IS SPLIT LIKE THAT OF A HARE. THE SCAR IS FROM THEM SEWING IT TOGETHER. I HAVE SEEN YOU COVER YOUR MOUTH WHEN YOU TALK. MRS. FENNEWALD SAID STOP COVERING YOUR MOUTH. INSTEAD YOU STOPPED TALKING. SHE SENT YOU TO THE OFFICE. MRS. FENNEWALD HAS THE HEART AND BRAINS OF A FLY. OH JEANETTE.

WHEN YOU WERE IN THE OFFICE SHE WROTE CLEFT PALATE ON THE BOARD. SHE WROTE HARE LIP. SHE EXPLAINED YOUR FACE TO US. WHEN YOU CAME BACK THE MEAN ONES KNEW WHAT TO CALL YOU. BUT IT IS AN HONOR TO BE PART RABBIT. WHEN THE BELL RANG YOU RAN FASTER THAN ANYONE. THE MEAN ONES YELLED IT. OH JEANETTE. IT WAS ME, ARNOLD, WHO NAILED A NAIL IN MRS. FENNEWALD'S BACK TIRE.

OOOOOH!

ARNOLD!

YOU LIKE HER.

SHUT UP. DON'T EITHER

I WILL NOT

BY LYNDA "How 'bout them Government tests with Radioactivity?" BARRY ©1993

I SOCKED JIMMY BUDREAU FOR YELLING HARE LIP AT JEANETTE THE HAIRLIP AT THIRD RECESS. THE SECRET IS OUT. EVERYONE KNOWS I LOVE HER. I SAID NO I DON'T I WAS JUST DOING MY NOBLE DUTY FOR PEOPLE WHO ARE DEFORMED AND JEANETTE THE HAIRLIP, HARE LIP, WHATEVER IT IS, SHE HEARED ME. HEARED ME SAY DEFORMED.

I WILL NOT...

FORGET ABOUT HER FORGET ABOUT JEANETTE JUST FORGET ABOUT HER KICKING ME HARD IN THE LEG AND THEN JUST STARING AT ME WHITE CROOKED SCAR AND STRETCHED OUT SIDE OF THE LIP. THE FIRST TIME SHE EVER TOUCHED ME WAS A KICK IN THE LEG SO FORGET THE HARE LIP FORGET JEANETTE IF SHE CAN'T APPRECIATE TRUE LOVE. I GOT A BRUISE ON MY LEG FROM HER KICK ON ME WITH HER WEIRD HARD SHOES. A BRUISE THAT LOOKS LIKE ABRAHAM LINCOLN.

I will not

..USE VIOLENCE TO SOLVE MY PROBLEMS.

AND ARNOLD? YOUR SENTENCE IS "I WILL NOT TALK BACK TO MRS. FENNEWALD."

HOW COME EVERY STORY EVERY BOOK EVERY MOVIE TURNS OUT BETTER THAN LIFE IN REAL LIFE? IN THE MOVIE OF ME AND JEANETTE THERE'S A KISS OF SPLENDOR A MAGIC KISS FROM ME AND HER LIP GOES NORMAL AND THE HARE LIP FLIES ONTO OUR MEAN TEACHER MRS. FENNEWALD WHO SAW JEANETTE KICK ME AND SAID JEANETTE GO TO THE OFFICE! AND I SHOUTED NO! AND GUESS WHO ALSO GOT SENT TO THE OFFICE?

THAT'S NO FAIR MRS. FENNEWALD.

I BEG YOUR PARDON?

JEANETTE GOT A LONGER SENTENCE THAN ME.

FINE. ADD THE WORD "ENCYCLOPEDIA" TO YOUR SENTENCE. SATISFIED??

IN THE OFFICE IT WAS JUST ME AND JEANETTE SITTING ON HARD CHAIRS WAITING. I WASN'T ABOUT TO TALK TO HER AND SHE WASN'T ABOUT TO TALK TO ME. WE GOT TWENTY MINUTES AFTER SCHOOL FOR ONE WEEK. NOW ALONE IN ONE ROOM WILL BE ME, JEANETTE AND HER ROYAL MEANESS, MRS. FENNEWALD. US WRITING 200 SENTENCES MRS. FENNEWALD PICKS. I WILL NOT. I WILL NOT. I WILL NOT EVER STOP LOVING YOU JEANETTE. I WILL NOT EVER STOP LOVING YOU JEANETTE. I WILL NOT EVER STOP LOVING YOU JEANETTE.

I will not use violence

(ENCYCLOPEDIA??)

BUT THAT DON'T MAKE NO SENSE!

THAT DOESN'T MAKE ANY SENSE!

SEE? I KNOW!

ARNOLD ARNESON!!!!

THE KISS OF THE HARE LIP

BY LYNDA "WHAT HAPPENED TO THE GRUTZ CHILDREN?" BARRY '93

I, ARNOLD A. ARNESON BEING OF SOUND MIND AND BODY DO HEREBY IF I SHOULD DIE GIVE ALL MY **COLLECTIONS** OF EVERYTHING TO JEANETTE THE HARE LIP OF MY SCHOOL. I, ARNOLD A. ARNESON BEING OF SOUND MIND AND BODY DO ADMIT IT...

I KISSED JEANETTE BEHIND PORTABLE THREE. THE KISS OF JEANETTE THE HARE LIP WAS INCREDIBLE.

SHE CHASED ME I THOUGHT SHE WAS GOING TO KICK ME AGAIN, I DUCKED BEHIND PORTABLE THREE WHERE WE ARE FORBIDDEN TO GO IT IS FORBIDDEN YOU COULD DIE BACK THERE FROM EATING POISON BERRIES YOU COULD DIE BACK THERE FROM HAPPINESS. SHE SAID CLOSE YOUR EYES. WITH HER HAND COVERING HER MOUTH SHE SAID CLOSE YOUR EYES.

AND SHE KISSED ME. JEANETTE PART RABBIT KISSED MY LIPS. THEN I SAID CLOSE YOUR EYES AND IT WAS MY TURN. MY TURN TO MOVE HER SHAKING HAND AWAY FROM HER MOUTH AND KISS HER STRANGE AND BEAUTIFUL LIPS.

INCREDIBLE SCARY!

BY LYNDA "LA SONORA DINAMITA!" BARRY ©93

<u>What you gonna be for Halloween!?!</u> INCREDIBLE IDEAS by your host ghost the incredible Scary Marlys!!!

Excuse me But Boo.

Look I'm FLOATING

ONE idea for a number one great costume is make a <u>WIG</u> OUT OF orange marshmallow Peanuts! Sew them together! Old ones Work Best! The smell Will make You scream.

Deadly fumes

Would You like to Bite my LUSCIOUS Hair?

use candy corn for vampire teeth

Make a marshmallow Hula skirt to go with it and For your top use two Bowls of that nasty hard candy your aunt always tries to make you eat when you come over but its all stuck together. Dump it out. Two Perfect Bosoms! tie them on you!

KISS ME YOU FOOL!

tie → the BOOBS ON WITH STRING

SEW THE MARSH MALLOWS IN LONG STRINGS

BEFORE IT WAS JUST STUPID CANDY

AFTER IT IS PART OF YOUR ALLURING FIGURE!

NOW GLUE OLD GUMDROPS TO YOUR SHOES!! ESPECIALLY THE GREEN ONES! GUESS WHAT? YOU ARE <u>VERY</u> SCARY NOW!"

ANOTHER CLUE TO SCARYNESS IS TO LOOK LIKE YOUR GUTS ARE COMING OUT. You can make very good fake guts with wet Bread and red food coloring in Saran Wrap

EXCUSE ME WHY ARE You running its just my guts hanging out!

AHH! ITS WAY TOO realistic!

SEE HOW GOOD IT WORKS?

Instructions
1. put bread without crusts in some water.
2. Squirt on food coloring.
3. put it in baggies
4. Saran wrap them around you
5. Lift up your shirt like its no big deal! Go "what? what's the matter!"
P.S. For extra weirdness put in hot dogs! For extra extra Weirdness put in canned peas!

Advice to GIRLS!

I know theres some girls liking to look all perfect + beautiful on Halloween. They pick Princess, Ballerina, Bunny, and many lame things. Take my advice! LOOK UGLY! It is very Great for your mind! Finally you can relax!

TRY Black Stuff IN YOUR TEETH

AND A UGLY WIG AT LEAST!

REMEMBER <u>HALLOWEEN</u> <u>IS</u> <u>NOT</u> <u>A BEAUTY</u> <u>CONTEST</u>! Love, Marlys

Advice to BOYS!

I know there's many Boys who want to Go as a lady with a Bra, high heels and panty hose. Take my advice! DO IT!! It is very Great for your mind!

OH MITCH YOU LOOK SO TERRIFIC!

OH MARLYS I FEEL SO TERRIFIC!

I LIKE YOU AS A BOY BUT YOU ARE ALSO VERY GORGEOUS AS A LADY!

REMEMBER STUFF YOUR BRA VERY BIG!! HAPPY HALLOWEEN!

123

By LYNDA "LEE "SCRATCH" PERRY "CHICKEN SCRATCH" ROUNDER RECORDS" BARRY ©1994

ASSIGNMENT: IMAGINE YOURSELF IN A PLACE YOU HAVE ALWAYS WANTED TO VISIT. WRITE ABOUT IT AS IF YOU WERE THERE.

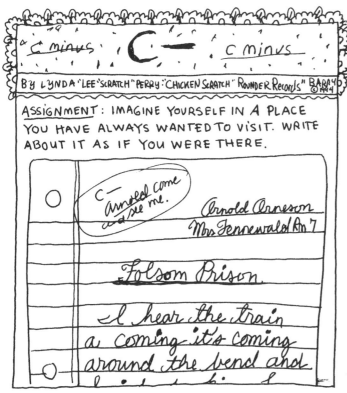

C— Arnold come and see me.

Arnold Arneson
Mrs. Fennewald Rm 7

Folsom Prison.

I hear the train a coming it's coming around the bend and

I told the cops I didn't do it. They did not believe me neither did the judge. Next thing I knew I was in this cell and I had on striped clothes and eating nasty food that they shove under the bars. I banged on the bars with my cup about starting a riot!

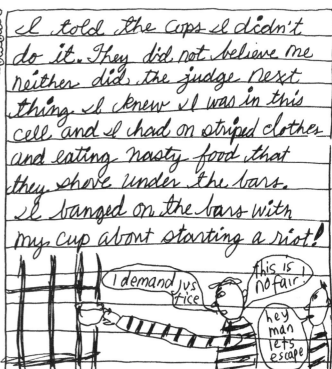

I demand jus-tice

This is no fair!

hey man lets escape

A guy in my cell had a perfectly carved gun out of soap. Realistic in every detail except for it was orange. "So what" he said lets bust out! "OK" I said and he freaked out the guard!

Arnold this is not a word!

I did not ask for illustrations!!

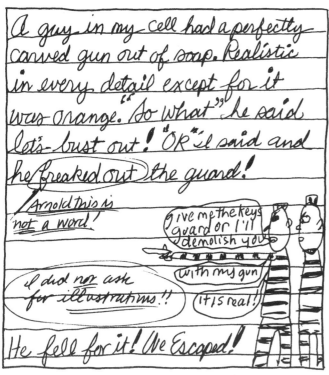

give me the keys guard or I'll demolish you

with my gun

It is real!

He fell for it! We Escaped!

We jumped on the train that goes by our prison! We stole out-fits from the rooms for disguise! I dressed like a lady and almost got away with it but I got busted by my deep voice! Then it was back to Folsom Prison. And the moral of this story is it did get proved I was innocent of my crime but then I had to stay in prison for escaping!!!! The End? No! I will get free!!!!!!!!

·D·O·N't·e·a·t· Weena

BY LYNDA ·ORDER CHRIS WARE'S NEW COMIC BOOK FROM / BARRY © 1994 / FANTAGRAPHICS · SEATTLE, WASHINGTON

ASSIGNMENT: WRITE A BIOGRAPHY OF A HISTORICAL FIGURE YOU ADMIRE. TELL US WHY.

(F) Arnold this is not what I asked for and you know it!	Arnold Arneson Mrs. Tennewald Rm 7

Morlocks vs. Eloi

My historical figure is in the future it is in the greatest movie of all time called The Time Machine where first a guy sends a cigar into the future then his own self.

What is a Morlock? a evolved human where the evolution crudded out in the year 802,701 and they live under the dirt and eat people called Eloi who are innocent and stupid because they don't know they are food and one is beautiful named Weena don't laugh that is her actual tragic name. In the future people have bad names.

Morlocks got white hair, no shirts, hairy legs and they look terrible when they decay in super fast motion while the guy is escaping with weena. and they got red eyes!!!!

My historical figure is the time machine man who was from around 1895 and the people laughed they said it couldn't be done. When you travel through time you turn invisible, that has always been one of my main thing to learn. When he gets to the future he figures out the morlocks are eating the Eloi.

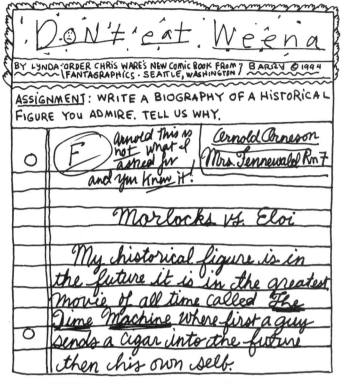

mmm—mm GOOD!

hey how come you always get the arm?

But Let's Eat

Shut up, Boy this is finger licking good eloi

Weena Next

He climbs down to the world of the Morlocks and grabs weena then they jump on the time machine and push the wrong button and go into the future and thats where you see the Morlocks head go Rotting off then my mom said go to bed I never saw the ending. I admire the Time Machine man for his smartness, his courage and his girlfriend. If you take points off because I can't remember his name it's OK. The End ??!!! maybe not !!

Yours Truly

Arnold Arneson

125

ROOM 14

BY LYNDA "BIG STAR · ALEX CHILTON · ON RYKODISC" BARRY © 91

Its supposed to be bad to hate people duh I know. the entire world knows. But I sincerely hate Mrs. Fennewald and she also sincerely hates me and It is also supposed to be bad to lie It's a lie to say I do not hate Mrs. Fennewald.

SCHOOL SECRETARY

But if you asked her Mrs. Fennewald do you hate Arnold Arneson she would say no! How could you even say such a thing I love all my children a double lie she lies about hating me lies about loving me our worst minute of every day is having to see each other but her, she will lie about it.

Mrs Holman. Our school secretary. She is decent →

Arnold?

Do you want a book to read?

ARNOLD?

Mrs. H LMAN

NO. THANK. YOU.

YOU SURE?

I. AM. SURE.

Like people lie all the time about people they hate. Does lying make the hating decent? NO. Does it make the hating go away? Mrs. Fennewald makes me sit in the office now every recess. She says I do not deserve a recess. I hear her in the teachers room laughing. It's because she loves me so much I sit here.

GO TO HELL MRS FENNEWALD

ARNOLD REMOVE YOUR JACKET. GENTLEMEN DO NOT SIT INDOORS WITH OUTDOOR JACKETS ON. It's Her →

I ASSUME YOU CAN HEAR ME UNLESS YOU WENT DEAF WHEN YOU LEFT MY CLASS

If someone treats you terrible and can control you your life your recess you start hating them. If you tell the truth of it they say you are special and if you don't watch out it will be special ed. The room with all the special haters. The room with the ones they won't let us play with. All boys. Room 14. You can see them staring out the window. Staring at us. I hate you Mrs. Fennewald. I hate you. Sincerely. totally.

IS HE GIVING YOU ANY TROUBLE MRS HOLMAN?

NO. NOT ARNOLD. I'VE NEVER HAD ANY TROUBLE WITH HIM, MYSELF.

MRS HOLMAN!!! MAY I SPEAK TO YOU?

history

BY LYNDA "ITS OK TO READ 6 BOOKS AT ONCE" BARRY © 94

Mrs. Fennewald called my Mom who had to go in for a special conference which my mom even my mom said that lady is stuck up I said See mom See can you blame me for WHACK! Mom goes across my face. WHACK! You little smart ass.

What mom what. What do you mean what You want to end up in juvinile if thats your plan I'll drive you down there myself swearword swearword swear But Mom don't mom me you want to end up like Timmy. No. Yes you do. No I don't either. Well you are sure acting like it damn it Wheres my damn cigarettes I could choke you right now do you know that. Here they are Mom heres your cigarettes. WHACK!

You just keep it up just keep it up You'll be like that damn Timmy. No I won't. You bet you won't I'll kill you myself first. She is giving you one more chance then you are out. She's sick and tired of you Arnold. I know mom. She was sick and tired of me when she first met me mom. I don't know why you have to be like this. Look at Arna. She's a girl mom. WHACK. Mom! What did I say that time dang mom. Whack!

Now I am in my room. Now I hate everyone. Now I hear a tap on my door. I don't say nothing. Then the door opens. My perfect Sister Arna. Did I say she could come in? No. Arnold Arnold are you ok. Did I say for her to ask me that? No. Did I ever once say for her to come close to me? WHACK! Mom! Arnold hit me! Mom he hit me for no reason Mom! Wrong. It was for a reason. It was for the history of all reasons.

127

The very Pink Flowers

BY LYNDA *AFRICAN ACOUSTIC fom Original Music ←LABEL" BARRY©94

Theres this kid I shouldn't even be hanging around him name of Jim. Jim Jimmy Jim. The fire lover. The lover of things on fire. The lover of lighter fluid and Charcol wizard. Jim Jimmy Jim. When his mother calls him he runs the other way and me I follow.

He says his sister is a stupid idiot and thats why he has to burn her nightgown behind the school. Jim Jimmy Jim has her nightgown in a pay N save bag with matches and Ronsons lighter fluid. His sister is a stupid idiot for going out with Hector Milonga a cop car comes by us keep acting normal says Jim Jimmy Jim. His sister let Hector. His sister let him. Stupid Stupid Idiot.

He pulls the bag open and hands me the nightgown hold this he says. His sister is 17 I can smell the girlness I can smell the girlness in my hands Give it he says. His sisters name is Joanne. Oh oh Joanne. Hey! Give it! says Jim Jimmy Jim and grabs it and stares at me. I look down. He piles some leaves he lays down the nightgown of Joanne the little pink flowers of Joanne.

LIGHTER FLUID LIGHTER FLUID BACK UP back up here goes. Jim Jimmy Jim can light a match in one try. Back up he says. here goes. Fire. Bright Fire. Oh. Jim Jimmy Jim stares at it with no blinks. HEY! SomEone shouts HEY! I take off running. Jim Jimmy Jim just stands there. The pink flowers of Joanne. The pink flowers of joanne burn and burn in my head. They are burning now. Right now.

I ADMIT IT

BY LYNDA "HEY I HAVE A NEW BOOK CALLED: 'IT'S SO MAGIC' HARPER COLLINS" BARRY ©94

I admit I am only friends with Jim Jimmy Jim because of his sister. I admit I only go on missions with Jim Jimmy Jim because of her who is 17 her who is sneaking at night to see the forbidden Hector Milonga who speaks spanish who sings spanish who sings to her

Soy del barrio del alto yo soy aquél que no miro con quién tengo que pelear y a quien en el milongvear ninguno se puso a tiro I can't help it if you don't understand the words Hector dances to in front of the hypnotised Joanne. They are under the streetlight Hector holds his arms up and turns his head Jim Jimmy Jim ducks in the bushes and pushes my head down too. Jim Jimmy Jim the lover of fire.

Jim Jimmy Jim with the drops of gasoline hes been kyping slow from Mitchells gas at night almost got enough he whispers. Hector Milonga takes the beautiful Joanne in his arms her stackedness her stacked ness Almost got enough says Jim Jimmy Jim to burn Hector Milongas house down. Soy del barrio alto yo soy aquél que no miro con q vien tengo que pelear. Joanne Joanne. She is on fire.

He keeps gasoline in this ←

MILK BARN

Afterwards we follow her down Horton across 22nd, 23rd, 24th to the cutoff to the alley we are quiet she doesn't know we see every thing her climbing up the tree the tiny pink flowers for a second both me and Jim Jimmy Jim are burning she gets to her window she goes inside. I will kill him says Jim Jimmy Jim. He will die. By next week I will have enough to do it. Joanne is dreaming. On a soft pillow fires of hot dreaming are lit up in her. Oh to touch her even once.

FIRE
FIRE
FIRE

Jim Jimmy Jim is burning

BY LYNDA "Are Julie + Smokey Coming to New Orleans?" Barry ©94

Excuse me Excuse me your name is Hector Milonga right? He looks at me. You're the boyfriend of Joanne, right? He really looks at me. We're standing by the bus stop. He is going to work. He works at Providence Hospital. Janitor. I know everything about him from spying with Jim Jimmy Jim. Excuse me it's important, I say.

the stored up gasoline

I tell him how Jim Jimmy Jim is burning. How he has saved enough gas to burn all of Hector Milongas house down and his plan is to do it that night that very night all because Hector Milonga touched the sister of Jim Jimmy Jim. I swear to god I say. The bus comes. The bus leaves. Hector stays on the bench looking at me. He lights a cigarette and looks at me. Can a guy say another guy is handsome without being a fag?

the matches

Hector Milonga has the darkest eye parts and his hair is blacker than I've ever seen. I look down. He asks me am I joking him. He has an accent. No I say. Call the police I say. It's happening tonight. No police No police says Hector he holds his hands up and shakes them like a head going no. No. No. You my friend he says. I nod my head. I want to say I am your anything. I want to say I am you. The bus comes. You my friend he says. He gets on.

him ⟶

That night Jim Jimmy Jim Comes over to pick me up. I'm supposed to spend the night. I tell mom to say I can't. Why? she says. Just cuz I say. Arnold she says. Why. Jim Jimmy Jim is at the back door. Please mom I say. He's knocking. Hey! He says. Hey Arn! Hey! Mom stares at me and then goes into the kitchen. I listen hard for the words that excuse me from Jim Jimmy Jims last secret mission.

130

Hector

by LYNDA "Cuarteto Patria on CoraSon. COCD106" ← SOGOOD! Barry©94

The music coming out of Hector Milonga's house is very beautiful It's the first warm night and the windows are open and we can see an old lady with white and black hair in braids all wrapped around her head She is bringing dishes to the table we can see Hector Milonga laughing and eating and she laughs also.

In the yellow lit up square of the window they are laughing. Hey! says Jim Jimmy Jim Hey stupe Keep your head down you trying to get me busted? I am in the bushes with Jim Jimmy Jim I am on a mission with him now he has enough gas to burn the house of Hector Milonga down down down. The music coming out of that lit up house is so beautiful Hector Milonga gets up and dances with the old lady and The old lady dances back. Jim Jimmy Jim Checks his Matches.

Tonight is just practice. Tonight is just practice for the day Jim Jimmy Jim pays Hector back for touching The beautiful Joanne. The beautiful sister of Jim Jimmy Jim who no one must ever touch he lights a match in one try and we wait. We wait until every light in the house goes out. Time? Says Jim Jimmy Jim. I look at my watch. 11:57 I say. Jim Jimmy Jim writes it in a notebook next to 11:54, 11:44, 12:02 He has been watching many days.

Hector Milonga is a man. Hector Milonga has a job. Hector Milonga should never have started it he started it he deserves it says Jim Jimmy Jim. Another Match. Let's go says Jim Jimmy Jim and then the sound of feet in the dark. We freeze. The sound of pink feet walking in the dark the pink feet of Joanne move slow to the house of Hector Milonga. Hector Hector whisper Joannes pink lips. Hector. I will kill him whispers Jim Jimmy Jim then both of Them at the exact same second whisper his name. Hector.

131

R.E.D. SPARKS FLYING

BY LYNDA "RAGDALE SO LONG RAGDALE" BARRY 84

I hear fire trucks. Did Jim Jimmy Jim burn Hector Milongas house down like he Said he would? I hear sirens trail down that way. I get up and put on my shoes. My sister Arna catches me. Where you going? No place. Go back to sleep. I go out the back door.

The stars are bright and powerful through the berzerk black branches of trees. I'm running to where the red sparks are flying. To the choking smoke. Three more blocks but I can already tell then blam on the back of my head blam I am on the ground then kick kick on my head and side Jim Jimmy Jims shoe kicking you told you told you warned them I'll kill you then kick kick again

Then I don't know. Jim Jimmy Jims feet running and the cold sidewalk under me. The stars are bright and powerful through the berzerk black branches. I smell smoke. See red sparks flying and then I am gone for awhile and when I come back there is mom and there is Arna and there is a nurse with a shaver and a doctor with a needle 16 stitches on the back of my head it was a brick arna said

16 stitches in the shape of a J for Jim Jimmy Jim who did not burn Hector Milongas house down because I did warn Hector and Hector had his friends waiting outside in a circle. no Jim Jimmy Jim didn't burn Hectors house he got mad and burned a different house instead. One nearby. One lady died.

132

·B·E·I·N·G· ·I·L·L·E·G·A·L·

BY LYNDA "BLACK ACE · the Boss Carol. Rounder 374" BARRY ©94

Juvinile is where Jim Jimmy Jim is and back to where he was born is where Hector Milonga is supposed to go because he is illegally here and the police asked so many questions about why Jim Jimmy Jim wanted to burn Hector Milongas house down they asked me and asked me and asked me.

Hector Milonga has dissappeared the police say the grandma lady at the house where he was says he doesn't ring a bell she doesnt know a Hector Milonga. I remember Hector Milonga if that is even his real name the police says they are like roaches they scatter that quick when the lights come on. Jim Jimmy Jim is in Juvie for Arson that murdered a lady.

And I told and told and told because I didn't know that Hector Milonga was illegal I didn't know there was such a thing as a person being illegal. Hector, if you are ever reading this I swear to god I would have never busted you to the police if I had known the busting was possible. Also the thing with Joanne the sister of Jim Jimmy Jim is also illegal Hector. She is 17 Hector. Jim Jimmy Jim is in Juvie.

And my mom is dragging me to Sears to buy a suit because I'm in trouble and when you are in trouble you need a suit. They are trying to figure out how much guilty I am. I knew about the matches. I knew about the gasoline. I knew Jim Jimmy Jim. The lady at Sears turns me to the three mirrors. You're going to be a heart breaker someday. She pats my shoulders. I see Mom crying. I'm a heart breaker now. I'm a heartbreaker right now. Hi Hector from Arnold wherever you are.

133

'CELL' #1

BY LYNDA "TRUST THE INSECT" BARRY © 1994

I have to do perfect I have to do all my homework I have to get along with the evil mrs. Fennewald. the Judge says do this or you go to juvie with the famous juvinile delinquent Jim Jimmy Jim #1 arsonist the 'cell membrane controls the flow of materials in and out of the cell.

cell membrane

~~Nucleus~~ Jim Jimmy Jim

Cytoplasm

The cell membrane is what surrounds the cell that Jim Jimmy Jim is sitting in right now in juvie where I will be if I don't do perfect do all my homework <u>Cell Structure</u> by Arnold Arneson due tomorrow every living thing whether plant or animal is built of cells which are the units of life as we know it and if you hang around Jim Jimmy Jim you'll end up in one cell single cell cell cell cell the word cell looks so weird to me.

Cell-mem-brane

CYTOPLASM OF THE J.D.

I WILL   GET YOU ARNOLD

~~NUCLEUS~~ Jim Jimmy NUCLEUS

they don't know if single celled things are plants or animals they say cells climb a ladder and we are sitting at the top of the ladder we are number One we are incredible we are the champions of cells the book says we are the winners of the contest of evolution our cells helped us figure out fire which is weird considering Jim Jimmy Jim. Only things with cells burn.

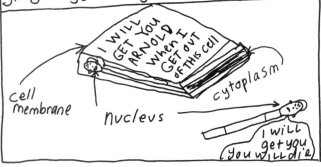

I WILL GET YOU ARNOLD WHEN I GET OUT OF THIS CELL

cell membrane

nucleus

cytoplasm

I WILL get you (you will die)

The lady made of cells in the house made of cells that Jim Jimmy Jim set on fire. The lady made of cells and now Jim Jimmy Jim is in a cell and they judged me and judged not exactly guilty. I hung around Jim Jimmy Jim but I never lit no matches. Do your homework says the judge do perfect every minute three hundred million cells die in your body and are replaced mostly replaced. Do perfect says the judge. Do perfect and forget about it.

when I get out you will die

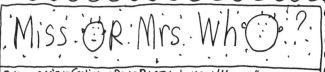

Miss OR Mrs. Who?

BY LYNDA "THE GENIUS OF DAVE BARTHOLOMEW!!!·EMI" BARRY ©1994

The lady made of cells who died when jim jimmy jim set her house on fire, who was she? Nucleus Cytoplasm endoplasmic reticulum who was she? Mom says don't ask I walked past the house where it was where it was you can see the fireplace and concrete steps and somewhere her bones + teeth

hello — — arnold

shut up my sister Arna says you are giving me the creeps don't talk about the dead ladys teeth shut up Arnold they are in a box they are under the ground by now which grave yard which one because I would like to know is it the one by Volunteer Park I keep thinking that is the graveyard where the lady made of cells got ditched.

29 bones of the skull
teeth =
incisors
canines
premolars
molars
wisdom

hello— Arnold

Don't ask says Mom and she hid all the newspapers and said no to reporters who wanted my words for a story on juvinile delinquents like jim jimmy jim everyone wants my words on jim jimmy jim the #1 Arsonist killer my same age and I want words on the lady made of cells if I had busted Jim jimmy jim to the police she would still have nucleus cytoplasm endoplasmic reticulum. That's what the judge said.

theres 2 bones missing

hello arnold

please find them arnold I need them

young man he said. I could have prevented it if I went to the proper authorities. Not exactly guilty. I want to know who she was. All I need is her name just her name. Miss or Mrs who? then I'll walk in the graveyards I'll start at the one by Volunteer park and I'll walk and walk until I find her. Not exactly guilty. Not exactly guilty. I need to explain that part to her.

yoo hoo arnold — — over here!

135

No One Understands Monsters

BY LYNDA "I LOVE WNUR EVANSTON ILLINOIS" BARRY ©94

D+

Arnold Arneson
Mrs. Fennewald Room 7

Be More Understanding
(of Monsters)

Alot of times when monsters first appear on earth the people try to kill them. Examples:

Mixed-Up Zombies: This fortune teller threw acid in their faces for no reason and they turned Zombies and she kept them in a cage and her stacked sister teased them then they

escaped and of course tried to kill people.

the evil Carmelita — the mixed up zombies

Gorgo: He looks like Godzilla but a volcanic eruption got him out of hibernation and a guy saw him and died from just looking at him because he was so scared but who got blamed. Gorgo got blamed.

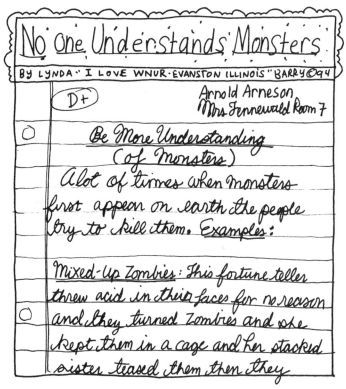

Dagora: They were outer space jelly fish who loved eating diamonds. The people got mad and killed them all by making them crispy and hard. Just for stupid diamonds.

The Sun Demon: A scientist messes up an experiment and turns radioactive and everyone hates him and he can't control himself when a guy is mean to a lady then he beats up the guy then the guy gets a gun then the radioactive mutant kills the guy and a dog then gets killed

just for messing up a radioactive experiment which could happen to anyone. He gets shot in the throat.

The Hot Heela

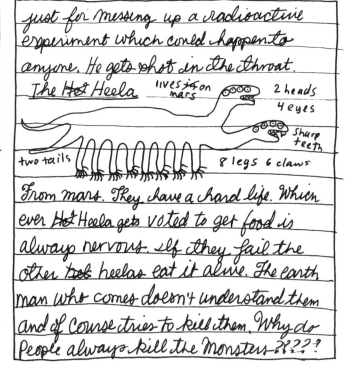

lives on mars — 2 heads — 4 eyes — sharp teeth — two tails — 8 legs 6 claws

From mars. They have a hard life. Which ever Hot Heela gets voted to get food is always nervous. If they fail the other heelas eat it alive. The earth man who comes doesn't understand them and of course tries to kill them. Why do people always kill the monsters??????

WILL YOU SHUT UP?
BY LYNDA "HAITI" CHÉRIE · MÉRINGUE · CORASON COCD107 · BARRY ©94

I love my brother which he would say shut up to if I ever say it which I said it once which he told me to shut up because of, which did hurt my feelings but I didn't show it because he hates that.

Arnold Arneson is my brother the one they are blaming at school for that lady who died in the fire lit by Jim Jimmy Jim Arnold did not do it Arnold didn't he did not. that's how I got my first bloody nose a girl named Marie at the monkey bars would not shut up about the great Arnold Arneson my brother so I socked her in the gut so she socked me in the face and kicked my leg with her red boots because she thinks she's a cowgirl.

And my face got a bloody nose and she begged me not to tell because she has a perfect record. we went in the girls' can to wipe the blood she said she liked my red heart necklace, that it would go perfect with her clothes, could she wear it, the red heart necklace I got from Arnold my brother who found it on upper field of Selmer Junior High where he wasn't supposed to ever go.

He gave it to me he said it didn't mean nothing so don't think nothing, here, have it, he said. It's a thing I hide because I never want the one who lost it to see it on me and say give it back. Please please let me try it on said Marie our most popular girl, it's incredible it matches me more than you, said Marie who undid it from my neck. Will you shut up about my brother? I said. Will you? Marie said if I let her keep it over night. Just one little night then she swore she would give it back.

137

Marie the Liar

LYNDA "HAITIAN RARA on Smithsonian Folkways" Barry©qu

Don't ever let marie borrow nothing of yours she will say she lost it She accidently lost it and you will never get it back and she will never feel bad about it because she has a perfect record Marie stole my red heart necklace Marie the liar Marie the Cheater.

YOU WERE STUPID TO LEND IT TO HER IN THE FIRST PLACE.

I KNOW, MOM.

Marie who pretends she's your friend until some one gives you attention especially a boy then she will put you down because she needs all the boys especially the boy you secretly tell her you secretly like named Charlie who you would never have a chance with but Marie would have a chance with. Marie I know you have my red heart necklace.

NO USE CRYING ABOUT IT ARNA. IT'S YOUR OWN DAMN FAULT.

I'M NOT CRYING, MOM

Marie has a perfect record of never getting in trouble I want to hate Marie I want to hate Marie but since first grade I have always worshipped Marie She told me Charlie matched her better than he matched me that is why. And everything matches Marie better than it matches me She told me that secretly I was her best friend and pretty soon she would tell the world.

I TOLD YOU THAT THING WAS WORTH MONEY IF YOU LET ME HAVE IT WHEN I ASKED FOR IT I'D STILL HAVE IT.

I KNOW, mom

Since first grade I have always worshipped marie and given her everything of mine or she took it and I have tried to stop worshipping her but it is hard because Marie is the beautifullest and most incredible of all the girls since first grade I have wanted to be her best friend she said to shut up about the necklace because she accidently lost it Marie the Liar Marie the cheater please don't ever stop liking me.

YOU KNOW YOU KNOW. YOU KNOW EVERYTHING, DON'T YOU?

138

Look at that tree

By *Lynda* "You just need a bucket and 2 sticks" Barry © 94

My whole life people been saying look at that tree look at that tree I think that I shall never see a poem as lovely as all my whole life people been saying that and for what because I looked at the tree and didn't see nothing.

Once I did see a squirrel running in the top branch and with my Daisy I shot his little ass. From my window up here. And it's true the birds used to come and sing until I shot their little asses too. With my Daisy. With my Daisy rifle I have shot the asses off of everything that came near that tree and I have shot the tree itself on slow days. Today is a slow day and that tree is dying.

I think that I shall never see a poem as lovely as money. The leaves from the real tree of life. Wish I had me some. A poem as lovely as a tree with money hanging down all over it. I think that I shall never see a poem as lovely as Cable TV. Man come and chop down two trees because they was messing with the cable now there is only one left and it's blocking my view of the corner of the action.

I think that I shall never see the reason they don't chop that tree. Except for that one night I got so very high. A mellow high. That night I made <u>good</u> friends with my tree it was my good buddy could hear it talking. "Study me. Study me." And I was. And I <u>was</u> getting knowledge because that was <u>good</u> <u>weed</u>. It told me how all the other trees didn't make it and it was the <u>last</u> <u>big</u> <u>daddy</u> and I start to cry until my brother ronald come up and slap the side of my head and point it back to the cable. I think that I shall never see. I think that I shall never see.

139

WHY DON'T YOU PLAY MUSIC?

BY LYNDA "Do You Like old Beautiful Scratchy records" BARRY © 1994

Dance little baby child and the baby child does. Look at him jumping to the music. What happened between you and music? Dance little baby child dance.

On the rolling seas of life music is a gold and silver spangled boat rocking with you. Look at that baby child. What happened between you and music? The man took it away from you and left you standing like you standing now uh huh watching the baby child dance. Why you smiling like that? Why you grinning when you watch him rocking on the rolling sea?

What you remembering? A time when you didn't know you didn't know how. Look at that baby child toss itself and turn. Why the man want all the music? Why he say you can't and he can? Why don't you play music? Watch that baby child beat his spoon. Why you so afraid? Why you think you can't? Why the man want all the music? Why don't nobody play music no more? Watch that baby child beat his spoon.

Once upon a long time ago you could hear people singing. Singing with the rolling. Said Jean Toomer in Cane: "God's body's got a soul. Bodies like to roll the soul. Can't blame God if we don't roll. Come brother, roll. Roll!" Watch that baby child jumping in his bright spangled boat. Snatch the music back. Beat your spoon. Swing your **Starry** hammer. You know why he want all the music. Snatch it back! Come brother! Roll. Roll!!

BLAM BLAM

on the Way Home

BY LYNDA "AUTO BINGO" BARRY ©1994

I hate my brother. And my sister. And my mom. And my dad. If you only knew how much I hated them you would never say you don't really hate them you're just mad at them that's them over there at the Dairy Queen picnic table eating ice cream I told them I'm staying in the car with the windows rolled up they said Fine.With.Us.

HAVE YOU DUG

I hate them I hate them I hate them the only thing I wanted In life was to stop at Wall Drug. We stopped there on our way to vacation and there was a rattle snake (real) (dead) in plastic covered in a clear dome of plastic for $3.97 which I didn't have which none of them scrounges would give me then on vacation my grandma gave me $5.00 and I saved that $5.00 and the scrounges knew why I was saving that $5.00.

WALL DRUG?

It is such a long boring road flat, flat, all the way to Wall drug but to me It was worth everything because the rattle snake was going to be the star of my life How long 'Til wall drug How long til Wall drug my brother and my sister both scrounge heads don't care about wall drug so they didn't wake me up when the signs went 20 miles 15 miles 10 miles 5, 4, 3, 2, 1 and then Dad, who I hate, passed it and Mom, who I hate, let him.

DAD MAKE HIM SHUT UP!

You want to walk home?

YES.

To them a rattle snake is nothing. To all of them licking white ice cream over there at the picnic table a (real) (dead) rattle snake is nothing. In a clear dome of plastic. that was going to be the best thing I ever owned. I am never going to sleep in front of them again. and I will always hate them for this as long as I live World without end If you only knew how I felt you would never say some day I will forget all about it.

I'M GOING TO MAKE YOUR FATHER STOP THE CAR!

DO IT MOM

NOW WE'RE 206 MILES PAST WALL DRUG

I am babysitting

BY LYNDA "Birds singing in the backyard trees" Barry © 94

How many wheels does the truck have let's count those wheels, one, two, and my little brother counted the wheels counted sixteen wheels on a half smashed tonka that was supposed to be indestructable that my other brother said nothing was indestructable and got the hammer. counted 16 wheels on a truck with no wheels.

It's summertime summertime and I am babysitting I am out under the clothes line watching the baby count invisible wheels while my other brother sits in front of the TV screaming Nothings on! Nothings on! I hate this! What's the use of this if nothings on! And then our dog pushes open the screen door walks out into the yard and throws up.

He throws up crayons and a truck goes by in the alley and there is a lot of dust and the baby starts coughing and then starts counting truck wheels over again One two fourteen sixteen one hundred and our dog hears something and shoots out of the yard barking Let's count those wheels says my little brother who we call the baby even though he's almost three Let's count those wheels he must have saw that on TV

Fix me something to eat! my other brother shouts I'm hungry! he shouts I'm starving! I'm starving! I can't get full! Nothings on! Fix me something! He's shouting from the front room. I lay in the grass and watch a bee claw at a dandelion between the baby and the dog barf. Under the flapping clothes I can look straight up and see the moon out in the hard middle of the day. Let's count those wheels. yes yes Let's count those wheels.

cut

BY LYNDA "TALK to YOUR Neighbors" BARRY © 1994

Mom told me a million times don't touch razor blades but I stole a pack and I hid them in my hiding place and I opened the perfect paper wrapping and I picked one up and I don't know how I don't know how because I hardly felt it. But then red blood red blood gushing.

and I was screaming and mom was at work and I was screaming and running out of my fort and up the path and onto 24th and a lady slammed on her brakes and jumped out of the car What happened? What? She took my hand and asked and I kept crying to keep from explaining.

You gonna need a couple stitches where's your house at where's your mama at and I snatched my hand away and tore back down the path with the lady calling after me shouting every word of come back. What would the Indians do in this situation? What would the Indians do when their mother was going to kill them? Wrap it in leaves.

I ducked into my fort at the bottom of the dump ravine. Still the lady's voice calling. I tore off leaves and wrapped my hand like it was the medicine man who told me to. The razor blades and the perfect paper were looking at me. I was squeezing my hand that was still gushing blood and the razor blades and perfect paper were just cracking up laughing.

143

BALLS

LYNDA "Kevin Kawula drew last weeks strip" Barry © 94

Summers getting boring. I wish for school. Don't tell nobody I said that unless you want to see my body dead from everyone on my street. Summer is getting boring though. nothing happens besides me getting my ass kicked again. Oh and the library. Going to the library.

UH...

YOU'RE DEAD BY ME!

I'M KILLIN' YA.

That's where I read the weiner of an elephant weighs sixty pounds. Next time someone tries to kick your ass say that to them before they do it and they will halt. and then say I will tell you more x-rated facts if you be my friend and maybe they will say OK like the evil Kim did. A guy called Kim from 24th street who didn't beat my ass because of the elephant weiner knowledge.

wait.

a butterfly has 12,000 eyes.

so?

an elephants brain weighs 16 pounds.

So? I'm still killin' ya.

I know how much his weiner weighs.

Prove it.

In anchient days a man had to put his hand on his balls if he was swearing to tell the truth but if a squid eats its balls it will die. Kim said show me where it says that. If you're lying I'll kill you. Show me. We walked to the library. I got the book. I pointed to the sentence but a magic happened on the sentence where the word testicles was, it changed to tentacles.

also, you know pigs?

their weiners are curly.

what about the weiners of fish.

Psych.

no. swear.

I told Kim tentacles was the anchient word for balls and he believed me and said why would a squid eat its own balls and I said not so loud! the librarian! Kim said oh and we walked home. He said if I was lying about tentacles being balls he would kill me. I put my hand on my balls and said I swear. Tonight I'm asking my dad is there a way we can move to a different town as soon as possible.

COME ON. TELL ME.

well.

I'LL kill you if you lie to me.

Fish weiners are fascinating.

They don't got weiners. YOU'RE DEAD!

144

I KNOW!

BY LYNDA "MAN I DIG JAZZ ON WNUR: EVANSTON "BARRY©94

I KNOW ALL THE MONSTERS. DRAGULA, THE GREAT VAMPIRE STAGULA, DRAGULABA, THE GREAT VAMPIRE KNOWN AS SMAGULA, BLAM! MY BROTHER TRIES TO KNOCK MY BLOCK OFF. SAY IT RIGHT! HE SCREAMS LOUD IN MY EAR DRUM. SAY IT RIGHT OR I'LL KILL YA! OK, I SAY. OK!..DRAC-U-BLA. BLAM! DRAC-U-LA, I SAY, OK? DRAC-U-LA. DRAC-U-LA. CRACK-U-LA.

I'LL KILL YOU! HE SAYS. BUT I KNOW ALL THE MONSTERS! FRANKENSTICK, THE SCUMMY, THE LEACHER FROM THE BLACK STABLOON BLAM! BLAM! I'M ON THE FLOOR I'M FIGHTING BACK BUT HE'S ON ME HE'S HANGING SPIT OVER MY FACE. SAY. IT. RIGHT. OK OK! FRANKENSTEIN. THE MUMMY. THE CREATURE. MAN LET ME GO! COME ON! AND HE GETS UP OFF OF ME AND I SAY WRANKENSPLINE AND RUN FOR IT.

I WHIP THROUGH THE KITCHEN STILL KNOWING ALL THE MONSTERS! THE KULFMAN! THE PLOB! WACK-U-LA! OW! YOW! OW! STUBBED MY TOE! OW! HAR HAR HAR MY BROTHER'S DYING LAUGHING HAR HAR SERVES YOU RIGHT! IT WAS THE MONSTERS, HE SAYS, THE GHOSTS OF THE MONSTERS DID THAT TO YOU FOR INSULTING THEM! OW. OW. DAG! OW. MY TOE IS SIDEWAYS!

WHAT THE HELL NOW? WHAT? MOM HAS THE GARDEN HOSE. I'M HOPPING OUT CRYING. MY BROTHER'S SCREAMING I DIDN'T DO NOTHING! HE STARTED IT! OW, MOM! MOM. OW! MY TOE, MOM, OW! DAMN YOU! SHE SHOUTS. AND GOES TO GET HER PURSE. HOSPITAL. MY TOE IS BROKE IN TWO. SEE? MY BROTHER SAYS, MONSTERS ARE REAL, HE SAYS. DON'T MESS WITH MONSTERS! I WAIT UNTIL MOM IS 3 FEET AWAY, AND I SAY YOU MEAN LIKE SPLAGULA?

145

.the .SIGN .FOR .THEM.

BY *LYNDA* in the triangle between the Blue and White Nile *Barry*

"What you doing stupid that's stupid god you're stupid," That's my sister talking that's my sister standing over me squawking, "It's September if you don't know stupe. You don't plant things in September." Squawk Squawk. I punch another hole into the dirt and drop a seed in.

last night I had a dream of flowers flowers flowers. "All's that's going to happen is the plants are going to die. you know? All's that's going to happen is as soon as it gets cold they are dead. Automatically. God you are stupid." Her feet just stand there and her legs just stand there. I punch another hole and the feet and legs finally run away. It was flowers flowers flowers, billions of them. Zillions.

If I could drop myself into the hole instead of the seed, hear me Our Father, for I am in need. My name is being shouted. The shouter is coming!! I'm faster with the seeds now, poking holes where they can't guess. My name is being shouted and the stick is knocked out of my hand. Last night I had a dream of flowers flowers flowers. It is true that I am stupid Mother. Yes. You're right. Yes. What was I thinking.

What was I thinking? In my secret mind? I was thinking it could happen. it could happen. morning glories, foxgloves, zinnias, sweet williams climbing all the way up over this house and that would be the sign.for them. Them who are coming, are looking for me and truly coming. The ones who know by flowers flowers flowers in the middle of November. The ones who know to take me away from here, and are looking for me.

146

the Bee Hospital!

BY LYNDA BARRY ☼ come on put up your dukes! ©95

There's a kid name of Monte 3 doors down who catches bees in a jar. he gives himself the contest of how many bees can he catch at once, then he screws the lid on, no air holes and leaves the jar in the sun. I want to put Monte in a jar.

FREDDIE

FREDDIE I'M GONNA CREAM YA!!

Anybody knows what he does is cruelty. Today I kyped his bee jar when he went inside to eat. I ran into our basement. The bees were fainted. I opened the lid and put 13 cotton balls in a shoe box and picked up the fainted bees with tweezers. Each one got a cotton ball bed.

FREDDIE YOU FAG YOU FRUIT LOOPS SISSY QUEER FAG COME OUT HERE SO I CAN CREAM YA!

Some looked tragically croaked. Some could still wiggle one leg. I put drops of water on them to wake them up more. I could hear Monte screaming my name. He can't prove it was me that took them. I went upstairs to watch TV. Later Monte made his mom come over and ask did I steal his bees. I looked all innocent and said no.

When the world was finally asleep I snuck down to the bee hospital. Except for one, all the bees were gone. But where were they? I opened the outside door and the moon made a blue path on the concrete. In the morning I am hoping they will find their way outside. Final Score: Monte 1, Bee hospital 12.

I SEE YOU IN THERE!!! COME OUT HERE BEFORE I COME GET YA!

SUPER Marlys Guide to Band-Aids

BY LYNDA BARRY LIVE FROM THE WAVE POOL AT THE DELLS.© 95

The #1 rule of all Band-Aids is <u>don't go</u> wasting them! They are <u>not</u> a toy! Unless you buy them with your own money. Then they are a toy. Because you get your say on them.

MARLYS! YOU WASTED ALL MY GOOD BAND-AIDS!

← VERY MAD!

BEFORE

NUHUH, I BOUGHT THEM WITH MY BIRTHDAY MONEY. OH.

→ SLIGHTLY EMBARRASSED.

AFTER

#2 rule is there is no such a thing as a ouch-less band-aid. So when you put a whole box of Band-Aids on yourself it's going to sting incredibly when you have to take them off. My #1 tip is: Go in the bathtub with them and do a soak-off. But don't let them go down the drain or you will get a massive clog which = <u>trouble</u>.

WHO CLOGGED THE DRAIN UP WITH BAND-AIDS?!

← very mad again!
• Hands ALL wrinkled from water→

I JUST PULLED the plug and they just accidentally flewdown!

#3 rule is: Be <u>very</u> careful about which toys you put band-aids on. Like say if it's pure plastic skin it's OK. But say you put the band-aid on the painted eye part? Chapter two is the whole eyeball peels off. And <u>forget fur</u>. Do not put a band-aid on <u>anything</u> with <u>fur</u>. It tears <u>all</u> the fur off. Even on a dog.

WHY DID YOU PUT Band-aids on Pookie?!

← VERY very mad!

Slightly → innocent!

I just wanted us to match!

The last rule of Band-Aids is <u>Do Not</u> Chintz out and buy the ones in the paper box! ALWAYS <u>BUY THE Metal Box</u>!!! Then afterwards you can use it for your treasures or a grasshopper or like some money, as a holder of your money. But <u>don't shake it in the car</u> too <u>long when parents are driving</u>! OK! Peace + Love + Right on power from the great Marlys !!!

MARLYS!!

← You MIGHT SAY FURIOUS!

↑ IN THE BACKSEAT→

Shake shake shak shake shake shake shake your boodie shake your boodie

JUST 10 MORE SHAKES, OK?

148

Super Marlys Guide to Mud!

BY LYNDA BARRY ❀❀ Ben + John G. are asleep. Shh. 🐸

Which would you pick to play with: ☐ Barbi or ☐ Mud? If you checked mud then probably you are incredible. If you checked Barbi then you need advice on how to get incredible.

TO MAKE MUD YOU DON'T NEED NO SPECIAL TALENTS. ONLY WATER AND DIRT.

IT'S GOOD TO WEAR YOUR SUNSUIT. IT'S GOOD IF YOU GOT AN UNLIMITED GARDEN HOSE.

←WATER   DIRT ↓

Of the ideas on how people were created I pick mud as the number 1 concept. That people came from mud. People are excellent to make from mud! Obviously God would never pick Barbi to play with if he could pick mud! Only people who have freakouts about getting dirty pick Barbi or boys maybe GI Joe.

NORMALLY YOU USE ROCKS FOR DETAILS. BUT I USE CHICLETS FOR TEETH. IT'S WASTING CHICLETS BUT IT'S FOR A GOOD CAUSE.

PAT   PAT   PAT

← IT'S OK TO MAKE YOUR MUD PEOPLE BIG!! EVEN STAND ON THEM!

Or maybe you got the bad deal of parents who will never let you get dirty. That is tragic. Like say if the mom and dad of god said he could never get dirty. there would be no world!

OTHER DECORATIONS ARE LEAVES, STICKS, and also squished MUDBALLS.

WHATEVER YOU EVEN GOT!

Then how can you ever know about the beautiful goodness of Mud? How bad it wants to **be** things. How bad it wants to get on your legs and arms and take your footprints and handprints and how bad it wants you to make it alive! Mud is always ready to play with you. Seriously you should try it! That is my great advice from marlys right on!

AND AFTER YOU'RE DONE, MUD **LIKES** TO BE BLOWN UP WITH THE GARDEN HOSE!

5... 4.... 3.... 2...

149

SUPER MARLYS GUIDE TO BE VERY POPULAR!!

by LYNDA BARRY & PRINCES HOT CHICKEN SHACK! © 1995

People ask me Marlys how did you get so totally popular? #1 answer is GIVE OUT CANDY to people. Give out lunch meat to dogs! (If you also want to be popular with dogs which is an excellent feeling!)

Chomp chomp thank you marlys you are great!

oh...

FOR YOU!

IT IS NOTHING!

AND make sure it is not bum scrubly candy like menthol or butterscotch or lunch meat with pieces of weird stuff mashed in it that you got two-for-one on sale. People always know when you are being skimpy.

wrong

HAVE SOME, Queen girl!

chomp. eeuu! These are nasty! I was going to invite you to my party but now forget it!

right

HAVE SOME, Queen girl!

CHOMP! Wow! will you please bring your bowl of candy to my party?

yes!

Other ways to be popular is tell people incredible compliments. Like for a dog you say "Good boy! Here boy what a good doggie, boy!" For a person you can go what long luxurious eyelashes! Or you always look so clean what is your soap?

For Boys say "what an incredible wart!"

or "you spit great!"

or "Dag what an incredible smashed-in thumbnail. It's so purple which is my favorite color!"

My sister Maybonne says I am plastic jive for wanting to even be popular. I told her she was looking incredible and gave her a thing of Sugar Babies. She said I was still plastic jive but let me sit on her bed with her and listen to the radio. What's wrong with being plastic jive if it turns your life so incredible?

CHOMP

DON'T TELL ANYONE I LET YOU DO THIS.

WANT SOME MALT BALLS?

150

SUPER MARLYS GUIDE TO RUNNING IN the SPRINKLER
BY LYNDA BARRY. MISSING that old Bison trail ©95

Sprinkler is such a gorgeous word and there are many kinds to run through.

there's the leaky flat snake which you can just jump over once if you don't want to get too wet or you can run the whole thing over and over!

It's the most gentle one. Good for shrimps

there's the twisty turner which is so magical the way it spins and interests dogs

you can jump it or dive under it and put your hand over one of the water holes and watch the other side go way high.

there's the built-in rich people's kind that you stub your toe on when you are illegally running on their property.

I COMMAND YOU TO REMOVE YOURSELF FROM MY LAND AT ONCE! GUARDS! TAKE AIM!

YOWA! YOWA! YOW!

this is the same kind as at the golf course so take my great advice of always look **down** while you are running for your life!

The number one sprinkler of all time is the swaying fan. you can run through it, you can do a close up with your face on it and feel the water jets, or you can do my favorite of just lay there and when it hits you, Scream!

Love always, Marlys

151

E·r·r·a·t·i·c··b·o·u·l·d·e·r·s·

BY LYNDA BARRY · What a sad day · © 1995

It was the nighttime guy on the radio who said it, We were all in the car after one whole day at this incredible park made by the ancientness of glaciers, and they kept on playing my sister's favorite band on a radio station that isn't normal for us.

What we saw by freddie Aug 9.

Kames (Caused by a glacier) It's high!

Four songs of it all in a row and my sister says that's the best radio station she ever heard and if only we could get that station where we lived, she was sad because it was already starting to crackle out. My brother freddie was asleep but he woke up after the radio guy made the announcement and my sister started crying.

Kettles   (you could get down in them!)

The guy that was just singing died, said the radio announcer, and then his voice was all fading and then the radio station was gone. My sister has all their records and her dream of life was to go to one of their shows, because there is natural love there. She told Freddie it was like if you turned on the radio and the real Santa was dead. Peace Santa. Love Santa.

Potholes   where you could trip!

My sister kept crying and I thought it was weird that Freddie started talking about the glaciers. How they changed everything. How there could have been a peace glacier and a love glacier that melted and left a beautiful place, a gorgeous place like where we were, then he reached over the backseat and got the rock he carried all day and gave it to Maybonne as a present for her sadness.

The most beautiful one I found

*RIGHTEOUS

by LYNDA BARRY ❊ SHE FLIPPED HER TURBAN ©1995

My Sister was making breakfast. She said "here are your righteous eggs, man." I said, "I wanted righteous french toast." She said, "Don't say righteous if you don't know what it means."

YOU'RE NOT RIGHTEOUS ENOUGH TO KNOW WHAT IT MEANS.

I said, "I know what it means. It means great." And she started laughing at me with her new way of laughing with her top lip stuck out, going, "Doy, Doy. Doy. Doy-a-hoy" which is another one of her new sayings she learned in the Dairy Freeze parking lot.

I said "Ever since you dyed your hair and got your new personality you have been so righteously stuck up." She started dancing and singing "Power to the people." If only she didn't look so beautiful. She got beautiful and I stayed the same.

She got new righteous friends and at school I was only being hated. My brother Freddie came in. He said, "Can I have some righteous orange juice?" and my sister smiled at him and said "Right On." I slid him my plate. I said, "Here have my righteous scrambled eggs, I don't want them anymore."

S'WRONG, MARLYS?

SHE'S RIDING A RIGHTEOUS BUMMER.

154

The Girl Next Door

LYNDA BARRY © 1995 THERE IS AN EVIL FISHBOWL!!!

One thing that is a noticeable weirdness in life is when someone whose guts you hated turns into your friend like Donna Dulaire the stuck up hog face crybaby from next door.

WELL HERE, HON. AT LEAST WEAR A HAT.

YEAH, OK.

It was freddie who first made friends with her because he has mercy inside of him for all living creatures even the ones that freak out when you turn their rock over, even creepy squirmy worm head Donna Dulaire who he just kept on saying "Hi" to until she just gave up and said "Hi" back.

HOW ABOUT SOME HOT COCOA?

YEAH, ALL RIGHT.

And then she was over at our house squatting in front of our TV and hogging down our food of Wonder bread and butter and powdered sugar sandwiches that Freddie kept piling in front of her and she always tried to talk with big wads in her mouth saying "Hi Marlys, Hi Marlys, Hi."

HONEY, IT'S ALMOST TIME FOR DINNER.

YEAH, I KNOW.

And after one week of her invasion you could say I got used to her and after two weeks my foot didn't want to kick her in the leg so bad and after three weeks she got big lumps in her neck and didn't come over and then it turned out she went in the hospital. And she's supposed to come home today. So that's why I'm waiting on the freezing front porch. So I can shout it: Hi Donna Hi Donna Hi!

HEY, SHE'S HOME!

HEY, EVERYBODY! DONNA DULAIRE IS HOME!

DONNA'S MOUTH

LYNDA BARRY ©1995 I LOVE ALEX CHILTON A LOT

There's different ideas about where the big red lumps on Donna Dulaire's neck came from. Her mom thinks it was from Donna sucking on Flubber or Donna chewing on Silly Putty or Donna biting all the hair off her Midge Doll and then sucking Midge's head.

Or eating the feet of her Barbi or eating every color of her play dough or biting up her Super Elastic Bubble plastic which it says right on the package <u>Do Not Eat</u>. But Donna says she can't help it. It is her tragic bad habit to try and eat her toys. And even my toys. She ate my little Chinese eraser doll and I bonked her on the head for it.

Mrs Dulaire's idea of how to cure Donna is no more toys. She has called our house to tell us Donna can't play with any toys ever in her life again after she swallowed 3 of Freddie's marbles. And now Donna looks so sad and lonely and she says please Marlys please just let me hold your Tressy Doll.

And then I look over and there's sudden wads of Tressy hair sticking out of Donna's mouth so I bonk her on the head again and that's when Freddie gets the idea to do a magic spell on Donna to help her with her problem. "But you have to be willing. Are you willing?" asked Freddie. Donna looked at him hard. She said, "OK if you will let me hold your G.I. Joe"

PUH-LEEZE?

Little Things

BY LYNDA BARRY. The Death of Atlas. © 1995

Donna Dulaire asked her mom could she spend the night at my house and the shouted answer was: "NO WAY IN HELL!" THen Donna asked could I stay over at her house and the same shout came out flying. Why does Mrs. Dulaire hate me so bad?

I was sitting on the plastic covers of their couch with my socks hanging over the plastic paths on their carpets. My shoes are not allowed inside. They bring dirt. Also, DON'T TOUCH ANYTHING! YOU MIGHT BREAK IT! Mrs. Dulaire has a lot of figurines.

Donna Dulaire came into the room with her eyes down. She gave me the news of I had to go home. I said Bye and she said Bye and on the frozen porch I jammed my shoes back on. In my pocket was a small blue and white cat that I shouldn't have took.

In my room there is a private cigar box with an incredible Spanish lady on the lid. I only ever take things that can fit inside. And I only ever take things from people who hate me. And the box is getting fuller. And when it is all the way full I will.... I will.... well I don't know what I will do.

157

The FALLING Leaves

LYNDA BARRY: "HE IS A SOCIOPATH BUT IT DOESN'T BUG HIM"

<u>Assignment</u>: Please write a description of the changes Autumn brings to the world around us!

<u>It's, Autumn, by Marlys!</u> <u>room 7!</u>

Well, first, most obviously, is the leaves! Colors, then, falling off, then, laying there! And, squirrels, digging!

And, my sister, getting busted, for, shoplifting! And, also, her, getting, illegally drunk, on, ripple, or, Boone's Farm, and, barfing! And, my brother, getting, socked in the face, on Halloween! And, it is, colder! And, now, it gets dark, very, very, very, early!

We, the people, are thinking, about, Thanksgiving! The pilgrims, and, Squanto! The birds, are, flying south! My sister, is grounded, until, Dec. 1! In, the play, we are doing, for assembly, I, have, to, be, a, vegetable! I, have, to, be, a, broccoli! I, get to say, "I, am so, delicious!"

My sister, says, she will, kill, herself, when, the, last, leaf, falls, from the tree, outside, her, bedroom, window! So, I, glued, 79, of, the, leaves, on! That, is, all, I, can, think of, to, write! The, End? By, Marlys!

B+ ☺ Good story, Marlys, but <u>watch those</u> commas!

OH, MARLYS.

STORY PROBLEMS
BY LYNDA BARRY ✿ THE BULLS! ©96

MRS. DULAIRE COMES TO OUR HOUSE TO SCREAM AT US EVERY 3 DAYS. SHE SCREAMS FOR 20 MINUTES EACH TIME. HOW MANY HOURS OF SCREAMING AT US DID MRS. DULAIRE DO LAST YEAR?

MONTE DULAIRE BURPS VERY LONG BURPS THAT LAST 7 SECONDS. HE ALSO BURPS SHORT ONES OF 2 SECONDS. HE BURPED 18 LONG ONES AND 17 SHORT ONES ON THE BUS THIS MORNING RIGHT IN MY EAR UNTIL I SLUGGED HIM. HOW MANY MINUTES OF BURPS DID IT TAKE TO GET ME VIOLENT?

EEERRRRRRRRPPP!!!

DONNA DULAIRE EATS GLUE THAT SHE SQUIRTS ON HER FINGERS. SHE ALSO EATS PASTE THAT SHE SMEARS ON HER FINGERS. IF SHE USES 1/125th OF THE GLUE BOTTLE AND 1/105th OF the PASTE JAR EACH TIME, HOW MANY HELPINGS BEFORE SHE BARFS?

MR. DULAIRE ONLY SAYS 6 WORDS A WEEK AND 3 OF THEM ARE SWEARS. HOW MANY SWEARS DID HE SAY IN MARCH AND APRIL? EXTRA CREDIT QUESTION: IF 30% OF THE SWEARS WERE AT ME FOR DRAWING CHALK HOPSCOTCHES ON HIS DRIVEWAY, HOW MANY SWEARS WERE LEFT OVER FOR HIS FAMILY?

#⊙!α*⊙#!!

159

THE MOST REMEMBERY VACUUM

LYNDA BARRY · MARDI GRAS MAMBO

You wouldn't think a certain vacuum cleaner could stay in your mind except if you ever plugged in the one my mom bought from a garage sale lady for $5.00.

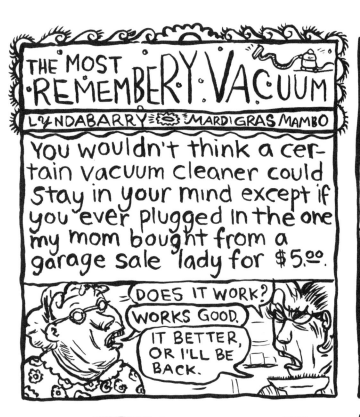

DOES IT WORK?

WORKS GOOD.

IT BETTER, OR I'LL BE BACK.

It is true it could excellently suck up the dirt, but it sounded like a screaming head and emitted a horrible choking smell that not even Lysol, Pinesol, and Spic'n'Span could conquer.

BEST VAC I'VE EVER HAD

LOOK AT IT GO!

EEUU!

MOVE.

BUT MOM! THE SMELL

THEN DON'T BREATHE.

TURNED OUT THERE WERE !!! TRAGICALLY DEAD ROTTED BODIES IN IT! HAMPSTERS TRAGICALLY CHEWED UP IN THE engine! I went back to the garage sale lady and asked her did she notice her pets were missing.

YOU FOUND MY MONKEY!!

NO.

um. no. I think it was hampsters.

YOU FOUND MY MONKEY, "LARS"!!

UH. NO.

Mom tweezered out the tragic chunks but the haunting fumes and the screaming stayed. For $5.00 mom still thought she got an incredible deal. I kept thinking of how weird it would be to croak in a vacuum cleaner. And was the screaming sound their ghosts wanting justice?

YOW!

THEY'RE BACK!

IT SHOCKED ME! THAT DAMN VACUUM JUST SHOCKED ME!

161

IF I COULD DO IT OVER AGAIN

by Lynda Barry © '97

If I could do it over again I would have never ate a whole bag of colorful mini-marshmallows before my turn in tumbling.

OH
OH NO I
I THINK I'M GONNA
DON'T LOOK!

I would have never picked to be the food when our class did Journey Through the Body for assembly.

OK! Will the digestive juices step forward and surround Marlys.

UM
MRS. VANDA
IS IT too late to change my pick?
DON'T DO THIS TO ME.
I BEG YOU.

I would never have ratted my hair up so intensely with the extra hold Adorn.

UH, MAYBONNE CAN YOU BRUSH MY HAIR OUT?
WHERE'S YOUR BRUSH?
UM
SEE... WELL, IT'S IN THERE.

And I would have never ever ever of kissed Monte Dulaire if I would have known the tragic results.

CHILDREN HI LIFE THE GOOFUS & GALLANT ISSUE

THE DOCTOR SAID IT'S AN ALLERGIC REACTION TO A VERY IRRITATING SUBSTANCE. WHAT COULD IT BE?

SCIENTIFIC MARLYS!

WONDERS (actual) OF the DEEP
CONVOLUTA Roscoffensis
BY Lynda Barry ©97 Happy B-Day JON G!

MARLYS and Skreddy 57 GO MICRO TO BRING YOU DETAILS concerning A MIND BLOWING little CREATURE.

"I'M LIKING THIS WATERY WORLD!"

"HEY, CONVOLUTA WHAT IT IS!"

CONVOLUTA IS A DINKY FLAT WORM THAT LIVES IN THE SAND ON CERTAIN SHORES. SHE LETS TINY SEAWEED LIVE INSIDE HER. SHE DOESN'T HAVE A MOUTH OR A BRAIN BUT HER LIFE VIBRATIONS ARE SO MELLOW. WHEN THE TIDE GOES OUT, SHE RISES TO THE TOP OF THE SAND AND GETS PHOTOSYNTHESIS LOVE.

THE SUN SHINES

CONVOLUTA'S INNER SEAWEED EMITS CHLOROPHYLL

SHE FEELS FINE FOXY AND FREE.

WHEN THE TIDE COMES IN, SHE GOES DEEP DOWN INTO THE SAND AND ACTS VERY SENSUOUS. WHEN THE TIDE GOES OUT SHE RISES AGAIN. BUT WHAT IS SO WILD ABOUT CONVOLUTA IS: SHE WILL DO THIS EVEN IN A FISHBOWL! SHE IS SO SENSITIVE, SHE CAN FEEL THE TIDE IN A MAYONNAISE JAR!

"THAR SHE BLOWS!"

HELLMANS

"DAG, CONVOLUTA!"

AND THE SCIENTISTS SAY HOW? NO BRAIN, EYES OR EARS OR SUDDEN BONG HITS THAT GIVE ENLIGHTENMENT. HOW DOES CONVOLUTA DO IT? SHE DIDN'T TELL MARLYS AND SKREDDY 57 BUT SHE GAVE THEM WONDER ANYWAY AND THEY WANTED ME TO PASS IT ON TO YOU.

"HEY! LET'S GO FIND THE CLOWN-FISH."

"YEAH. HE OWES ME MONEY."

DON'T FREAK IT'S ONLY NATURE

LYNDA BARRY ⚬☞ I LIKED AFTER BEAVIS BIT THE CACTUS

UM.

EXCUSE ME BUT IF YOU FREAK VERY EASY DON'T READ THIS. GO WATCH CARTOONS.

BECAUSE THESE ARE A FEW OF MY FAVORITE THINGS.

IN THE DISTURBING CATEGORY.

IF YOU DON'T LIKE EXTRA PINK DANGLES OF FLESH,

DON'T GO STARING AT THE STAR-NOSED MOLE.

NO BRAG. BUT.

I CAN DRINK 10 TIMES MY WEIGHT IN BLOOD!

LEECHES HAVE TINY DOTS ON THEIR HEAD THAT THEY USE TO DETECT HEAT, MOVEMENT, LIGHT AND THE MOST HORRIFYING SPOT TO ATTACH THEMSELVES TO YOU, AS THEY LOVE HEARING THE WORDS, "OH GOD! OH GOD! GET IT OFF ME! GET IT OFF!"

TERMITES

CAN MAKE 22-FOOT-TALL NESTS OUT OF THEIR SPIT, THEIR POOP, AND THE DIRT AROUND THEM. AND THE NESTS ARE SO HARD AND STRONG YOU NEED TNT FOR REMOVAL

I CAN'T DO THAT. CAN YOU DO THAT?

DAG. WHOA.

I SAY LET THEM STAY

GOOD THING THIS STORY PROBLEM IS JUST PRETEND!

SAY MONTE DULAIRE IS SCREAMING AT YOUR BROTHER SKREDDY 57 THAT HE IS A FAG. AND SCREAMING AT YOU ON HOW UGLY YOU ARE. THEN SUDDENLY THIS THING HAPPENS WHERE YOU CONTROL THE ROPE THAT IS HANGING HIM OVER THE PIRANHAS. OK. MONTE WEIGHS 74 POUNDS. A PIRANHA CAN EAT 2 OZ. PER MINUTE. IF THERE ARE 200 PIRANHAS, HOW MUCH LONGER DO WE HAVE OF MONTE?

LICE

JUST READING THE WORD FREAKS YOU!

WHY DID I HAVE TO COME BACK AS AN ECTO-PARA-SITE?

IT EVEN FREAKS ME!

IF ONLY I HADN'T CALLED FREDDIE A FAG. SOON THEY WILL APPLY THE DEADLY SUNTAN LOTION AND MY HORROR WILL BEGIN. IF ONLY I HAD BEEN NICER TO MARLYS.

AND I'M UNFREAKABLE PRETTY MUCH.

BUT LOOK HOW EVEN OUR LANGUAGE HAS LICE!

• "NIT-PICKING!"
• "GO OVER IT WITH A FINE TOOTH COMB!"
• "THAT IS LOUSY!" • "WHAT A LOUSE!"

AND "GUESS WHY MONTY BELIEVES IN REINCARNATION"

165

LORD LOVE A LUNGFISH

by Lynda Barry ©1997 oh ooo-La.!!!

GREETINGS AND DOWN WITH THE MAN AND WELCOME TO THE LUNGFISH HOUR OF POWER.

OUR ANIMAL BROTHER, THE LUNGFISH, IS A MAJOR MIND BLOWER IN HIS ABILITY TO GROOVE AND BE MELLOW IN SO MANY DIFFERENT SCENES SUCH AS · WATER · MUD · DRY MUD. · MUD THAT IS ALL CRACKED AND FREAKY.

WHEN THE WEATHER GETS VERY HOT AND DRIES UP THE LUNGFISH'S WATERY WORLD, HE DOESN'T BECOME A LITTLE JUNKIE CRAWLING ON A SHAG RUG, AND STEALING OTHER PEOPLE'S UNDERPANTS OFF OF CLOTHES LINES, AND SELLING HIS BLOOD AT A CLINIC LIKE A WINO. THAT IS NOT HIS STYLE.

HE DIGS A HOLE IN THE MUD

HE COVERS HIS EYES

HE PUTS HIS NOSE BY A LITTLE BREATHING HOLE

AND DREAMS HE IS IN A HOLLYWOOD MOVIE AND THAT HE IS THE STAR.

WHILE THE MUD GETS HARD AND DRY, SO DOES THE LUNGFISH. HE CAN STAY ALIVE LIKE THIS FOR YEARS, JUST SLEEPING AND DREAMING OF TEAMING UP WITH HARRISON FORD AND DANNY GLOVER IN: TWO MEN AND A LUNGFISH AN ACTION ADVENTURE AND LOVE STORY. LETS ROLL A CLIP:

NO. DON'T SPEAK. JUST SWIM AWAY AND DON'T LOOK BACK. I SHALL NEVER FORGET YOU.

WE'RE OUTTA TIME!

D.G.
H.F.

C'MON LUNGFISH! THE WHOLE PLACE IS ABOUT TO BLOW!

IF YOU DUG UP THE LUNGFISH HE WOULD LOOK SO WRINKLED AND HE WOULD BE SO DRIED UP THAT YOU WOULD FLASH ON THE WORDS: HE'S DEAD.

SPEAK TO ME

← HE'S SHRUNKEN LIKE A EARTHWORM CAUGHT ON THE SIDEWALK ALL DAY IN JULY

BUT AFTER A COUPLE OF DAYS IN THE RIGHTEOUS WATER, OUR LUNGFISH IS READY FOR LIFE, LOVE AND LUSCIOUS BUG TREATS.

JUST TALKING 'BOUT THE LUNGFISH!

CAN YOU DIG IT?

M.E.D.I.C.A.L CONDITIONS

+ NURSE MARLYS +

Lynda Barry © 97 ※ TAKE THE "EL" TRAIN!

HELLO AND WELCOME TO THE MARLYS MEDICAL MINUTE!

TODAY I'D LIKE TO TELL YOU MY FAVORITE CONDITIONS.

OW. OW. NURSE MARLYS! YOU ARE LEANING ON MY OPERATION! OW! GET OFF! OW!

THESE ARE REAL! NOT MADE UP! SO SIT BACK AND RELAX AND GET READY FOR...

TRAGIC NAME SYNDROME

WHERE THE PARENTS EITHER THINK TOO HARD OR DON'T THINK HARD ENOUGH ON WHAT TO NAME THE BABY.

SUFFERERS INCLUDE...

"WADLEY"   "MELVINETTE"   "TANGERINA-AMBER-GRIS"

"BRAINARD"   "SQUIDLEY"   "PETULA"

"GNARLENE"   "WEENUS"   "FREEBIRD"

NURSE MARLYS Rx: USE YOUR INITIALS INSTEAD UNLESS THEY ARE B.O., P.U., R.S.V.P.

BROMHIDROSIS (STINK FOOT)

WHERE YOUR FEET ARE VERY RASTY WITH ODORS OF HORROR!

SOMETIMES I HAVE THIS CONDITION ESPECIALLY WHEN MY EVIL COUSIN ARNOLD SNEAKS SMELL-O-RAMA ITEMS IN MY DRESS SHOES →

Nurse Marlys' Rx:
1. WASH YOUR FEET MORE ESPECIALLY IF YOU HAVE COMPANY
2. SOAK YOUR FEET IN ICED TEA.
3. SOAK YOUR FEET IN MELTED ORANGE POPSICLE FLUID
4. DIP YOUR FEET IN THE WATER OF GREEN FIZZIES.
5. CHECK SHOES FREQUENTLY FOR **FISH CHUNKS**

PTYALISM (TOO MUCH SPIT)

TRY SPONGE CAKE!

OK

LENTIGO (FRECKLES)

ALSO KNOWN AS MELA-MARLYS

METEORISM (IN 1934 THIS WAS THE NAME FOR IF YOU CUT ONE OR MORE)

WHOA!   KAHUTEK!   UM. EXCUSE ME.   SERIOUSLY

WELL THAT'S ALL WE HAVE TIME FOR! SEE YOU NEXT WEEK!

CLOWNISM (WHEN YOU GET YOUR FACE STUCK IN CLOWN-HEAD POSES)

WAIT! THE CURE FOR CLOWNISM!! WHAT IS IT!!?!

171

172

174

187

TRAILER PARK MARLYS!

THE MARLYS REPORT

AND NOW, ANOTHER VERY INCREDIBLE TRUE LOVE STORY FROM OUR TRAILER PARK.

THE DUCHEES' DAD SHOWED UP AFTER 7 YEARS OF WANDERING.

GO GET MOM.

HI KIDS! DON'T YA RECOGNIZE ME?

MRS. DUCHEE HIT HIM WITH A SKILLET.

YOW!

—BLASH!

SHE STILL HAD HARD FEELINGS ABOUT THE PAST.

YABBER! YABBER! YABBER! *#@!

HIS HEAD WAS GUSHING BLOOD.

OW OW

MRS. DUCHEE CALLED THE COPS, WHO WEREN'T THAT INTERESTED.

GET YOUR DAD A WASHRAG AND A BEER. GO.

THEY BOTH GOT VERY DRUNK.

SHABA BABBA SLUR

SPTH PTHH SLUR

WHEN THE COPS CAME, THEY WERE MAKING UP.

I WUV YOU!

I MITHED YOU!

HEY. HEY. HEY!

MRS. DUCHEE GOT EMOTIONAL.

YOU KEEP AWAY FROM MY HUSBAND!

OH CRIPES!

THEN MR. DUCHEE CALLED HER EVELYN.

EVELYN?

MY EVELYN!

WHO'S EVELYN?

TURNS OUT HE WASN'T MR. DUCHEE. HIS NAME WAS RODNEY CANEY.

THIS COURT NUMBER 71?

THIS IS 27

WRONG TRAILER.

OOPS

AND NOW SHE'S MRS. RODNEY CANEY.

NEXT WEEK: MORE TRAILER PARK NEWS!

LYNDA BARRY ©1998

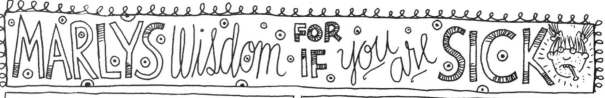

MARLYS Wisdom FOR IF you are SICK

1. LET ALL THE DOGS IN THE BED! THEY HAVE MAGICAL HEALER POWERS! IF YOU DO NOT HAVE PERSONAL DOGS, JUST BORROW YOUR NEIGHBOR'S!

I FEEL THE SUPERFRAGALISTIC VIBRATIONS!

2. WHEN YOUR EXCITED FRIEND WHO TALKS REALLY LOUD INTO THE TELEPHONE WANTS TO BLAB WITH YOU, SAY PLEASE CALL BACK LATER!

IT'S FOR YOU.

IF I TALK TO HER I WILL GO BERSERK

PLEASE WILL YOU TELL HER?

MARLYS GUESS WHAT YOU MISSED FOR LUNCH TODAY?!!

3. DO NOT ASK FOR YOUR MOST FAVORITE FOOD! IF YOU BARF IT, YOU WON'T BE ABLE TO EAT IT IN THE FUTURE FOR A LONG LONG TIME!!

MARLYS ARE YOU SURE YOU WANT FRUITLOOPS AND CHOCOLATE MILK FOR DINNER?

I. AM. SURE.

4. DON'T GET FREAKED BY THE VERY WEIRD DREAMS! MOSTLY IT IS JUST THE COUGH SYRUP!

HELP!

WHICH DRAWER IS IT, MARLYS?

ARGUS THE 100-EYEBALLED MONSTER FROM ANCIENT MYTHOLOGY WANTS TO BORROW SOME UNDERPANTS!

5. IT IS IMPORTANT THAT YOU CONTROL THE ENTIRE COUCH! EVERYONE ELSE JUST SIT ON THE FLOOR! ALSO IT IS YOUR RIGHT TO HOG THE TV!

CHUMP.

MARLYS IS A CHUMP.

SHUT UP!

JUST BECAUSE YOU ARE SICK IT DOES NOT MEAN YOU CONTROL THE UNIVERSE!

YES IT DOES!

6. IF YOUR COUSIN SNATCHES THE REMOTE CONTROL, CALL RESCUE 911!

YES, UM, I'D LIKE TO REPORT A TRAGICAL EMERGENCY PLEASE?!

A ROBBERY!

CAN YOU PLEASE COME RIGHT AWAY? MY SHOW IS ON!

LYNDA

BARRY 99

205

MARLYS AND FRED MILTON

CROCHETED-AFGHAN MARLYS

219

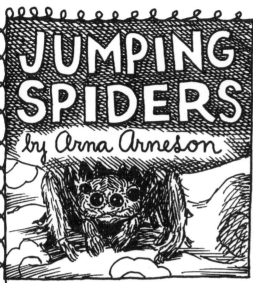

JUMPING SPIDERS

by Arna Arneson

SOMETIMES LIFE GIVES US SITUATIONS WHERE WE ARE CONFUSED AND FRIGHTENED ..... AND SOMETIMES THE JUMPING SPIDER COMES TO HELP.

WITH HIS BRIGHT FRONT EYES HE SEES ME LONELY.

ARTHROPOD ARACHNID SALTICIDAE ON MY PILLOW LOOKING.

PANORAMIC EIGHT-EYED VISION TAKES IN MY SCENE: MY AUNT SHOUTING. I WET THE BED AGAIN.

THE DOOR SLAMS. I MUST SLEEP IN THE WET BED TO LEARN MY LESSON. THE JUMPING SPIDER WAVES AT ME AND BOBS. BE A SPIDER.

BE A SPIDER-GIRL WITH ME. I WILL TEACH YOU ALL CAMOUFLAGE AND TURNABOUT DEFENSE. MIMIC ME. BE A JUMPING SPIDER-GIRL.

IN THE MORNING MY AUNT SHOUTS AT ME FOR CROUCHING ON MY PILLOW. I SAY NOTHING. JUMPING SPIDERS NEVER TALK TO HER.

MER-MONSTER MARLYS

My Walk to the Lake

IN THE SUMMER YOU CAN HEAR THE CARS GO BY. RADIOS PLAYING LOUD. TEENAGERS, TEENAGERS ON THE LOOSE. GOING TO THE LAKE. COMING BACK FROM THE LAKE. WILL THEY GIVE US RIDES? NO.

ME AND MY COUSIN ARE WALKING THERE BAREFOOT. IT'S STUPID, I KNOW. BUT MARLYS SAYS TO TOUGHEN UP OUR FEET WE MUST DO IT. THE STREET IS BLACK BURNING LAVA AND THE SHOULDER IS SHARP GRAVEL. ANOTHER TEENAGER GOES BY.

WE WILL GET KILLED FOR TAKING THESE TOWELS. IF MY AUNT FINDS OUT, WE ARE DEAD. WE KEEP RUNNING TO PATCHES OF SHADE ON THE ROAD. OUR FEET ARE ON FIRE BURNING. MARLYS HAS A DOLLAR. SHE SAYS, "REFRESHMENT STAND! REFRESHMENT STAND!"

I'M GETTING ME A FUDJYCUL AND A NUTTYBUDDY

WHAT YOU GETTING, ARNA?

BOMB POP. CREAMSICLE. OW. BARBECUE POTATO CHIPS.

WE CAN HEAR THE SHOUTING AND THE SPLASHING. THE WOODEN BOING OF THE HIGH DIVE ON THE RAFT. THE SMELL OF THE LAKE COMES CARRIED COOL UP OUR NOSES AND FINALLY OUR FEET TOUCH THE GRASS GRASS GRASS.

MADE IT!

AHHHH.

AHH.

Water World

ME AND MARLYS WERE AT THE LAKE ALL DAY JUST STANDING IN THE COOL WATER. WE SWAM UNDER WATER ACTING LIKE MERMAIDS. WE DID SOME UNDER WATER HAND STANDS.

WEIRD.

SEE?

YEAH.

WE SPENT ALL OUR MONEY AT THE REFRESHMENT STAND. WE FELL DOWN ON THE SLIME AREA BY THE WATER FOUNTAIN. THE CONCRETE THERE IS GREEN AND SLICK. MARLYS SAYS SEAWEED. IT'S MINIATURE DEADLY SEAWEED GROWING.

FEEL IT?

UH-HUH.

WE WATCHED OTHER PEOPLE FALL DOWN FOR AWHILE AND THEN WE STOOD IN THE WATER SOME MORE. THE SUN WAS GOING DOWN. A KID GOT LOST, HIS MOM WAS SCREAMING, THEN HE GOT FOUND.

FEELS SO CONVINCING.

IT WAS A LONG WALK HOME BUT THE STREET HAD THE COOLING SHADOWS LAID ACROSS AND OUR FEET DID NOT GET SINGED. MARLYS SAID, "ARNA. YOU FEEL THE WAVES? YOU FEEL LIKE YOU ARE STILL IN THE WATER?" WE STOPPED FOR A MOMENT IN THE LONG SHADOWS FEELING THE WAVES THAT KEPT MOVING US.

DAG. FEELS REAL.

SCHOOL

IF YOU HAVE EVER HAD A GOOD TEACHER, IT'S VERY HARD TO HAVE A BAD ONE. I THINK TO A TEACHER THAT'S BAD, KIDS ARE ALL THE SAME.

EACH OF YOU WILL STAND, SAY YOUR NAME, SAY MY NAME, SAY YOUR GRADE.

IN ORDER, NOW...

MRS. QUIRT WILL READ US THE SAME BOOKS AT STORY-TIME SHE HAS ALWAYS READ. FABLES WITH MORALS, CALLED MORALS AT THE END. SHE WILL WRITE THEM ON THE BOARD AND WE WILL COPY.

NO. YOUR NAME FIRST. THEN MINE!

NEXT.

CLAP!

MRS. QUIRT SAYS NO ONE WILL GET AWAY WITH ANYTHING IN HER CLASS. SAYS SHE HAS BEEN TEACHING LONGER THAN WE HAVE BEEN ALIVE AND SHE'LL BE TEACHING LONG AFTER WE ARE GONE; WE CANNOT SURPRISE HER.

EYES FORWARD!

NOT WITH AUTUMN OR WINTER OR THE FLOWERS OF SPRING, WAITING NOW QUIETLY IN ROOTS AND BULBS AND SEEDS. WAITING FOR THE PASSING OF THIS COLD, DARK TIME. MY NAME IS ARNA ARNESON. MY TEACHER IS MRS. QUIRT. I AM IN THE FIFTH GRADE.

RIGHT. NOW. LET'S DO IT ALL AGAIN.

L Y N D A B A R R Y '99

TWINS

I AM IN TROUBLE FOR STARING AT TWINS, TWINS IN OUR CLASS-ROOM, QUITE BEAUTIFUL TWINS, REGINALD AND RONALD CHOMDELAY.

MRS. QUIRT SAYS THERE IS NOTHING SPECIAL ABOUT THEM, IT IS SIMPLE BIOLOGY, NOTHING MORE, NOW WHO WAS MAGELLAN AND WHAT DID HE DO? HANDS?

SEE HERE, ARNA! YOU CAN'T FIND TWO ORDINARY BOYS MORE INTERESTING THAN A GREAT EXPLORER! EYES FORWARD!!

REGINALD AND RONALD HAVE DEEP BROWN SKIN AND PALE GREEN EYES. THEIR HAIR IS STRAIGHT AND SHINES. NOTHING AT ALL SPECIAL SAYS MRS. QUIRT. EXACTLY IDENTI-CAL MYSTERIOUS TWINS, SITTING BESIDE ME IN ROW 2.

NOTHING IN OUR LIVES CAN COMPARE WITH WHAT MAGELLAN SAW ON THIS JOURNEY.

MRS. QUIRT MOVES THE POINTER ON TIERRA DEL FUEGO AND I MOVE MY EYES TO THE TWINS. LET HER CATCH ME, I DON'T CARE. MRS. QUIRT IS SO WRONG ABOUT SO MANY THINGS.

COUNTING OUT

MRS. QUIRT SINGS HIGH AND MARKS TIME WITH HER FEET AND PLAYS AN INSTRUMENT CALLED A ZITHER WITH A THING CALLED A PLECTRUM. PASS IT ON.

HER EYES ROLL UP SLIGHTLY BEHIND HER THICK GLASSES, SHE SINGS 'HEY NONNY—NONNY' SOME KIND OF BRITISH SONG. SHE'S BEEN TO LONDON AND HAS SEEN THE QUEEN WAVING. HEY NONNY NONNY. PASS IT ON.

SHE HAS A MOLE BY HER EYE THAT SHE THOUGHT COULD BE CANCER SO SHE WENT TO THE DOCTOR BUT THANK GOD IT WAS NOT. SHE HAD AN UNCLE WHO MET WINSTON CHURCHILL. HE WAS NOT VERY FRIENDLY. PASS IT ON.

PLEASE, WHEN YOU SPEAK YOU MUST STAND BY YOUR DESK AND ANSWER CONCISELY, NO PERSONAL STORIES THAT WASTE CLASSROOM TIME. I DON'T CARE IF YOU LIKE ME, BUT YOU MUST RESPECT ME. I HAVE VARICOSE VEINS. PASS IT ON.

Lynda 1999 Barry

MOVING DAY

Lynda Barry © 1999

A HOUSE! A HOUSE! NOT A TRAILER BUT A HOUSE! MY COUSINS ARE YELLING AND RUNNING UP AND DOWN THE STAIRS. "OPEN THE DOOR!" SHOUTS MY BROTHER. "KEEP YOUR DAMN PANTS ON!" SHOUTS MY MOM. MAYBONNE SAYS, "IT'S A HOLE," AND MY AUNT WHAPS HER. WE ARE ALL MOVING IN TOGETHER AND I WILL ADMIT I AM EXCITED!

I TOUCHED THE DOORKNOB FIRST! FIRST ONE IN GETS FIRST DIBS ON BEDROOMS!

ONLY IN YOUR MIND!

NO.

YES!

"WHERE'S THE DAMN KEYS?" SAYS MY AUNT. "HOLY BALLS, DON'T SAY YOU LOST THEM ALREADY!" SAYS MY MOM. "YOU HAVE THEM!" "THE HELL I DO!" AND WHILE THEY DO THEIR USUAL BICKER ME AND FREDDIE RUN AROUND THE SIDE OF THE HOUSE AND INTO THE BACKYARD.

THAT'S A FORFEIT! THAT'S A AUTOMATIC FORFEIT ON PICKS OF BEDROOMS!

WHOEVER LIVED IN THIS HOUSE BEFORE US MOVED OUT BY HURLING IT ALL INTO THE BACKYARD. IN THE PILE WAS EVERYTHING: CHAIRS, BIKES, AN IRONING BOARD, CHRISTMAS PAPER. ALL RAINED ON. ALL WARPED. ALL RUSTED.

YOU AND ME ARE THE KING AND QUEEN OF THIS LAND OF TREASURE, ARNA. CLAIM IT WITH ME.

I CLAIM IT.

I CLAIM IT.

NOW IT'S OURS.

ABOVE OUR HEADS A WINDOW FLEW OPEN. MARLYS STICKING HER HEAD OUT AND SCREAMING, "IT'S A RIP-OFF!" SHE WAS CRYING AND SHE SCREAMED IT ABOUT THREE MORE TIMES BEFORE MY AUNT YANKED HER IN. FREDDIE TAPPED MY SHOULDER AND HANDED ME A CHEWED ON PLASTIC BANANA FROM THE DUMP PILE. AND I DON'T KNOW WHY BUT WE JUST STARTED LAUGHING AND JUST COULDN'T STOP.

YOU STUPID IDIOTS! WHY ARE YOU LAUGHING?! DONTCHA GET IT? IT'S TRAGEDY!

TRA-GE-DEE!

MARLYS! DAMMIT MARLYS! GET AWAY FROM THAT WINDOW OR I'M GOING TO WRING YOUR NECK!

235

WE ARE HOME

LYNDA   BARRY 1996

IN THE NEW HOUSE, WHICH IS AN OLD HOUSE WITH A BIG DUMP PILE BEHIND IT AND OTHER PEOPLE'S THINGS STILL IN IT, BUT IT IS <u>HUGE</u>, I MEAN HUGE WITH SO MANY WINDOWS WHO CARES IF SOME OF THEM ARE BROKEN, IN THIS NEW HOUSE WE CAN ALL HAVE OUR OWN ROOM BUT NO ONE WANTED THAT EXCEPT MAYBONNE.

AREN'T YOU EVEN GOING TO BE SCARED UP HERE?

OF WHAT?

HAUNTED GHOSTS.

NO.

MAN YOU GOT BRAVERY.

HER PICK OF BEDROOM WAS IN THE ATTIC WITH DANGLE LIGHT BULBS ON A PULL CHAIN. THE STAIRS UP TO IT ARE TINY AND STEEP. HER MOM HAS BAD KNEES AND IS FRIGHTENED OF FALLING." THE ATTIC IS PERFECT," SAYS MAYBONNE.

SURE GOT A LOT OF 'STENSION CORDS.

SO?

JUST SAYING YOU GOT A LOT, YA CRAB

I'M NOT A CRAB

IT DOES HAVE A FEATURE, A SMALL LITTLE DOOR THAT LEADS ONTO A FIRE ESCAPE SO DECREPIT. IT'S WOODEN AND SHAKEY AND THE PAINT'S PEELING OFF. "NO GOING OUT THERE!" SAYS HER MOTHER. MAYBONNE AGREES, THE TEENAGER AGREES. IT'S GETTING DARK AND THEN TIME FOR BED.

YOU TOLD MOM YOU'RE NOT GOING OUT THERE BUT YOU ARE BECAUSE I KNOW YOU ARE.

GOODNIGHT, MARLYS.

SO OBVIOUSLY.

FOR SURE TO SMOKE YOU ARE.

GOODNIGHT, MARLYS.

GOOD NIGHT, LYING SMOKER

AND MARLYS IS SNORING AND HOGGING THE BED, DOWNSTAIRS THEY ARE WATCHING JOHNNY CARSON. ABOVE ME SOFT FOOTSTEPS, THE SOUND THROUGH THE CEILING OF A TEENAGER HAUNTED BY A DOOR TO THE NIGHT. MY COUSIN MAYBONNE LIGHTS UP A SALEM, BLOWS GHOSTS TO THE DARKNESS, BE IT EVER SO HUMBLE, THERE'S NO PLACE LIKE HOME.

Silver Tone

LYNDA   BARRY '00

IN THE ATTIC MUSIC KEEPS ON PLAYING. IT'S THE SAME SONGS OVER AND OVER. THE TEENAGER HAS A WORLD UP THERE, MAYBONNE IN HER BEDROOM WITH HER SILVERTONE STEREO BLASTING.

OH FOR THE LOVE OF GOD. SHE'S PLAYING IT AGAIN.

IT'S THE MOSLEYS. THEY'RE FROM MILWAUKEE.

WHAT THE HELL DO YOU KNOW ABOUT MILWAUKEE?

MY AUNT YELLS FROM THE KITCHEN, SOME SWEARS AND A COMMAND, TURN IT OFF, TURN IT OFF!! SHE SHOUTS TO THE CEILING WHILE THE MOSLEYS SING. NOBODY NOBODY NOBODY NOBODY. NOBODY'S GONNA LOVE YOU THE WAY THAT I DO.

THE TEENAGER HAS NO RESPECT FOR OTHERS. IS SHE DEAF? THE TEENAGER IS SKATING ON THIN ICE. IS SHE AN IDIOT? DOES SHE THINK THE ENTIRE WORLD REVOLVES AROUND HER? WILL SHE ANSWER? WHO IN THE HELL, JUST WHO IN THE HELL DOES SHE THINK SHE IS? THE MOSLEYS SING NOBODY NOBODY NOBODY.

SHE CAN'T HEAR YOU, MOM. SHE CAN'T HEAR NO ONE WHEN SHE LISTENS TO MUSIC.

MY AUNT AT THE STAIR-TOP IS SCREAMING, ON THE LATCHED DOOR SHE IS POUNDING. OPEN IT! RIGHT NOW! OPEN IT! FROM HER PLACE IN THE CENTER OF THE COOL SPINNING UNIVERSE THE GIRL IN THE SONG HEARS A TAPPING AND A BUZZ. A WASP AGAINST A WINDOW-PANE. NOBODY. NOBODY. NOBODY'S GONNA LOVE YOU THE WAY THAT I DO.

237

WHAT NAME

LYNDA BARRY 1999

OUR MOMS SAID, "WE'RE GOING TO PLAY BINGO." ONE SAID, "IT'S BINGO NIGHT!" THE OTHER ONE SAID "SURE AS HELL IS!" MARLYS WATCHED THE CAR DRIVE AWAY. SHE SAID, "THEY AIN'T GOING TO NO BINGO."

THEY CALL IT BINGO BUT IT'S SOMEWHERE ELSE.

BLOCK IT, MAN. YOU'RE NOT EVEN TRYIN'!

I SORT OF AM.

BE SERIOUS!

WHY NOT JUST SAY THE ACTUAL NAME? IT'S SO CHUMPY TO KEEP SAYING BINGO, BINGO, BINGO.

MAYBONNE WAS IN THE KITCHEN SHOVING IN THE TV DINNERS. SHE SWITCHED THE RADIO FROM COUNTRY CAVALCADE TO THE NATION'S NUMBER ONE SOUL. MARLYS SAID, "YOU THINK YOU'RE BLACK." MAYBONNE SAID, "SHUT UP HUNKY." "OOO!" SAID MARLYS, "I'M A HUNKY. WOW."

WHATS IT SAY? 350°? 375°?

375°

BUT WHAT'S BO-HUNKY THOUGH? SERIOUSLY I HAVE HEARD BO-HUNKY AND ALSO BULL-HUNKY.

AND THERE'S A CANDY CALLED BIG HUNK AND A CANDY CALLED CHUNKY. NOTICE THAT?

"I'M A FAG," SAID FREDDIE, HE WAS SITTING ON THE STEP-STOOL. ARNOLD SHOVED HIM, "NO YOU'RE NOT, NOT NO MORE." ARNOLD WAS DOING CHARITY LESSONS ON KUNG FU TO ALL OF US. HE TOLD FREDDIE TO GO WITH DRUNKEN MONKEY STYLE KUNG FU AND HE WOULDN'T BE NO FAG. THEN HE DID A KICK AND A RIP CAME FROM HIS PANTS.

HIYHAA!

SHUT UP YOU GUYS!

RRRIP!

"WHAT'S ARNA?" SAID MARLYS, AND THEY ALL LOOKED AT ME. I WAS HOLDING A BOX FROM THE DINNER, THINKING ABOUT THE WORDS "SALISBURY STEAK," WHY IT SOUNDED SO GOOD BUT TASTED SO BAD. BUT WHAT IS IN A NAME. TO FOUR KIDS AND ONE TEENAGER LEFT ALONE ON A SATURDAY NIGHT, TELL ME, WHAT IS IN A NAME.

LIKE HOW ARNOLD'S DRUNKEN MONKEY AND I'M BIG HUNKY AND FREDDIE'S THE FAG AND MAYBONNE IS FAKE OUT BLACK, WHAT'S ARNA. WHAT ARE YOU, ARNA?

DUH!!

SHE'S PEE-BED, REMEMBER?

SALISB

Mysterious World

LYNDA BARRY '00

MYSTERIOUS WORLD, THE ATTIC BEDROOM OF MY COUSIN, SMELLING OF NAG CHAMPA INCENSE, NAG CHAMPA IS HER BRAND, SHE KNOWS THE PLACES TO GO TO FIND SUCH THINGS, I'VE NEVER ONCE ASKED IF SHE WOULD EVER TAKE ME, THE ANSWER IS TOO OBVIOUS.

SERIOUSLY THIS KIND IS WAY NICER.

THAT OTHER KIND SMELLED LIKE DRIED BONUS CAT PEE.

SHUT UP. I'M CONCENTRATING.

MYSTERY WORLD, HER DRESSER AND HER MIRROR, HER DRESSER-TOP THINGS, THEIR ARRANGEMENT. HOT CURLERS, A HAIRBRUSH WITH A BLUE SPARKLE HANDLE, THE LOCKED BOX WITH A KEY SO HIDDEN NOT EVEN MARLYS CAN FIND IT. THE BOX HAS JAPANESE WORDS AND PICTURES ON IT. SOMETHING LIKE: 猫の子の首の鈴がねがすかにも音のみたる夏草のうち, SOMETHING MAYBONNE KNOWS, SWEARS SHE KNOWS THE SECRET MEANING OF.

SEEN WHILE HIGH

HOT 'N' CURLEE

MARLYS THINKS THIS BOX CONTAINS THE ANSWER TO HER QUESTION. THE NAME OF THE BOY, SHE'S SURE THAT THERE'S A BOY, LOOK HOW CAREFULLY MAYBONNE IS COMBING HER HAIR, FOR SURE THERE'S A BOY. MAYBONNE SAYS NO, MARLYS SAYS LIAR, MAYBONNE KICKS HER OUT BUT LETS ME STAY. MARLYS SHOUTS I'M A TRAITOR FROM THE BOTTOM OF THE STAIRS. IS THERE A BOY?

KNOW WHAT'S COOL ABOUT YOU, ARNA?

YOU BARELY EVER TALK.

YOU ARE BARELY EVEN NOTICEABLE. THAT'S COOL.

IS THERE A BOY? THE ANSWER IS NO BUT YES. THE ANSWER IS NO NOT YET BUT VERY SOON YES BECAUSE SHE HONESTLY FEELS HIS VIBRATIONS. WHOEVER HE IS HE'S THINKING OF HER TOO RIGHT THIS SECOND, SHE HAS EXTRA PERCEPTION. THAT'S HOW SHE KNOWS. THE BURNING NAG CHAMPA SWIRLS TENDRILS OF SMOKE. "WHAT'S IN THE BOX?" I SAY. "YOU TALKED," SHE SAYS AND STOPS HER COMB, LOOKS AT ME AND POINTS TO THE DOOR. DISQUALIFIED. SHE KEEPS HER SECRETS. MYSTERIOUS WORLD.

DON'T TALK TO ME YOU TRAITOR-BUM.

SO DID YOU FIND OUT?

NO.

I SAID DON'T TALK TO ME.

239

SNOW GIRL

LYNDA BARRY ©

I WAS THE FIRST ONE UP. MY AUNT AND MY MOM GOT NIGHT SHIFT SO TIPTOE AND WHISPER AND TRY TO KEEP SILENT ABOUT THE GORGEOUS SUR-PRISE: IT'S SNOWING.

IN THE BLUE LIGHT OF MORNING IT'S FALLING SO PEACEFUL ON ROOF-TOPS AND WINDSHIELDS AND ONE DOG IN THE DISTANCE IS BARKING NOT VICIOUS BUT EXCITED AND WAGGY. IT'S SNOW.

MR. PASHRI OUR NEIGHBOR COMES OUT WITH HIS THERMOS, HE STARTS UP HIS CAR AND STARTS SCRAPING. A BREAK IN THE CLOUDS, ELEVEN SECONDS OF SUN THROW GOLD AND THROW GLITTER AROUND HIM. THE SPARKLE, THE SPARKLE, THE SNOW, MR. PASHRI! LOOK UP! LOOK UP! THE SNOW!

AT THE LAST MOMENT HE LOOKS ALL AROUND HIM, SNOW DRIFTING IN SUNLIGHT THAT FADES. A BARE SPOT WHERE HIS CAR WAS SLOWLY GOES WHITE. AND THE HOUSE IS STILL QUIET, SO GORGEOUSLY SILENT, I'M THE FIRST ONE AWAKE AND THERE'S SNOW.

SNOW! SNOW! SNOW!

WISH I MAY

LYNDA BARRY '00

ON THE STEEP HILL BY OUR HOUSE KIDS ARE DRAG-SLED RACING. MRS. COSHERA HAS CALLED THE COPS ON US TWICE FROM THE NOISE. SNOW JUST NATURALLY MAKES KIDS SCREAM.

AHHHHH AAAHHHH AHHHHH!!

AT THE BOTTOM THE WEENIE KIDS WATCH FOR CARS AND BEG FOR TURNS ON THE BIG INNER TUBE, THE ONE CALLED "GLAMOROUS GLENNIS" BUT GLENNIS IS ALWAYS HOGGED.

ALL CLEAR?!

NO! 'CAUSE WE THE PEOPLE ARE ON STRIKE 'TIL YOU LET US RIDE!!

FORGET YOU MARLYS! SOME ONE ELSE!

YEAH! ALL CLEAR!

THE HOGGERS ARE ALL BOYS, STRONG ONES YELLING, "1-2-3 PILE ON!" AND THEY JUMP ON PURPOSEFULLY HARD AND THEY CALL THEMSELVES COMMANDOS AND I WANT TO BE THEM SO BAD.

WIPE OUT!

OW!

BOINK!

I WANT TO FLY DOWN THE HILL ON GLAMOROUS GLENNIS IN A PILE OF LOYAL COMMANDOS. SPITTING AND STICKING TOGETHER AGAINST ALL WIMPS, ALL WUSSES, ALL GIRLS, ME. JUST ONCE TO BE A BOY, A BOY, THAT CERTAIN KIND OF BOY.

THE PERSEPHONE myth

LYNDA .... BARRY '00

ARNA. ROOM 2. READING. EXTRA CREDIT. MYTHOLOGY: WHY THERE IS WINTER. HADES WAS THE VERY OLDEN GOD OF THE DEAD BEINGS. HE HAD A DOG WITH 3 HEADS GUARDING HIS WORLD. ONLY DEAD PEOPLE COULD GET PAST THAT DOG. I WANT A DOG SO BAD.

MOM?

CHRIST, ARNA, WHAT?

READ MY REPORT YET?

CHRIST I JUST GOT UP, YOU KNOW?

GONNA READ IT?

HE CAPTURED A BEAUTIFUL LADY, A MAIDEN CALLED PERSEPHONE. IF I COULD BE AS BEAUTIFUL!! HER MOM WAS THE GODDESS OF ALL PLANTS AND WENT SO INSANE WHEN HADES STOLE HER AND MADE HER HIS QUEEN. I WOULD MAKE FRIENDS WITH HIS DOG. TRUTHFULLY I CAN MAKE FRIENDS WITH ANY DOG. I WOULD BE GODDESS OF DOGS IN MYTHOLOGY.

ACTUALLY I COULD READ IT TO YOU.

LATER.

I HAVE TO TURN IT IN TODAY, THOUGH.

GO GET MY LIGHTER, WILL YOU? IT'S BY THE BED.

AND DEMETER THE GODDESS MOTHER WAS SO SAD AND FURIOUS SHE WOULD NOT LET ANYTHING GROW. SO ZEUS SAID HADES HAD TO LET PERSEPHONE FREE. HADES WAS SAD AND EVEN THE THREE-HEADED DOG WAS SAD. AND THE BOOK DOESN'T SAY IT BUT SHE LOVED THAT DOG!!

OK? READY? IT'S ON MYTHOLOGY

I DON'T UNDERSTAND EVEN HALF OF THAT. GO READ IT TO MAYBONNE.

LET ME HAVE SOME PEACE ON MY DAY OFF!

IF HER GODDESS MOTHER WOULD LET HER HAVE A DOG BUT NO. SO FOR PART OF THE YEAR SHE STAYS WITH HER MOM WHO IS HAPPY SO EVERYTHING GROWS. BUT THEN SHE MISSES THE DOG AND GOES BACK TO HADES. HER MOM GETS SO SAD AND EVERYTHING DIES. IF I COULD JUST HAVE A DOG THERE WOULD BE NO MORE WINTER, IF SHE WOULD JUST LET ME HAVE ONE BUT NO.

PUT ON A HAT AND A SWEATER! IT'S COLDER THAN HELL OUT THERE

YOUR FAULT.

WHAT?

Sucker Punch

LYNDA   BARRY ∞

I HAVE READ THAT THERE ARE TOADS WHICH FREEZE UP IN THE WINTER, BECOME HARD AND COLD AS ICE, BECOME ICE ACTUALLY, TOADS FROZEN INTO POSITION BUT NOT DEAD.

HEY ARMPIT! HE SAYS YOUR GUYSES' DAD LIVES IN HAWAII, RIGHT?

STAND UP FOR ME, ARNA. GO ALONG WITH IT.

THAT RIGHT?

IN ANTARCTICA THERE ARE FATHER PENGUINS STANDING STILL IN FREEZING WIND AND DARKNESS, TWO MONTHS OF NOT MOVING WITH AN EGG BALANCED ON HIS FEET. THE ANTARCTIC FATHER IS BRAVE.

IT'S HONALULA IS WHERE HE LIVES, RIGHT, ARNA?

YOU WATCHED "HAWAII 5-0" LAST NIGHT, IS ALL. DOY!

RIGHT, ARNA?

'BYE, YA LIARS!

AND TOO THERE ARE THE FLOWER BULBS BURIED NAKED AND ALIVE ALONG WITH → *magicicada septendecim,* BORN IN A **TREE** BUT CLIMBS DOWN, DIGS DOWN, STAYS UNDERGROUND FOR 17 YEARS.

YEAH. LIKE HE'S BRINGING YOU TO HAWAII. GO SURFIN'. YEAH.

HE IS.

I'M TALKING TO ARMPIT. WHERE'S YOUR DAD, ARMPIT?

THERE'S A PICTURE OF MY DAD, SQUINTING IN THE SUMMERTIME BEFORE MIGRATION. HE WAS A LAUGHING SAILOR-MAN. FOLLOWED THE SUN. THE WINTER WAS FOR OTHERS, FOR SUCKERS, FOR CHUMPS.

THANKS A LOT, MAN! WHAT A GREAT SISTER! WHAT A **GREAT** FAMILY I GOT! DAD WAS RIGHT FOR LEAVING!

YEAH.

LOHA.

T.V. BLACKOUT

LYNDA — BARRY '01

YOU CAN'T TALK TO MARLYS WHEN SHE'S WATCHING TV. IT'S A LAW.

HEY, MARLYS. DO YOU KNOW WHERE MY---

SHUT UP! IT'S ON!!

YOU CAN'T TALK TO HER AND SHE WON'T TALK TO YOU BUT SHE WILL TALK TO THE TV.

HE'S NOT A DESPERADO, YOU IDIOT! YOU HAVE THE WRONG MAN, SHERIFF! ASK THE PADRE!

THEY CAN'T HEAR YOU MARLYS.

PINCH

OW!

IF YOU KEEP QUIET SHE SOMETIMES FORGETS YOU ARE THERE AND YOU MAY HEAR SOME INTERESTING THINGS.

OH ALFREDO. THE SHERIFF, HE IS BAD. OUR LIVES ARE SO IN DANGER. WE MUST FLEE.

OH ALFREDO. I AM NOT AFRAID TO DIE.

KISS ME, ALFREDO! KISS ME LIKE CRAZY!

LATER, WHEN YOU SAY THEM BACK TO HER, SHE WON'T HAVE ANY IDEA OF WHAT YOU'RE TALKING ABOUT. SHE TALKS TO THE TV BUT SHE NEVER REMEMBERS WHAT SHE SAID.

KISS ME ALFREDO!

WHY DO YOU KEEP SAYING THAT TO ME?

THE SHERIFF HE IS VERY BAD.

WHAT ARE YOU EVEN TALKING ABOUT?

244

Old Yeller

LYNDA   BARRY 00

ANY DOG. I THOUGHT I COULD MAKE FRIENDS WITH ANY DOG BUT SOMETIMES THE PEOPLE WON'T LET YOU. THERE IS THIS ONE OLD MAN.

#@✿# YOU! GET AWAY! MY DOG DON'T LIKE ⓒ✦;✿# KIDS! I DON'T WANT NO $✿#!@ LAWSUITS WHEN MY DOG TAKES YOUR@#//#✿ FACE OFF!

HE HAS A BEAUTIFUL BIG PUPPY, A SAINT BERNARD ON A TIGHT, SPIKED CHOKER-CHAIN. SHE WANTS TO PLAY SO BAD. SUCH A WAGGY-TAIL DOG LEASHED TO SUCH A GROWLING OLD MAN.

WHY DOES HE WALK HER TO THE SCHOOLYARD EACH DAY AT THREE? HE KNOWS THERE WILL BE CHILDREN. CONFUSING OLD MAN WHO HAS FORGOTTEN KINDNESS AND NEVER LETS HIS DOG REMEMBER FOR HIM.

YOU'RE WORSE THAN MY #!@◎✦ EX-WIFE! CAN'T TAKE NO FOR AN ANSWER!! YOU HAVE NO #✿ii@8# RIGHT TO ASK MY DOG'S NAME!

YEAH BUT WHAT'S HER NAME, THOUGH?

MY COUSIN SAYS I'M STU-PID TO KEEP TRYING. THAT MAN WILL NEVER BUDGE. BUT HIS DOG KEEPS WAG-GING HER TAIL WHEN SHE SEES ME. IF SHE CAN HOPE THEN SO CAN I.

✦#!!@s KIDS! ALWAYS WANTING TO PET MY @$✦!!# DOG! KEEP AWAY, YOU HEAR ME?!

OK, MISTER! SEE YOU TOMORROW, THEN.

✦#!!@$#✦!!!

See-Through

LYNDA BARRY '00

SOME PEOPLE ARE JUST NATURAL JUVENILE DELINQUENTS. LIKE MY BROTHER ARNOLD WHO GETS CONSTANT URGES TO BREAK THINGS.

DEAR LORD THAT WAS SO KEEN OF YOU TO GET JEFF KRILL BLAMED FOR THOSE WINDOWS I BUSTED.

ALSO THANK YOU FOR NO ONE KNOWING IT WAS ME THAT CLOGGED ALL THE TOILETS IN THE BOYS' CAN. AMEN.

OTHER PEOPLE ARE JUST NATURALLY SMART, LIKE → MARLYS, GETTING ALL As IN EVERY BOX ON HER REPORT CARD EXCEPT CONDUCT AND RESPONSE TO CRITICISM.

EXCUSE ME LORD FOR KICKING THAT ONE GIRL LOUISE IN THE LEG FOR HER ALWAYS RANKING ME DOWN AND FORGIVE HOW MUCH I ENJOYED IT.

ALSO THANK YOU FOR MY 100% IN EXTRA-CREDIT SPELLING ESPECIALLY ON THE WORD TONSILLECTOMY. AMEN.

AND THEN THERE ARE GENTLE PEOPLE LIKE FREDDIE WHO GETS PUSHED AROUND, LOVES NATURE, ALL NATURE, EVEN GREENISH MOLD ON WHITE BREAD.

DEAR OUR FATHER PLEASE REVEAL TO ME THE SECRETS OF FUNGI ESPECIALLY WHERE I MAY FIND SPECIMENS OF STINKHORN, WITCHES BUTTER AND CRAMP BALLS. IT'S FOR A PROJECT.

AMEN. OH. P.S. ALSO THAT GIRL LOUISE IS STILL SOCKING ME IN THE STOMACH WHEN NO ONE IS LOOKING REMEMBER I MENTIONED HER?

AND TOO THERE ARE THE BACKGROUND PEOPLE. THE ONES LIKE ME WHO ARE JUST NATURALLY SEE-THROUGH EXCEPT SOMETIMES TO DOGS. MAINLY I THANK GOD FOR DOGS.

ALL OF THEM. INCLUDING BIG FEROCIOUS, TINY YAPPY, MIXED, PURE, OLD, SMELLY, SLOW, FAST, ANY, ALL, EVERY.

THANK YOU! YOU KNOW WHY FROM YOU KNOW WHO.

AMEN.

246

Gemma

LYNDA BARRY '00

CHURCH BELLS RINGING, DING-DANG-DING, A CARDINAL, RED IN THE GRAY TREE TOP TANGLE, IS CALLING WITH A LOW-HIGH SOUND. FREDDIE SAYS, "HERE COMES SPRING."

THE SNOW IS OLD AND DIRTY AND STARTING CARS WHINE IN THE MORNING, NOT WANTING TO TURN OVER. DEAD ICICLES STILL HANGING BUT FREDDIE SAYS IT'S CERTAIN, IT'S MOVING DOWN THE RAILS, SPRING'S VIBRATION.

YOU GUYS BETTER COME INSIDE 'ELSE YOU'RE GONNA BE THE FROZE-OFF HINEY PEOPLE!

IF YOU DON'T KNOW IT, THEY GOT THE "EXPOSED FLESH" WARNINGS ON THE RADIO!

BRANCHES SNAPPED BY ICE-STORMS LAY STILL IN CROOKED PATTERNS. FREDDIE LIFTS ONE, POINTS OUT THE TINY REDDISH GEMMA, SAYS, "LEAVES AND FLOWERS, ARNA. THEY'RE LITTLE BUT THEY'RE HERE." THE MAIL-MAN WALKS BY IN EARMUFFS.

CRIPES, YOU KIDS SHOULD BE INDOORS, WEATHER LIKE THIS.

YOU 337?

HUH?

YOUR ADDRESS. 337.

OH. YEAH. HERE.

US MAIL

"SPRING IS COMING," SAYS MY COUSIN AND HIS TEETH BEGIN TO CHATTER. SIX CROWS PICK AT SOMETHING FROZEN IN THE SNOW. THEIR JET BLACKNESS MAKES ME DIZZY OR MAYBE IT'S THE COLD. SPRING IS COMING, I BELIEVE IT, BUT FOR NOW LET'S GO INSIDE!

DAG! 'BOUT TIME! COME ON! MAYBONNE MADE MARSHMALLOW TREATS AND THAT "INVASION OF THE BODY SNATCHERS" IS ON AND MOM'S GONNA GET MAD, FREDDIE, THROW THAT STICK BACK OUTSIDE.

Valentine

Lynda Barry '00

SHE'S IN OUR ROOM WITH GLUE AND GLITTER, RED RED PAPER AND BLUE HANDLED SCISSORS, SHAPING LEFT VENTRICLE AND RIGHT, FOR SOMEONE, SOMEONE, WHO?

SHOULD I USE SILVER GLITTER OR RED? YOU PICK.

SILVER.

NO, RED.

IN THE DOORWAY ARNOLD TEASES, CHANTING OUT DIFFERENT BOYS' NAMES, TELLING MARLYS IT IS HOPELESS, THE WHOLE SCHOOL THINKS SHE'S A SPAZ.

MIKE R! MIKE F! KEVIN! DON! ED! MIKE B! MATT! LOUIS! DANIEL THE AUSTRALIAN!

DAVID I! GARY! ANDRÉ! BEN! TOM! JOHN! ELMER! KOTOMICHI OKUMA! AM I RIGHT?!

MARLYS FOLDS AND SNIPS UNTIL SHE GETS THE HEART JUST RIGHT, ASKS HOW TO SPELL "ANONYMOUS" THEN SHE WRITES IT OUT IN GLUE. GLITTER SPARKLES, GLITTER FALLS, SHE TAPS THE EXTRA OFF, SOME GLINTS FALL ON HER SANDWICH BUT SHE EATS IT ANYWAY.

A MAYONNAISE AND RED GLITTER SANDWICH. EVER ATE ONE? IN FRANCE THEY ARE SO POPULAR.

PSYCH.

NO PSYCH. SERIOUS.

ARNOLD SAYS NOBODY WANTS HER HOMEMADE VALENTINE, A HEART SENT BY ANONYMOUS IS GOING IN THE TRASH. MARLYS WAVES IT SO THAT THE SPARKLES CATCH THE LIGHT, SAYS IF HER HEART LANDS IN THE GARBAGE, WELL, IT WON'T BE THERE FOR LONG.

IF THEY THROW IT AWAY, NO BIG, IT STILL COUNTS. IT STILL TOTALLY COUNTS.

YEAH, BUT WHO IS IT FOR?

YOU.

248

ANGEL MARLYS

ABOUT the AUTHOR

I'M A DOG LOVING PERSON, BORN IN 1956. I'VE ALWAYS LIKED TO DRAW AND WRITE, AND ONE DAY IN 1986 I MADE THE COMIC STRIP CALLED "THE NIGHT WE ALL GOT SICK" WHERE I SAW MARLYS FOR THE FIRST TIME. SHE'S HAD A HUGE IN-FLUENCE ON ME EVER SINCE. ALTHOUGH MY OWN CHILDHOOD WAS VERY DIFFERENT FROM HERS, SHE'S HELPED ME MAKE SOME SENSE OF THINGS THAT I NEVER HAD WORDS FOR BEFORE. SHE BECAME THE IMAGINARY FRIEND I'D ALWAYS WANTED. I HOPE YOU ENJOY THIS COLLECTION OF HER STORIES. I'M SO HAPPY TO HAVE SO MANY OF THEM ALL IN ONE PLACE AT LAST. Lynda Barry